THEN I CHOOSE A HORRIBLE END

Marina Meier

eBook ISBN: 978-1-7641211-0-1
Paperback ISBN: 978-1-7641211-1-8
Hardcover ISBN: 978-1-7641211-2-5

Cover design by Yulia Zaitseva
Copyedited by Halley Sutton

First Edition

Published by Svitlo Press
svitlopress.com

To fear.

To the one I had to battle.

To the one I learned to befriend.

To the fear that helps me at work,

and the one that keeps me awake at night.

To you, my fear — who finally became Alicia's.

CHAPTER 1

A lone streetlamp bathed the overgrown bush in light. The bush rustled.

So did whoever was hiding in it.

Alicia Brooks stared through the living room window. Was it her imagination?

Half an hour ago, she had woken in the middle of the night, heart pounding as if it might break through her ribs. Messy hair clung to her face, and her sweat-soaked hands feverishly gripped the sheets.

The image of her nightmare lingered in her mind — a rotting pig's snout stitched to a human body. The ringing in her ears slowly faded, and the contours of the bedroom solidified. The dream began to dissolve, sinking like mist into her subconscious, settling over the heavy knot of fear in her mind.

Alicia and her boyfriend, Jack, rented a two-story house in southern Chicago. It was a small suburban area with stereotypically successful, wealthy, and morally suffocating neighbors. Cookie-cutter houses, identical lawns. Despite the proximity to high-crime areas, Hunter could compete for the title of the dullest neighborhood in Illinois. Nothing dangerous could ever happen here. Nothing criminal. Nothing...*right?*

Even half-asleep, Alicia looked striking. Her naturally curly blonde hair had been flattened by the pillow. The moonlight poured through the wide window, highlighting her blue eyes, like two round sapphires, on a thin face. Her silk nightgown had lifted slightly, pulled up by her stiffened nipples.

Alicia glanced at the clock — 4:30 a.m. Another panic attack had interrupted her sleep cycle. She craved cold, fizzy water, her dry throat still echoing the scream from her nightmare. Alicia quietly got out of bed and walked down the dark hallway, using her iPhone's flashlight to guide her. She descended the stairs to the living room, flipped the light switch, and looked out the window.

The window where fear lived. One of them, at least.

Why even look? Surely it was just her imagination?

A childhood memory whispered an old legend. How empty, night streets could lure an unsuspecting passerby in the spring. "Come for a walk," the bare trees would beckon. "Come look," the shimmering stars might invite. "Are you here? Step closer."

The guest's eyes would catch a sharp movement, unable to identify the running animal in the darkness...a dog? A fox? Or was it...wait, a person crawling on all fours?

A woman??

What was in her mouth? Something long, covered in grayish-yellow scabs and oozing blisters, dragging on the ground, struggling to keep up with her front legs...or hands.

A tongue? Was that her tongue??

Those wild eyes would get closer and closer. Then the

"woman" lunged at the guest, wrapping her arms around them, shoving her rotten tongue down their throat. She had only one goal — to strangle anyone who dared to gaze into the heart of darkness.

"I imagined it," Alicia mumbled to herself, staring out the window. Her slender legs were covered in goosebumps from the cold floor. She was trembling. "God, that doesn't exist! Surely, there's just a stray dog hiding in the bush. An ordinary mutt."

Alicia was too scared to move. Too scared that if she turned her back on the stupid bush, she'd realize it wasn't a dog. She'd hear it. She'd see the creature from her childhood nightmare notice her and leap on all fours to kill her. The wind picked up, shaking the bush even more. Alicia held her breath and clenched her fists.

Her phone screen lit up. She almost dropped it in surprise.

"Breathe, just breathe slowly," she whispered, exhaling deeply.

She'd learned that trick during her first therapy session. "First, take a deep breath!" the poster of a smiling guy at the entrance proclaimed. Like it was a dentist's office, not that of a psychologist.

Along with the breath, logic came to her aid. All this wasted time and a near-panic attack — was her little night trip really worth it? *Silly girl.* She turned her back to the window and opened the fridge. Inside, a liter bottle of San Pellegrino. Holding the cold plastic bottle between her knees, Alicia struggled to twist the cap. She poured a full glass and downed it in one gulp. The water froze her brain and shattered her panicked thoughts.

As she left the room, Alicia glanced back at the window once more. The bush wasn't moving anymore. There was nothing special about it. Just a bush.

Alicia returned to the bedroom and quietly shut the door behind her.

"Ali, you okay?" Jack's sleepy voice came from the bed. He propped himself up on his elbows, eyes half-closed.

They had been together for a couple of years now. The first time she'd jumped up in the middle of the night, Jack had been seriously scared. Alicia had sat with her head bent toward her chest, muttering something incoherent. He'd shaken her shoulder — no response. Later, remembering a school lesson about sleepwalkers, he gently laid her back in bed. By morning, it turned out that Alicia wasn't a sleepwalker at all: she remembered the night's events, but had been so terrified that she couldn't control herself — she couldn't speak, couldn't get back into bed on her own. That was how Jack had been introduced to her panic attacks.

"Babe, are you okay?" he repeated when she didn't respond.

"Yes, yes, I'm fine now," she said. "Let's go back to sleep."

Alicia slipped under the cool blanket, pleased with herself. Tonight, she had conquered her fear on her own, even if not right away. Small steps, and the panic attacks would disappear forever.

Jack's soft snoring came from the pillow. She touched his warm cheek with her fingertip — he twitched but didn't wake. Her hand traveled from his temple to the top of his chestnut hair, and she leaned down to inhale the scent of his menthol shampoo. Her favorite. The feather duvet on his side had shifted, exposing his muscular abs — evidence of his thrice-weekly gym visits. Alicia wanted him. To wake him. To kiss him. She moved in so close that his warm breath tickled her lips, but then she changed her mind. Why ruin his sleep?

They were grown adults now, and those fleeting bursts of passion were for teenagers.

Girls in the office whispered about Jack when discussing ideal husband material. Young, but already in a management position at one of the city's leading architecture firms. Refined sense of humor, strong critical thinking skills, financially savvy — Jack had all the qualities society deemed desirable. Oh, and of course, a good salary.

They'd met at a LiveSafe company party. A loud event celebrating the company's birthday. It was an open-air bash, with live music, an open bar, buffet, and unlimited drinks.

Jack Sylvan, not yet promoted but already the life of the party, was smiling as he debated politics with the father of the company's founder. Alicia Brooks, a freshly unemployed graduate, was scanning the room for useful connections and listening to gossip from her best friend, who had brought Alicia along as her plus-one.

Alicia didn't believe in love at first sight — that pink, fluffy, made-up-by-American-screenwriters kind of love. But when she saw Jack in the crowd, she felt something. Not weak knees, and no, her tongue didn't get tied. Her heart didn't skip a beat. Alicia felt something more substantial coming from the guy — charisma, in the way his expressions played out; energy, pulling people, like flies, into his web of conversation; and something else — she felt that he noticed her, too.

Jack caught her eye, and his lips curled into a smile. A gold, floor-length dress with a lace top and long sleeves — not easy to approach, if not for the high slit running up her leg, exposing her slender thigh. She was the first to check him out, but when he turned to her, she didn't look away. She held his gaze for a couple more seconds, then turned her back to the bar, and walked away. She wanted to play.

And she won.

That evening, they talked late into the night, only realizing how much time had passed when the musicians began packing up their instruments. Before they parted, he called her a cab and got her number. That's how Ali made the most successful connection of the night.

The warmth of the memories finally eased her into sleepiness. Alicia yawned and nestled into her pillow. Even asleep, Jack saved her from her dark thoughts. Snuggling up to him, Alicia fell asleep instantly.

Chapter 2

The bedroom was already filled with bright sunlight when the phone rang. An alarm was unnecessary in this house — Jack's workday didn't start with coffee but with phone calls. He stirred and woke up.

"They could at least let us sleep in once," Alicia muttered.

"Clients don't wait," Jack noted logically, rubbing his sleepy eyes with fingers. He unplugged the phone, cleared his throat, and, still in his underwear, walked out of the room.

Ali, frustrated about the lost hour of sleep, reluctantly got up. Even though the panic attack hadn't lasted long, the feeling of exhaustion bored into her head like a thin needle. And to top it off, Jack's annoying clients, who called before eight in the morning — she was tired of it.

Running through the names of Jack's clients in her mind, silently cursing them, Alicia walked into the bathroom. She brushed her teeth and went through her morning skincare routine: eucalyptus-scented cleansing foam, toner, serum, and a matte moisturizing cream. Then she skillfully applied primer, foundation, concealer, bronzer, and highlighter. Opening the blush compact, she tapped her cheeks twice with an egg-shaped sponge.

Ahead was a short workday, followed by a long-awaited trip to the mall with Katie. Before summer, the friends always went shopping, grabbing push-up shorts, cotton sundresses, and sexy tops. Alicia loved rewarding herself for maintaining her summer body, while her friend...well, her friend rewarded herself just because.

Katie — Alicia's "BFF" since university — was a typical, ordinary girl. The kind you could meet at a club, dance with all night, and by morning, forget her face. She wasn't exactly well-shaped — flat both front and back. Almost transparent hair barely reached her shoulders and then went its own way. Katie tried (she really did), but she only looked beautiful when there wasn't a girl with more spark around. When God sprinkled ingredients for her appearance, He ran out of raisins.

Their friendship survived university competition, personal income ups and downs, and even living together in a small apartment. Besties forever. They shared everything: sex partners, dirty gossip, salary sizes. There was only one topic they almost never touched, and Alicia was incredibly glad about that.

***

It happened during their second year at university. Ali and Katie were renting a tiny apartment near the architecture building. The seeds of their friendship were just sprouting, and one day, they had an important presentation for a quarterly project. Ali, not finding her friend at home, assumed she'd spent the night at some guy's place — nothing serious. In their youth, they swapped boys and were swapped by them.

But Katie didn't show up for lunch. The "Physics and Modern Architecture" presentation loomed like a dark cloud of failure, and Katie, who was responsible for the final paper, was unreachable. With no better options, Ali got Katie's parents' address from the class rep and headed there, hoping to at least find the printouts.

On the way, she managed to listen to her favorite album *Prism*. The Black family's home was in the Riverdale area, which had only recently been absorbed into the city limits. As a student working part-time at a call center, Alicia couldn't afford a taxi, and even the train ticket cost her a cup of coffee and a sweet bun from the university cafeteria. She mentally cursed and simultaneously hoped to find her friend at her parents' house. She had no other options.

If Ali had known what awaited her, she wouldn't have gone. If she had known, she would have done every report on her own.

The Blacks' apartment building was slowly falling apart. People still lived there, but the bricks of the once-massive building had crumbled in places, and all that remained of the fire escape were rusty railings. Alicia passed the dusty, abandoned concierge desk — no one had stood behind it for god knew how many years. The elevator was "temporarily" out of order, as indicated by an equally old, moldy sign. Ali pulled out a scrap of paper with the address and obediently started climbing the stairs.

Her confidence drained with each step, and by the time she reached the right door, it was gone. The building might have been unkempt and rundown, and even a broken elevator could be chalked up to the high-crime neighborhood, where your chances of becoming a victim were high. But a door, where people lived, should never look like that. The lower half of the door, covered in dark gray vinyl leather, had been gnawed in places. Above, where the rats hadn't reached, the fabric hung in uneven, ragged strips, revealing the rotting wood beneath. There was no doorbell.

In her mind, fear of uncertainty — who knew what kind of creature could live in a creepy block like this — battled with fear of expulsion. The latter won. It always did at that age. Alicia couldn't afford to retake the class without a serious reason. She swallowed hard and knocked on the door with her foot, carefully avoiding the rat droppings.

"Ali? What are you doing here?" The door opened slightly, and a female silhouette peeked through the crack.

Behind her, the hallway was swallowed in darkness, with no light source in sight.

"Katie, we have an important presentation in an hour and a half about —" The door slammed shut in her face, only to reopen fully a few seconds later. From the darkness emerged a girl, barely resembling the smiling roommate she knew.

"Oh, Ali, I'm sorry, I completely forgot to tell you," Katie said.

Her dirty hair had grayed and blended into the wall. Dark, puffy circles stained the pale skin under her eyes like smeared watercolor. Her face was swollen from crying, so much so that Katie looked like a drunk at a train station.

"I'd invite you in, but...I have to stay here today. I'll bring out the printouts, okay?" her friend continued.

Alicia felt torn. Common sense urged her to grab the materials and head to the station; if the train arrived on time, she could still make it by the middle of class. But leaving her friend in this mayor-forgotten place didn't feel right either.

Alicia stepped into the doorway and hugged her roommate with one arm.

"Katie, I'll stay with you. Tell me what happened."

And Katie poured everything out. A sick mother and how the illness had turned a caring woman into a shapeless being over the course of a few years. Katie spoke in abrupt bursts and pauses, wiping her face with the dirty sleeve of her sweater. Alicia nodded, stroking her friend's head, but inside, she was fake. She hadn't suspected a thing. And worse, the urge to leave hadn't disappeared. Alicia felt disgusted. Disgusted by standing in the hallway that reeked of sour pickles, sweat, and urine. Disgusted by the loud groans of the old woman in the other room. Disgusted by her own self-pity. Disgusted by her fear.

A loud knock interrupted Katie's monologue, and she rushed to the far room. Ali, trying not to breathe, looked around.

The faded gold wallpaper smelled of dampness, with patches of fuzzy black mold in the corners. Four doors led off the hallway — two near the entrance and two at the far end, where her friend had run. Between the doorways, light squares were visible on the walls, remnants of once-hanging portraits or family photos. Alicia lingered a moment by the front door, trying to inhale the smell of the stairwell. Biting her lower lip, she followed Katie.

***

"What were you dreaming about when you woke up again in the middle of the night?" Jack asked over breakfast. They'd hastily fried eggs and were finishing off the lukewarm coffee.

Alicia shook her head. She had hoped he wouldn't remember, and sharing her childhood nightmares and silly fears about a bush seemed stupid. *It was just a bush!*

"I don't even remember anymore, sorry for waking you," she waved it off.

Jack gave her a skeptical look, frowning. The quality of his sleep had improved since their first year living together, but once or twice a month, he still noticed when Alicia woke up scared in the middle of the night.

"It's not that you woke me up, it's that you're skipping your regular sessions with Ms. Dancy. You said it yourself: there's no benefit with breaks."

"Jack, it's the end of the quarter. I can't think about anything but work."

"So, you woke up because of work?" His deep wrinkle smoothed out.

"Of course, Jack," Alicia smiled. *Silly dream!*

"You know, babe," Jack hugged her from behind. "You can take sick leave, and I can pass your project to another consultant while you rest. I'm the big boss, after all."

Jack winked and laughed, but Alicia rolled her eyes. Every time he told her she could take a break and someone else could take over her work, it made her angry. How could she accept that she was easily replaceable and that anyone could do her job? Even if it was true.

"No, I don't need sick leave. I'm fine. I'll schedule a session for tomorrow."

"Alright." Jack kissed her on the cheek. "I've got a few calls to make, see you downstairs in the car in twenty minutes."

After Jack's promotion to head of the department, she'd tried to resist the constant phone calls intruding on their personal life, but eventually, she gave in. Half of Jack's job was endless communication. More responsibilities meant more money. Everything had its price.

Alicia nodded and loaded the plates into the dishwasher. Jack hadn't been scared off by her "condition," and after her first wake-up from a panic attack, he had convinced her to start therapy to stabilize her mind. He firmly believed that all problems in the head could be cured through conversations with specialists.

The sessions were varied: sometimes they involved long talks, sometimes half-hour meditations (during which Alicia often dozed off), and occasionally, deep hypnosis to relive anxious memories and reshape them. This was called "memory falsification." Alicia had tried to learn how to practice it on her own. The idea was to revisit a nightmare in a calm setting and live through it again, explaining the supernatural with real things. For example, drawing a stray dog near the damn bush. Easier said than done.

Alicia leaned against the wall, closed her eyes, and began breathing slowly. Counting the seconds. Feeling the tickling air on her tongue.

"One, two, three," she exhaled. "One, two, three," she

inhaled. "One, two, three."

The imaginary room appeared before her, along with the view of the avenue. Inhale. Night, streetlamp. Exhale. The bush next to it. Inhale. A black mutt. Exhale. A mutt, barely visible in the darkness. The boxwood bush. Inhale...

Outside, a gate clattered, pulling her attention away — the image of the dog blurred in her mind. In its place appeared the creature. A woman, or something resembling one, on all fours with a reeking tongue dragging along the ground. Searching. Hungry. Turning around...

Alicia opened her eyes. She hadn't rested enough to face the nightmare again.

CHAPTER 3

The red rays of sunset, like an almost-ripe apple, filled Ali's office. She had spent the entire day running between the client and contractors, avoiding unnecessary conversations with her colleague, Cole Church. He had already managed to spoil her mood early that morning when he gleefully informed the client on a group call about a bulk discount for the next phase.

The project team was small: a manager, a contractor, and two consultants — Ali and her hated competitor, Cole. They were supposed to work as a team, but Jack had quietly hinted to her that the success of the quarterly presentation would determine the future of the consultants — one of them was certain to get a promotion to manager. Somehow, Cole had caught wind of this, too, and was now going out of his way to outshine Ali in front of the wealthy client. Teamwork was out of the question.

Alicia yawned widely, not bothering to cover her mouth, and glanced at the clock — it was already five. Stretching in her chair, she sent a text message:

```
Jackie, I'm going shopping with Katie now.
              Dinner tonight?
```

Almost immediately, she received a reply:

```
Ok. I'll stop by the pizzeria and grab a
   four-cheese pizza for tonight. Xxx
```

Her friend was already waiting in the lobby, standing right under the company logo. It was Katie who had introduced Alicia to the fateful corporate event that had both spiced up her personal life and jump-started her career. But ironically, Katie herself had no serious relationship, and after a few years at the company, she hadn't received a promotion, either. Things just hadn't worked out for her.

Did they love each other as friends? Of course. But was there room for envy? Undoubtedly.

The mall next to the office was huge, far larger than the local ones in their neighborhood. Right at the entrance was a small stage with a quartet of young violinists. A sign at the foot of the stage read *Charity Concert for Leukemia*. They played well, but the sound occasionally dipped, and the speaker would crackle annoyingly.

Upbeat music played in Sephora, bringing neither sadness nor nostalgia. The girls immediately headed to the makeup bar — a small island in the center where they could grab any sample and test the products.

Ali grabbed her favorite nude lip gloss and applied it. Lately, stylists had been raving about the natural makeup look, which she always pulled off so well.

"Can I help you with anything?" a friendly girl with a name tag that read Sakura asked them.

"We're just looking," Katie said, popping out from behind a

mirror with one eye already done in makeup.

Ali snorted and shook her head. Sakura smiled knowingly.

"The nude shade suits you well but try adding a hint of passion with this red lipstick," the consultant handed a tester to Ali. "It goes perfectly with your sapphire eyes. And it won't smudge when you eat."

Without thinking, Ali wiped off the previous gloss with cotton pads from the counter and applied the red shade using a disposable brush. Smacking her lips, she stepped back from the mirror.

Sakura was right. Her smooth, perfect lips didn't just stand out — they seemed to blur the background around her. Ali tucked strands of hair behind her ears and turned to the side. The focus on her lips didn't shift.

"It suits you perfectly," Sakura confirmed.

"Take it, Ali. Take it," Katie popped out with both eyes now fully made-up. "You look stunning. And I've picked out a new palette, look."

With fresh makeup and lighter wallets, the girls wearily stumbled out of the store. The concert had already ended, and the musicians were packing up their instruments. Small children had started climbing onto the stage and tugging at the violinists' legs.

"We've barely been to Sephora, and I'm already exhausted," Ali muttered.

Katie waved dismissively. It wasn't shopping if it was just one store.

"We're going there," she pointed to the glass storefronts with large red "Sale" signs.

The store had discounts on every third item, but apart from the cashier, who was lazily playing on his phone, there were no customers. He didn't smile or even bother to take his feet off the counter when they walked in. Ali ran her fingers over the sweaters hanging on the racks. Terrible quality. Katie, lured by the promise of low prices, grabbed several identical silk blouses and rushed to the fitting room.

"Ali," Katie called from the fitting room after half an hour. "I picked a couple of blouses, two shirts, and a gorgeous dress. Now stop wasting time and pick something to try on, too. Come on, I need one more item for the discount."

Ali smirked but got up from the pouf and approached the skirt section. Who doesn't love a discount?

A sea-blue leather skirt caught her eye. Ali pulled it into the light and ran her finger along the seam. Compared to the sweaters, it was decently made. Nylon, polyester. Made in Bangladesh. $49.

"You've convinced me, Katie, I'll try the skirt," Ali said, and stepped into the central fitting room.

For nylon, the skirt fit well and didn't clash with her style. Ali twirled in front of the mirror in the fitting room, adjusted her hair, and winked at herself. She tried to sit down. Strike a pose. Not bad — she could take it. She unzipped the back, and the skirt fell to her feet. Ali bent down to pick it up when she noticed, in the reflection, a silhouette behind the curtain.

Tall. Broad. Motionless.

"Katie," Ali called quietly. "Is that you?"

The figure didn't move.

"Katie," Ali raised her voice, worried now. "Why are you

just standing there?"

"Huh? I'm getting dressed, what do you want?" Katie's voice came from somewhere nearby, several fitting rooms over.

Alicia tensed. The silhouette clearly didn't belong to her short friend — it was a tall man. Someone was still standing behind the curtain, even after Alicia's anxious question. She cautiously scooted toward the wall on her haunches, leaning to see the feet of the figure standing there.

Nothing. He must have been farther back than the gap allowed her to see, but why did the shadow on the curtain seem like it was within arm's reach?

She froze, too afraid to move closer. Something about the figure gave off an unnatural sense of dread. The complete stillness, the long, pointed right hand. No, not just a hand, Ali realized. He was holding some long object.

Ali stood up from her crouched position, covering herself with the skirt like a fan, and grabbed a wooden hanger with her right hand. If she could strike him with the metal hook, the creep wouldn't have it easy. Slowly, she approached the curtain, ready to swing her improvised weapon.

Katie suddenly appeared in front of her, blocking her view of the store.

"What's with your face? Why are you holding a hanger? Did you see the price on that skirt and decide to run for it?" Katie laughed at her own joke.

"Uh-huh," Alicia tried to force a smile.

She stepped past Katie and looked over her shoulder, searching for the person who had been standing there a minute ago, holding something in his hand.

No one was there.

"Maybe you should put something on before stepping out into the store, madam? No need to flash your underwear, huh?" Katie asked, glancing back as well.

"M-m-m, I thought I saw someone standing here."

"There was no one, stop making things up. Hurry up and get dressed, they close in half an hour."

An hour later, a grumpy, middle-aged taxi driver of Middle Eastern descent pulled up in front of a brick house, and Alicia made her way toward the front door along a decorative path laid between boxwood bushes. The light was on in the living room, meaning Jack was already home.

She quickly took off her outerwear, along with the large shopping bags filled with her new purchases and almost sprinted toward her boyfriend. There was no point in keeping anything bottled up — Jack's words would, as always, calm her down.

Jack was sitting at the wooden kitchen table, holding his phone to his ear with his shoulder. Both hands were busy rummaging through a stack of papers — contracts and agreements piled on the table from his work bag.

"Jackie, hey, I —" Ali began in one breath but immediately fell silent when she saw Jack free one hand to press his index finger to his lips.

"That sounds great, Gabe, but what external resources will we have?" he asked into the phone, placing his other hand over his chest and shaking his head at Ali.

He pointed at the phone, his lips forming a silent apology. Ali nodded, disappointed, and Jack gave her a mini-bow before heading upstairs, still on the phone with his ever-demanding client who had no regard for personal time.

Alicia glanced around the now-empty room and quickly pulled out her phone to text her therapist.

CHAPTER 4

The practice on North Way Street was a portal from the busy Chicago office building to a secluded cabin in the woods. It was spacious, with a soft sofa and two matching armchairs in the middle of the room. The windows were covered with a special tinted film that cast everything in a yellowish hue — even on rainy days, it looked like the sun was shining. On the beige wall hung a composition of three paintings: early autumn trees covered in golden leaves and an orange-tinged landscape symmetrically receding into the distance. Fragrant incense sticks filled the air with the smell of pumpkin spice latte and cinnamon.

On the opposite wall stood a tall cabinet filled with various statues and figurines, gifts from grateful clients. They were all different sizes and themes, seemingly odd together, yet each one added to the atmosphere of the room, as if boasting how many happy people had left this office.

Ms. Dancy had been working as a psychologist for twelve years. A well-groomed woman around forty, she never allowed herself to face clients without styled hair and light makeup. Her main rule was "the client comes first," and she was ready to accept visitors in her office even in the middle of the night — for an additional fee, of course. An emergency consultation was billed at triple the normal rate, and within half an hour of payment, Ms. Dancy would offer a cup of decaffeinated herbal tea and start taking notes in a personalized matte notebook with the client's initials.

Alicia had arrived early for her morning consultation before work. She had tried to start a conversation with Jack in the car, but he was so overloaded with work from the night before that he spent the entire drive persuading a skeptical client to double the project's budget.

Sitting on the hot, sticky couch in the lobby, Alicia nervously twirled her hair, trying to put herself in her boyfriend's shoes and think about how she would prioritize things. The potential project promised great profits for the company, but Alicia hadn't been going to therapy without good reason. After all, therapy had been Jack's idea after what happened on Halloween a few years ago, when they had been dating for only a couple of months.

***

That year had been cold, often rainy. In honor of the pumpkin holiday, Ali and Katie had thrown a themed party at a house rented by their classmates. Without a proper heating system, they used all sorts of ways to stay warm: from portable heaters to cheap liquor, which the students indulged in almost daily.

The house had five bedrooms for each resident and a huge

living room. Bryan, a burly guy from downstairs, had pushed the IKEA sofas against the wall to make room for dancing. While Ali was pulling out dusty cardboard boxes with pumpkin, witch, and hairy spider decorations, Katie was unpacking bags of snacks and counting the pizzas for the night — half a pizza per person. The alcohol selection was left to the boys.

By evening, people had started to arrive. The sober ones came early to help hang up decorative cobwebs. The street was filled with all kinds of creatures: zombies and skeletons, superheroes and villains, wizards and clowns, and even someone's child dressed as a beer bottle.

Jack had also come, and he wasn't alone. Alicia had begged him to bring someone for Katie, for a double date, so he had invited Adam — an intern from his company who wasn't the brightest but was always up for a party.

Soon, the empty pizza boxes overflowed the metal trash can and piled up on the kitchen counters. Someone had carefully removed the olives and, finding no better place, had simply laid them on the sticky table — a fly was already crawling over them. The once-sober guests had almost emptied the alcohol supply and hit the dance floor, while those who came from other parties had lost the ability to stand.

"Babe, that lifeguard costume looks amazing on you," Jack said, hugging her waist as they moved away from the dancing, beer-spilling crowd.

"Thanks," Alicia grinned mischievously. "You haven't even seen the extras that came with it. I left them in the bedroom, I can show you later."

Jack cleared his throat and licked his lips.

"Shall we go take a look?"

"There you are!" Adam appeared behind them, spreading his arms to drape them over both their shoulders. "I've been looking for you guys."

He hiccupped, drowning out Jack's disgruntled grunt.

"Katie and I," he continued, glancing around. "By the way, where is she? Katie, Kaaatie."

Katie appeared out of nowhere, like a genie from a lamp.

"You were looking for me?"

"Yes, there you are," Adam let go of Jack and Ali — her shoulder was already aching — and pulled Katie into a hug. "We've come up with a brilliant idea and we really want to share it with you."

With that, he pulled a small, transparent bag with colorful tabs from his pocket.

The neighborhood kids were already fast asleep when Ali opened her eyes and stared at the ceiling. It was breathing. Like a sleeping animal, its belly slowly rising on each inhale and even more slowly falling on each exhale. The whole ceiling was one giant furry belly.

She opened her eyes again, for real this time. The ceiling was perfectly normal, though the paint was peeling in places. She winced from the pain in her head after the strange stuff from Adam's bag. She hadn't noticed how much time had passed or where her boyfriend had gone. Alicia lay in her bedroom, still dressed as Pamela Anderson from *Baywatch*, trying to piece together the events of the last few hours. Katie crawled on the floor, laughing. Adam rummaging through a box of Halloween masks. Jack…

"Jackie?" she called softly.

Ali sat up and rubbed her eyes. Was her boyfriend still in the house? Or had he already left? Where had he gone?

The door opened.

"Jackie, I was just..." she began but fell silent.

It wasn't her boyfriend standing in the doorway.

Ali gasped and blinked several times to shake off the effect of the drug, but the figure didn't disappear. The person with the pig's head was still standing in the doorway.

The dirty-pink, wrinkled snout moved in time with his breathing. Coarse black hair stuck out unnaturally. A dark brown spot covered the right ear, while the left was a gaping hole — as if someone had bitten off a chunk. The creature snorted.

Ali couldn't take it anymore. She screamed at the top of her lungs before losing consciousness.

By the time Jack heard the scream from the next room, a dazed Adam had already pulled off the realistic mask and was standing there, shifting nervously like a dog that had done something wrong. Jack shoved him aside roughly and knelt by the bed.

"Alicia?"

He took her cold, sweaty hands in his and whispered again: "Ali?"

Jack brushed his hand over a large, damp spot on the bedspread and placed his palm on her forehead. Feverish.

"What did you do?"

Adam didn't immediately realize the question was directed at him. He caught the searing glare of his boss and began mumbling incoherently about a mistake in finding the right room.

"Why did you put that mask on, you idiot?" Jack roared, his voice filling the room.

"What's going on in here?" Albus, another housemate, sleepily poked his head through the doorway. He looked at Ali, then at the slow-witted intern, and his eyes widened. Adam continued to fidget on the spot and even tried to back away but was paralyzed by Jack's burning stare as he called for an ambulance.

***

Her thoughts were interrupted as the wooden door opened.

"Ms. Brooks, good morning. How are you feeling today?" Ms. Dancy asked with a smile. No surprise, she was in the office bright and early. Ali suspected that the therapist might actually live in the building.

"Sorry for arriving early." Alicia stood up from the couch.

"No worries, I'm happy to see you anytime. Come on in."

Alicia sat down on the left side of the soft sofa and crossed her legs, watching as the woman was running her finger over the spines of the hardback books on the shelf labeled "B."

"And here's your personal journal. Would you like tea or coffee?" Ms. Dancy turned around.

"No, thank you. I'm in a rush to get to work. It would be great if we could start and finish early, please."

"Of course, Ms. Brooks. Your wishes are always my priority." The therapist wheeled over a cherry wood table and opened the journal engraved with *A. B.* "So, what would you like to discuss today?"

Alicia wrapped her arms around herself and began telling her about the bush incident, then about the strange vision in the fitting room. As the words spilled out, her story sounded no more serious than the fantasies of an eight-year-old, but the therapist kept a straight face, nodding and taking notes.

By the time the story ended, Alicia felt relieved. It was always like that — just releasing a bit of her worries, sharing a fraction of her problems, made things lighter. Together, they worked through affirmations, engaged in neurographic art, and soon their time was up. Ms. Dancy saw her to the door.

"Thank you for the productive session today, Ms. Brooks. I highly recommend taking a sick day to recover. Mental health should never be sacrificed for work. I'll send the bill to your account — there will be a small surcharge for the out-of-hours consultation. Have a great day."

CHAPTER 5

Ms. Dancy, if asked, would not have approved of her client working right after a session. But no one asked her. Ali, though a regular in therapy, naively enjoyed the immediate effect after the sessions and neglected the required home practices.

The office reception was chaotic. The "coffee girls," as they were called in the inner circle, clucked around the coffee machine, waving their hands at each other and at the red light that had replaced the usual three green ones. They resembled nervous moms who couldn't figure out whose kid was the first to suggest smoking, deciding that the loudest would be right.

Jacqueline, usually occupied with Facebook, was hurriedly typing something on the keyboard of her work computer. Under layers of powder and brown eyeshadow, which by the end of the day migrated from her lids to under her eyes, she greeted clients at the reception desk. She was almost fifty, but she told everyone different numbers. For the women in the office, she was under forty, and for the interns, no older than thirty-five. Though the front desk had a dress code, it seemed to apply only to the coffee girls. Jacqueline didn't bother with a name badge and always wore a deep neckline, proudly declaring she didn't want to hide her "natural assets."

Alicia had only one question: which boss was Jacqueline sleeping with?

Behind her stood a couple of men in blue uniforms. The taller one had "Fixers Chi" written on the brim of his cap — one of the big maintenance companies that serviced office buildings. The men were talking to each other while Jacqueline nodded. They towered over her on either side, and all three were staring at the monitor when Alicia approached.

The woman, whose makeup hadn't moved yet, lifted her head, and her face took on the typical "hello, my dear friend" expression, which was part of her job.

"Oh, Lia, sorry, I'd love to have coffee with you, but we've got a disaster here."

"Hi, Jaque, what happened?" Ali asked, returning the same fake smile. She never liked it when people butchered her name.

"You wouldn't believe it — the power went out last night, and everything's gone haywire. Security systems, internet access points, even the coffee machine — it all needs to be reset, so the boys are here to help us out."

Jacqueline pouted her filler-enhanced lips and turned to the "boys," who were at least twice Alicia's age. The shorter one glanced at the cleavage in front of him but quickly averted his eyes. It was hard to tell if he was embarrassed or just unimpressed with the surgeon's five-hour job.

Ali stifled a laugh.

"Have you seen Cole today?" Jacqueline turned back to her, having sufficiently graced the men with her attention.

"No."

"He looks suspiciously happy. He rushed past without saying hello," she pursed her lips. "And I heard Mr. Wales is visiting the office today."

Alicia's smile faded.

Cole had been background noise to Alicia until the day he decided to undercut her on the project and gain Mr. Wales's favor entirely for himself. LiveSafe had pretty decent principles and mostly treated its employees fairly, but there was one unspoken rule: only one person per team would be promoted at the end of the quarter. If the project, of course, was a success. Otherwise — only one would be fired.

For Alicia, this project was more than just an opportunity for growth. She was racing ahead of her peers, climbing the career ladder while falling in love with what she did. Even a mini-project or a tiny task brought her a fountain of colorful emotions. In tough times, the fountain spewed black and gray, but the darkness always evaporated, leaving behind a rainbow.

The project for Mr. Wales had divided Alicia's career into "before" and "after." When it succeeded (and there was no other option), she would become the youngest lead consultant in the company.

Ms. Dancy had warned her several times about the unhealthy relationship she had with work, advising against total immersion in her career at the expense of her mental health, but Ali had always brushed it off. It was easy for Ms. Dancy to say, with her own psychology business in a fancy downtown office. Alicia, on the other hand, was carving her path from the bottom. Well, almost from the bottom.

Nodding a couple of times out of politeness, Ali confidently headed toward the elevator and didn't even notice when she bumped into Jack.

"Hey, babe, you're already here?" He wrapped his arm around her lower back and kissed her on the cheek.

"Don't do that here, I've told you. Everyone already thinks I'm getting paid because I'm sleeping with you." Ali coldly removed his hand. Her head was pounding harder now. She needed a pill.

Her finger pressed the gleaming button on the wall. The glass elevator, as if waiting for them, opened its doors. Jack wanted to keep talking, but he noticed they weren't alone.

The man inside the elevator was one of the "Fixers Chi" workers. Without greeting them, he stood there, staring at the floor.

"Good morning." Jack stepped into the elevator first, pulling out his sky-blue laminated pass from his jacket pocket.

Almost all levels in the building were tightly secured and wouldn't work without electronic access cards of varying levels, from sand-colored to dark-blue, symbolizing which floors were accessible to the cardholder. Jack was only one promotion away from the top floor.

After the beep, Ali pressed the buttons for nineteen and twenty-third floors. Trouble never comes alone, and this day had already gotten off to a bad start. She wrapped her arms around herself, watching through the crack of the closing elevator doors as the coffee girls swarmed Jacqueline. Well, at least trouble wasn't hers alone.

Glancing sideways at her boyfriend, she noted with dissatisfaction that he had already buried himself in work, rapidly typing out messages. Alicia didn't like it when he showed some affection in front of colleagues, something she had mentioned more than once. Jack naively believed that people came to the office solely to work, despite Ali trying to explain to him that at least a third of the staff had been hired to satisfy the eyes and other body parts. But Jackie acted like he was born yesterday.

"We only have professionals here. We don't have time for office flings and indulgences during work hours," he would shrug, not noticing the torrential rain of envy that poured over Alicia every time they passed through reception.

The elevator was moving *unbelievably* slowly.

In the perfectly polished reflection of the doors, she studied the man in the back of the elevator. His dark blue, heavily patched uniform hung on slumped shoulders. The "boys" from reception smelled of laundry detergent and cologne, but this man hadn't been given a new uniform. His cap looked even worse, crumpled and with gray stains, the inscription barely legible. Around his neck hung a worn-out lanyard with a yellowed access card. The elevator had already passed the first five floors — beyond that, he had no access. Just as a suspicious thought crept into her mind, he lifted his head.

Rage? Anger?

His gray eyes glared at her through the reflection with hatred.

But why? Who are you?

She wanted to say something, to turn around, and even push him, to make him stop drilling a hole in her mind.

The air was thick with the sharp smell of chemicals and

something sickeningly sweet.

The walls of the elevator swayed before her eyes, the floor jolted, and Ali, swaying, leaned against the wall. Her clammy skin left marks on the glass. The elderly janitor would definitely wave her rag in displeasure again.

"Hey, hey, Ali, what's wrong with you?" Jackie's sharp voice broke through the fog in her mind, and the walls of the elevator steadied.

She felt a warm hand on the back of her neck and opened her eyes. She tried to inhale but couldn't at first. Jack stood over her, frowning, pressing the door-open button with his other hand. The screen showed the nineteenth floor.

"Do you need a doctor? Fresh air?"

"It's stuffy..."

He wrapped his arm around her neck — a familiar hold, the way he used to carry drunk friends — and they stepped out of the elevator.

To the right was an internal staircase with a sign nailed to it that read "Fire Exit" and a sofa. Not big enough for a tall man to lie down on, but it was just right for Ali.

Her head was pounding. More than anything, she wanted to silence the throbbing in her temples with Panadol or something stronger, but her office seemed an unreachable goal at the end of a hallway lined with white wooden doors.

Squinting from the pain in her temples, she glanced back over her shoulder.

The man was staring at the floor, but something told her he was smiling.

CHAPTER 6

"Are you sure you're okay?"

Jack hovered over her, one hand resting on the armrest.

"Yes." Ali reached out and touched his cheek — clean-shaven and smelling fresh. "I just needed something sweet to eat. Thanks for looking after me."

Alicia lay half-reclined in the stiff leather chair, her lower back almost sagging toward the floor. She pushed away the rolling table loaded with protein bars, overripe bananas, and a pack of salt-and-vinegar chips — everything Jack had managed to find on the floor. Ali decided not to mention the little incident in the elevator. Her splitting headache, Ms. Dancy, that irritating colleague, and, if she added a geomagnetic storm to the mix — it was a miracle she had made it through the morning.

"I thought you fainted. And I still think you should take the day off."

"No, Jackie, I just dozed off. It's important for me to finish Mr. Wales's project myself, and if Cole takes over...I don't even want to think about it." Ali clenched her fist until her knuckles turned pale. "You know me, I'm deeply invested in my work."

There was no way she could let Cole win. He wasn't getting any victory. Just because he'd been active in the office today didn't mean the battle was won. All she needed was to recover with some sweet tea and a snack. Then, she could find out why the client had shown up unexpectedly.

Ali watched as Jackie recalled Mr. Wales — a hefty man with a thick mustache, always dressed impeccably. Mr. Wales had already built two new developments with their company, working closely with Jack, and now he was aiming for a larger project — a residential complex with private spaces for the tenants. The project was so big that the company had doubled the staff involved.

"Alright," Jack's phone rang. "I've got to head to a meeting, babe. If you feel bad again — I'm always a call away."

Always, unless your phone is busy with work, she thought, but waved him off with a smile.

The office, though small like the others on the floor, was still her private space behind a closed door. The high ceiling made it feel more spacious, but if she added even one more cabinet, there'd be no room to get to the desk. Still, the floor-to-ceiling window let in plenty of daylight, boosting her productivity. Besides the desk, her "quarters" housed a fabric chair, a mobile drawer for personal items, and the leather chair where Alicia now rested.

LiveSafe had toyed with the idea of open spaces a couple of times but always decided against it.

"We don't want to violate your privacy," management had once declared in a company-wide email.

Alicia finally turned on her computer. In the corner of

the screen, work emails started flying in. The latest one was from Mr. Wales. Alicia clicked it open, reading through the thread, and smirked. Cole had invited the client via email and hadn't bothered to copy her in, but fortunately, Mr. Wales had addressed his reply to both of them, along with the attached email thread:

> Hello, Mr. Church and Ms. Brooks,
> I hope you had a good weekend.
> How are things with you?
> Thank you for the invitation to the office.
> I'm happy to meet with you today at 2 p.m.
> See you then, Charles Wales.

Ali raised her fist in a triumphant gesture. She still had at least three hours, but if she skipped lunch, she could get everything done. Cole's little scheme was clear from the email history, and now it was time for her move. A spark lit in her mind, and the idea was ready — she just needed to take it and act.

She grabbed her phone, sent a short message, and launched a program on her computer. When her phone beeped with a new message, Ali didn't even glance at it. She already had more to show at the meeting than her rival had done in a week.

* * *

At 1:50 p.m., Alicia was adding the final strokes to the whiteboard in the meeting room. The space seated up to five people and was equipped with everything needed to encourage clients to spend as much money as possible. A brand-new

Samsung TV was mounted on the wooden wall. A cooler with ice and eco-friendly paper cups stood nearby, and photographs of completed projects and awards — the pride of a dozen employees, both current and former — decorated the walls.

Cole wasn't there yet, but knowing him, he was probably waiting at reception, looking out for Mr. Wales. He lacked the professional skills or brains that Alicia had, so he tried to curry favor any way he could. *Pathetic.*

Ali poured herself some cold water. A green cartoon bunny with a wide grin stared up at her from the cup. It hopped on its hind legs, beneath the words "protect nature." *Even the cups were different*, she chuckled. In the staff kitchen, they used the cheapest, environmentally harmful plastic ones.

The door opened. Two men entered. Even a child could tell who the successful millionaire was and wasn't. Mr. Wales, dressed in an understated Prada suit, had the latest Rolex on his wrist. Cole was his complete opposite. His face was speckled with stubble, like wet sand had been thrown on him. *Red-red, freckled* — the words popped into Ali's mind. His shirt was tucked into gray pants, and underneath it, a white undershirt peeked through. The collar of his shirt was stained from daily wear and even bleach couldn't get it clean anymore.

"Good to see you, Ms. Brooks." The hand with the Rolex extended to meet hers.

"How was the drive? No traffic?" Alicia shook his hand, wearing a polite smile.

Behind the client, Cole gave her a ridiculous bow and smirked. *Idiot.*

"I don't want to waste a minute of your valuable time, Mr.

Wales, so I'd like to share some good news," Cole said as he circled the table, glancing at the blank side of the whiteboard. He spread out a long sheet of paper, facing it toward himself, and continued.

"Your idea for a pool makes sense, but if we build it in the green zone on complex grounds, we risk wasting money if it's not used. The solution is..." he paused dramatically, making Alicia fight the urge to roll her eyes. "A rooftop pool. We can reduce the terrace and electronic barbecue areas to make room for the pool. With a rooftop, we'll kill two birds with one stone — it'll be warmer from the sun than at ground level, and the view will be better, motivating people to use it more often."

Charles Wales sat with his fingers interlaced, nodding approvingly before turning to Alicia. She wondered if he truly didn't notice the competition between them or if he was simply pretending. Either way, it worked to his advantage — two heads were better than one. He should have seen Alicia's potential by now, but being a closet anti-feminist, maybe he wasn't ready to hand the project over to her "delicate" shoulders.

Ali sensed her moment and stood up.

"Good thought, Cole, but I can't fully agree. On the rooftop, people will be exposed to the high UV index that Chicago experiences during summer. And we'd be reducing the rooftop space for something that will sit unused for seven to eight months of the year," she said, theatrically flipping the whiteboard to reveal a cross-section drawing of the building. "But a pool on a dedicated floor won't sit empty. With the opportunities we have to dedicate an entire floor to it, we can also include a children's pool, so adults can feel more comfortable without splashing and noise around them. In winter, the area will be heated, keeping the water at a consistent temperature. And if tenants want to enjoy the view, we can put a jacuzzi on the roof, which will be in demand even on a cool autumn evening."

Charles Wales stood up and slowly approached the whiteboard. In the hastily drawn sketch, the pool was shown just under the roof, with its own quick-access staircase. The jacuzzi wasn't in the drawing — Ali could see him realize she must've just come up with that. *Clever,* she thought she could read in his eyes.

"Good ideas. I'm glad we're moving forward," he said, looking at the two consultants, who were waiting — for praise or for a decision. "Ms. Brooks, please prepare the cost estimate for the pool and update the plans with your changes to the project. I'd like to see it by the end of the week. Mr. Church, I trust you'll assist Ms. Brooks in this."

Cole nodded, drilling holes into Alicia's temple with his stare. She, not bothering to hide her victorious smile, offered her hand for a shake.

She'd beaten him.

CHAPTER 7

"You played me cleverly."

They walked down the corridor after seeing their "ticket to the future" off to the underground parking. Cole unlocked his phone and pulled up a message from Alicia:

```
Pool? Sure :)
```

He showed her the screen, impressed that she had figured it out.

"Next time, make an effort to copy me on the email."

"Don't be mad, you've already won. How about we grab lunch together? We can discuss *your* idea and split the work."

Alicia nodded without hesitation. Working with him, especially on her idea, wasn't something she wanted, but she couldn't ignore Mr. Wales's instructions. Besides, what kind of professional would she be if she couldn't separate her emotions from her work?

"Let's go eat, but I'll choose the place."

"Deal. You know, I've always liked strong women," Cole said, holding the door open for her as they left the office.

The cold wind slapped them in the face.

This March in Chicago could rightfully be called the fourth month of winter. The Cloud Gate was covered in three layers of snow. In a few bald patches, the snowy ground reflected back. Laughing schoolchildren were running down the hill, with a screaming mom behind them, waving hats in her hands.

Cole pulled his hood over his head and pointed across the street. Alicia nodded, exhaling a puff of steam. Usually, they went to The Loop, but today, neither of them felt like braving the weather, so they headed to the nearest place for brunch.

"You can pick the place next time, Brooks. The cold will devour us before we reach a hot meal."

If there's even a next time.

They were seated at a corner table after a short wait. The place was packed, though most of the patrons only had steaming cups of coffee, hiding from the freezing weather outside.

A waitress approached them with paper menus. Her shirt matched the checkered tablecloth, and her name tag read "Anastasia." She wasn't quite a high schooler anymore but was still too young to be working during the busy hours of the semester.

"Terrible weather. Will you be having brunch or something from the mains?"

She placed the menus in front of them.

"Sweetie, we'll have two continental brunches and two glasses of wine," Cole handed her the menus, but instead of dropping his hand, he kept it there, brushing her freckled fingers.

Anastasia flinched, quickly turned, and hurried toward the kitchen. Alicia, watching the little show, snorted.

"A bit of flirting — research shows — raises people's endorphins," Cole said, sprawling comfortably on the bench.

"Maybe it's because they didn't have you in the study."

He laughed again, but Alicia didn't smile.

"Ali, Ali, look at us. You and I, like an old couple in a silver marriage. Why all the negativity when we get things done faster together than anyone else could alone?"

Alicia shrugged — she couldn't argue with that. Their first consulting duo in the company had outperformed productivity metrics and was even vying for the title of Breakthrough of the Year. Competition (not the healthy kind, but who cared) spurred quick solutions to complex problems. If one got sick, the other stepped in. If one didn't answer, the other was already on the phone. Can't come in? Die and get out of the way of those who can. The company was run by strong hands.

Anastasia brought their meals, and without raising her eyes, hurried back into the depths of the restaurant. Cole rubbed his hands together. The smell of hot soup enveloped them the moment the bowls were placed in front of them. They slurped, clinked their spoons, but the topic of the project never left the conversation.

Alicia, poking at the cooled chicken breast with her fork, laid out information about her research into aquatic structures. Cole listened and nodded, mechanically spearing boiled potatoes and sending them into his mouth. When needed, he could be a good boy.

Cole paid the check for both of them and even left a thirty percent tip. Anastasia mumbled her thanks and disappeared into the back. It wasn't the best lunch, but the project progress couldn't help but brighten their spirits. From the idea emerged a shared vision and, perhaps, even a bit of mutual respect. Having sketched out a rough plan in the notebook and assigned the responsibilities, they bundled up against the snow and headed back to the office to transfer the results into the main project draft. Now they were back in the same boat.

* * *

That evening, Alicia took a taxi home — Jack was once again working late in preparation for the quarterly presentation. Although they paid him double for overtime, it was the idea that drove Jack more than the money.

Alicia locked the door from the inside and dropped her beige bag from her shoulder. It hit the floor with a clatter, the corporate laptop inside protesting, but she didn't even look back. She kicked off her boots, which had rubbed her heels raw, and without bothering to line them up by the wall, headed deeper into the house.

She didn't like being lonely at home. *In solitude, not loneliness*, she corrected herself in Ms. Dancy's voice. To avoid waiting by the window for Jack to come home, Alicia had promised to dedicate time to herself: a bubble bath and an anti-aging face mask. Round, with cutouts for the eyes and nose, that smelled like fresh cucumber. Instagram ads hadn't lied — nothing smelled fresher.

As she passed the guest bedroom, Ali jerked her head so hard her neck cracked. A shadow. She slowly shifted her gaze, holding her breath. No one was sitting on the bed. What she'd mistaken for a person turned out to be two gift bags for the successful presentation, kindly purchased by Jack.

Ali rubbed her sore neck and closed the bedroom door. After a brief hesitation, she returned to the front door and checked the handle. Locked. For the third time, she hurried down the corridor, sat on the couch, tucked her legs under her, and sent Jackie a message. Forget the bath...To pass the time until he came home, she reached for the TV remote and gripped it so tightly that blue veins stood out on her skin. The trembling stopped.

Jack arrived when she was already dozing on the couch. She jumped at the sound of the door slamming. Her stiff back protested, and her stomach growled in sympathy. *The Late Late Show With James Corden* greeted them from the TV. Ali turned down the volume and got up from the couch.

"Hey, babe, how are you? Sorry, I wanted to come home earlier, but..." he spread his arms. "But I grabbed some pizza on the way home for dinner, if you haven't cooked anything."

He walked over to the table to set down the cardboard box, which was still steaming. Alicia stood on the other side of the table, arms crossed over her chest.

"You promised to be home earlier," she said, ignoring the wafting smell of bacon and nodding toward the clock on the stove: 10:17 p.m.

"I was waiting for the pizza." Jack smiled softly.

"Three hours?" Her stomach growled again, and Ali swallowed involuntarily.

He didn't respond, only pulled out clean plates from the kitchen cabinet and poured kombucha into the glass cups. He opened the box with "Giordano's" printed on it and served the pizza. Alicia, still standing with her arms crossed, glared at him.

"Let's start dinner, and I'll tell you everything. You'll understand why I was so late today," he said as he pushed the plate toward her.

"Well, convince me."

It turned out his reason for being late was indeed valid, and Alicia instantly hated it.

In celebration of the end of the first quarter, the company was organizing a business trip to Los Angeles. Most of the time, sponsored trips were planned to out-of-town sites, less often to conferences. Jack had already been to New York, Miami, and even Los Angeles already thanks to his clients (Alicia hadn't yet reached the level of business trips, but she always tagged along). This time, Jack was being sent to Los Angeles again, and though the company usually didn't mind employees bringing plus-ones, this time, it was strictly a business-oriented trip. All travel expenses had already been budgeted for the fiscal year, meaning there was no wiggle room for Ali to join. Nothing personal. Strictly business.

The main goal of the trip was to expand the office. Some major clients had long hinted at interstate collaboration in California, and LiveSafe had finally secured sponsors and resolved the last legal issues. The only detail left was which employees would be lucky enough to work in the sunny city. With Jack's excellent reputation, he was at the top of the list.

But no one had asked Alicia, and now she was angrily biting her lip. Move away from friends, family, and the life they knew...for what?

"I know how important it is for you to make that

presentation on time, and I'm ready to help right now."

"What does that mean?"

"We'll have time to prepare, but after your presentation, I'll need to be at the airport."

"Jack, are *you* planning to move?"

He clasped his hands together on the dining table. The cooling slices of pizza in the box didn't look as appetizing anymore. She could see on his face that he had hoped to enjoy dinner in a good mood, saving the heavy conversation for the morning. But he gave in. He liked Chicago, and moving wasn't in his plans, but what stung him the most was her reaction.

"Ali, there isn't even an office yet," he tried to soften the blow, despite the seriousness in her eyes. "It's too early to make any decisions, but I don't want to refuse on the first day —"

"Why are you making decisions for us?"

"I'm not making decisions. I'm exploring opportunities," he said, trying to calm her down.

Alicia twirled a strand of hair around her finger. She had grown up in Chicago and, without any fancy education, was already earning a good living at a young age. The prospects in the city were good, but not the best, and even if she considered Los Angeles for a moment...well, there could be something worthwhile in it. But today, she didn't have the strength to think about it. Ali rubbed her tired eyes and buried her fingers in her hair.

Sensing a moment of weakness, Jack stood up and approached her. Placing both hands on her shoulders — tense like stones — he gently squeezed and began to massage them. Her body began to relax — her shoulders dropped, her back rounded. He leaned in and kissed the top of her head. Inhaled. She knew that pause — like he was memorizing her scent, mixed with the remnants of sweet perfume. Then, another exhale, slower this time. His breath skimmed her skin before his lips found her neck.

She let out a soft moan. His stubble was a little prickly. Slowly, his dry lips touched every inch of her neck. Warmth spread through her body. Ali tilted her head toward him and kissed him straight on the lips.

James Corden, now silent, was already saying goodbye to his audience when the sounds from the bedroom finally quieted.

CHAPTER 8

She was walking down the office corridor that seemed to stretch endlessly. The giant, empty walls pressed the space in, like squeezing a balloon. Something dark stirred at the far end of the corridor. And Alicia could feel it. Quickening her pace, she began swinging her arms harder, breaking into a run — away from it. But her feet barely moved. Running in place. Useless. The desired door — the only exit — kept moving farther and farther away. The walls were nearly closing in, and the darkness was almost upon her when Alicia felt a sharp kick in her knee. The door began to dissolve along with the corridor, and a moment later, Ali was lying in bed. Her knee ached, and the one who had kicked her was still asleep. Frustrated that Jack had ruined her chance to open the door, she yanked the blankets onto herself and turned away.

But she couldn't fall back asleep. The morning sun was already peeking into the bedroom through the gap in the floor-length curtains. Forty minutes remained until the alarm. Biting her lower lip, she got out of bed with no intention of covering her still-sleeping boyfriend. She slipped on her terrycloth slippers with the massaging insoles and tiptoed into the bathroom. Yawning widely, Ali peeled off her pajamas and underwear and stepped into the shower.

Hot water cascaded from her head to her feet, waking her up as effectively as cold water would — exactly what she needed for a productive start to the day. Shivering from the sudden goosebumps, she remembered what day it was. The first quarterly presentation. After an intense week of preparation, the day had finally arrived. She gave herself two light slaps on the cheeks. The panic washed away with the soapy water down the drain, replaced by a fresh sense of focus. If she concentrated solely on the presentation, everything else would be shoved onto the deepest shelves of her mental closet.

The alarm went off in the bedroom just as Alicia was finishing her makeup. Smokey gray shadows gave way to sharp eyeliner, and her bitten lips were hidden under scarlet lipstick. Her golden hair, gathered into a bun, revealed striking white-gold drop earrings. Winking at her reflection, Alicia, feeling upbeat, headed purposefully toward the kitchen.

She turned on the TV, which silently played a morning cooking show. People in aprons bustled about, flipping pancakes and generously dusting them with powdered sugar. As if that amount of sweetness wasn't enough for the day, they drenched everything in maple syrup.

Jack came downstairs, still in his pajamas, but with his hair styled and freshly shaved. The morning paper was already lying at the front door. He continued to pay for delivery out of habit, remembering how his father had resisted online news until the very end and always started his morning in the yard with a cup of overly sweet cheap coffee. Jack gently picked up the unopened newspaper and headed to the kitchen.

"Good morning. You look stunning," he said as he kissed her on the lips.

Alicia smiled. "I'm making bacon and omelets for breakfast, and the coffee is ready."

"Tomorrow afternoon, I'm heading to the airport, and about the move..."

"I think we should put off that conversation until you return," Alicia interrupted, pouring coffee from the French press.

Behind her, the bacon was sizzling and popping on the stove.

"Maybe, but I don't like to leave things unsaid. But you're right, there's no rush. The deal could fall through." He wrapped his arms around Alicia, but she caught something in his eyes — like he was more worried about the company than about her.

They stood in silence for a while, broken only by the crackling oil. Jack took the wooden spatula from her hand.

"You smell too good. You don't need the scent of bacon clinging to your skin."

After breakfast, they loaded the dirty plates into the dishwasher and got into the car. The office was just a short drive away — eight miles — but the entire city was at a standstill. Even the newly-built wide roads didn't help the rush hour gridlock.

Alicia scanned her notes and slides on the tablet, mentally repeating the three- and four-digit numbers. From time to time, she asked Jack questions. In his position, he didn't need to present projects or report on every stage, but having gone through it all before, his advice was invaluable.

"Shall we stop for coffee on the way?" Jack asked.

"Hmm?"

"Let's stop at a café on the way," he repeated.

"No, no, we haven't arrived yet," she said, lifting her head but keeping her eyes glued to the printed words on the papers. "We can't be late."

"Come on, we still have nearly an hour."

"Jack, no! If I'm even a little late, Cole will take over the whole presentation, and then my promotion will be down the drain," she snapped, her lower lip showing faint bite marks.

Jack nodded silently. Alicia knew her unhealthy competition with Cole had earned his respect, though he had once mentioned that Mr. Wales had pushed things too far. Of all the managers, Jack had been the only one to oppose having two equal consultants working on the project. When his request was declined, he was politely asked not to interfere in other people's projects for personal reasons. For Alicia, that hint had been enough.

Despite Alicia's pessimism, they arrived with half an hour to spare. As they approached the parking lot, she quickly darted to the main entrance while Jack went to find a free spot. The parking lot was packed like sardines, and he had to go down to level minus three to squeeze in his Mercedes. After turning off the engine, he headed to the conference room.

Alicia stood among the other presenters, already radiating confidence. There were eight of them in total, each showing their nerves in different ways: a tall guy gnawed his nails, a plump girl twirled a finger through her red curls, Cole jiggled his bent leg with the rhythm of someone pumping an old sewing machine. Most of the executives had already gathered around the large round table. The coffee girls, having finished their morning tasks, huddled in the corner, giggling quietly. When Jack entered, the four of them fell silent for a moment, then started whispering excitedly, but he didn't glance their way. Ali's face revealed no signs of anxiety. Her posture was straight, and her smile was calm, though holding it all together wasn't easy. She met Jack's gaze for a moment, then purposefully looked down.

She was ready.

***

Alicia and her friends entered the dimly lit room. On a small stage stood a girl with a pathetic imitation of gemstones and makeup far too heavy for her age. Her nearly exposed chest threatened to spill out of the sheer, sequined dress toward every passerby. She gripped the microphone stand and tilted it slightly, like she'd seen in jazz movies, singing "Strange Fruit" in a thin voice. A song that had nearly driven its original singer to the grave. The young wannabe compared herself to Billie Holiday, ignoring the silent question lingering among the guests — how a Berklee graduate, from one of the best music colleges, had sunk to performing in a dive bar for hungry, drunk men.

The group headed for the only long table that seated eight. The place wasn't exactly popular, so it was no surprise they were lucky enough to find a spot for a large group on a Friday night in the city center. Alicia squeezed herself deep into the sofa as the others shuffled closer. Someone put their elbows on the table, only to pull them back immediately — the sticky, beer-soaked surface hadn't been wiped since the last guests left.

"Hey, miss," Jack raised a finger, but the waitress didn't hear him over the wailing of the wannabe jazz star. "Hey, excuse me, miss."

She continued looking at her phone, her back to the security camera in the ceiling corner.

"I'll go get her," Cole said, slid out from the table and headed for the bar.

Alicia, seizing the moment, turned to her boyfriend, but didn't get a chance to speak.

"Not inviting him would've been rude, babe," Jackie said, shaking his head.

"Who cares if it's rude or not when he shouldn't be here in the first place," Katie interjected. As Alicia's best friend, she didn't even need an invitation — she just showed up. And tonight, there was a reason.

"Here's to the promotion." Jack raised his chilled glass half an hour later. "On behalf of the company and the board of directors, I congratulate Alicia and Cole on their historic dual promotion!"

"Hip hip, hooray!"

Glasses clinked in a joyful search for their fellow glass friends. Alicia let out a quiet sigh. You'd think it was a moment to celebrate, to be happy. But it was hard to enjoy green grass when her neighbor's grass was greener. Even with her promotion to project manager, she felt just as lousy as she had that morning when she was still a consultant. Cole had done well enough, but he was nowhere near Alicia's level, and his promotion only devalued her own. It felt like kindergarten, where Santa gives

presents to good kids, bad kids, and even the average ones —
and there's no coal in sight. Everyone gets the same gifts.

The sweet taste of victory faded from her lips.

CHAPTER 9

Spring in Chicago was capricious. By day, it embraced you with sunbeams carrying the scent of cherry blossoms. By night, it bared sharp little teeth, refusing to release you from its icy grip. After the warmth came fierce, cold rains — sometimes with snow.

On that Saturday morning, the couple on Perry Avenue didn't want to get out of bed. They turned away from each other, pretending to sleep, both lost in their thoughts. The conversation about moving had been put on mute until after the work trip, which was set to begin with a Delta flight that afternoon.

The bed creaked as Jack got up. Alicia squeezed her eyes shut tighter and pulled the down comforter up to her chin, as if that would help her steal a few more minutes of sleep. Jack, trying not to wake her, quickly left the room, unaware of how her eyelashes fluttered and how uneven her breathing was.

She heard him go downstairs, followed by the sound of water flowing through the pipes. Alicia cracked her eyes open, adjusting to the sunlight flooding the bedroom. Her favorite time of day was always the morning. Despite the early wakeups, morning always did its job — it arrived. The dark, hidden night slipped away with the dawn, and morning followed close behind: sometimes sunny, sometimes rainy; bright or gray; filled with the shrieks of schoolchildren or the songs of crimson parrots.

As much as Alicia tried to enjoy her weekends, the thought of Jack's seven-day, six-night work trip wouldn't leave her mind. To avoid spiraling into an extended panic attack, she'd invited Katie over. Her friend had immediately agreed, not so much for Alicia's mental health as for the chance to hang out and eat well. But Katie didn't understand her the way Jack did. She joked sarcastically about the uselessness of therapists and the "quirks they make up for money," but she was the only option Alicia had to stay with her for so long.

There was no point in staying in bed any longer when the smell of frying hash browns wafted up the stairs and knocked on the bedroom door. Slipping into her slippers and robe, Alicia followed the scent.

In the middle of the dining table was a bag. A paper, eco-friendly bag, made from eighty-four percent recycled materials and only two percent trees — a Gucci bag.

"Good morning, darling," Jack said as he turned away from the stove, the oil in the frying pan sizzling behind him. "That's a gift from me. Congratulations on your promotion!"

Alicia reached into the bag and felt something soft and velvety. She grasped it with her fingertips and pulled it out. A flash of red satin appeared from the bag. She stood up straight and held the fabric in front of her. A long, red dress.

"Wow!"

It was *the* evening dress, a design Coco Chanel herself had come up with! Released this year! It had been shining in every targeted ad, but sales were still closed to the general public. Only for a select few.

Jack smiled.

"Try it on before breakfast? It should fit you perfectly."

"Thank you, thank you, thank you!" she squealed, running off to change.

Jack chuckled contentedly. He had told her the gift was the least he could do before his long absence, especially when the reason for the trip was so significant. He'd noticed how upset she was about the double promotion, so even before the celebration at the bar, he had used his connections to order the dress for her. It had arrived early in the morning, left on the doorstep with the newspaper, like a regular Amazon delivery.

"Jackie?"

He turned at the sound of her voice, a silent question frozen on his lips. His eyes flickered over the endless array of sparks. Alicia, in that red dress, radiated pure sex appeal.

The neckline playfully hugged her full chest. The fabric was stretched so tightly that Jack couldn't have pulled it away with his fingers to check if she was wearing a bra.

Her bare shoulders accentuated her slender neck, which lacked a gold chain, a gemstone necklace, or even the marks left by rough kisses from impatient teenagers that had once ringed her neck, years ago.

Without a single wrinkle at her waist, the dress flared into a long floor-length skirt. Alicia stepped forward, and the skirt parted, revealing a smooth, toned leg perched on a small heel.

She lowered her eyes mischievously and turned to the side, accentuating her hips wrapped in fabric.

She placed her hand on her waist. The tips of her fingers ran downward, signaling that there was no underwear beneath.

***

After breakfast, which consisted of instant oatmeal with chocolate-like chunks (the hash browns had burned in the pan and had to be thrown out), Jack went to pack his suitcase, leaving Alicia alone at the wooden table with her phone. The oversized men's T-shirt hung loosely on her bare body, covering her hips like a grandmother's nightgown. The dress, neatly folded over the back of the kitchen chair, the Gucci bag beside the coffee cup, and heart-shaped chocolates in glossy wrappers — it was an aesthetic she wanted to capture under an Instagram filter.

The neighbor's dogs started barking when the car pulled up to the house. Jack and Alicia held each other tightly. They stood in silence, listening to each other's breathing, accompanied by the faint beeping of the phone, which was diligently counting every second of the taxi's idle time.

"Well, it's time for me to go, darling."

"Good luck."

Jack grabbed his suitcase and opened the door.

"Hey, taxi?"

The short driver stepped outside and waved. He hurried over to the front door to grab Jack's luggage.

"Heading to the airport?" He smiled, revealing his crooked,

double-rowed teeth.

Jack nodded. With the hand that wasn't holding the phone, he took Alicia by the chin and kissed her lightly on the forehead, as if checking her temperature. Meanwhile, the phone gave a sharp notification — double the fare for waiting more than five minutes. The driver's smile widened, and his mouth began to resemble a chessboard.

"I'll text you when the plane lands."

The driver placed the suitcase in the trunk. Two men, one tall with perfect teeth, and one short, who couldn't afford good dental insurance, drove off in the same car. America — the land of opportunities for everyone, as long as everyone looks out for themselves.

***

One episode bled into the next, and the next, and if it hadn't been for the phone call, Ali would have continued living on Netflix. She reluctantly hit pause.

"I'm on my way out," Katie cheerfully announced.

"Pick up some wine on the way, please."

"Um, yeah, I —"

"I'll transfer the money now."

"Okay!" her friend's voice turned cheerful again.

Alicia leaned back against the headboard. The days when friends pooled their money for the cheapest bottle of wine and discount cheese were long gone. LiveSafe paid Jack well, and Ali could spend her entire salary on herself. The same couldn't be said for Katie, whose expenses — after taxes and her mother's care home — crammed in alongside spending on her personal brand and alcohol. Thoughts turned sour, and Ali sneezed twice. She sent a bit more money than needed, rewound the show a little, and turned off the TV. There was enough time to take a shower and tend to her recently appearing wrinkles.

Ali stepped into the shower and pulled the door closed. After a brief resistance, it shut — the landlord had promised to fix the door "within the contractually required minimum repair timeframe" — anywhere from one to six months. She turned the faucet to hot and dipped her foot under the water. Cold water slowly drained away, forming tiny coin-sized puddles in the uneven floor. Once it was warm, she jumped under the spray. Swaying her hips like in a Latin film, Alicia began singing — well, half-singing, half-yelling — her favorite song, "Roar."

Water poured over her stomach and legs, running away with her monthly utility bill. After another RO-AR, in the pause between lyrics, she caught the sound of floorboards creaking twice. *Where did that sound come from?* She silently turned off the water with one hand, straining to listen. Somewhere, water continued trickling through the pipes, droplets falling from her wet hair and splattering onto the floor. The bathroom door was locked, as always when she was home alone. *Nothing suspicious,* she reassured herself.

A few minutes later, she was lathering her hair with the water off and without any singing. The urge to dance along to Katy Perry was gone. The noise returned when she turned the water back on. Ali stretched tall, like a Royal Guard on duty. She could hear the creak of the floor, but now prolonged, as if an uninvited guest was confidently moving further. *Just the wind blowing across the floor.*

But her mind had already leaped over the small stream of self-assurance, and her hands switched off the water on their own. She wrapped a towel around her still-soapy hair like a turban and covered herself with its larger counterpart. Her wet feet slipped into slippers, picking up the lint inside them as she quietly stepped out of the bathroom.

The first floor was empty and still. The windows were open, the curtains fluttering in the breeze like monarch butterfly wings. *Just the wind,* Ali thought, when a rustling noise came from outside the front door. She jumped, strands of hair escaping the towel and chilling her back as they dripped down. The doorbell rang.

"Wh-who's there?" Alicia's voice was weak.

The doorbell rang again.

"Wh-who's there?" she asked, louder.

"Wine delivery, geez."

Ali exhaled, dropping her tense shoulders, and opened the door.

"Wow, why are you answering the door soaking wet in a towel?" Katie squeezed past her startled friend into the doorway.

"I was in the shower."

"Well, next time, don't lock the door before your bath when you're expecting me. No one's going to break in during the middle of the day. Now go and put some clothes on, I'll open the wine."

Chapter 10

Alicia placed the fourth bottle of wine on the small round table.

"Pour it," she said playfully and sat on the carpet, crossing her legs.

Katie grabbed the bottle with both hands. Red wine flowed into the glasses like a river, filling them to the faded line left from the last drink. Katie tried to place the bottle back on the cork coaster from IKEA, but she missed. The Australian fruit-berry Shiraz hovered in the air for a moment before toppling over, spilling directly onto Alicia.

"Shit."

The white tank top quickly turned into a large pink stain. Alicia spread her hands in a futile attempt to catch the spill, but the cold liquid slipped through her fingers like a sieve. The wine continued to drip, resembling a weak hose spray, until almost the entire bottle had soaked into her worn jeans and the wool rug beneath her. Alicia blinked, looking around through her hazy, wine-induced gaze, while her sticky hands slowly caught up with the scene. She found the bottle, tilted her head back, and pressed her lips to the neck, drinking deeply — until she choked. Katie jumped up to pat her back, but Alicia stopped her with a wave of her hand. She coughed, tossed the bottle aside, and wiped the wine from her mouth with the back of her hand.

"The rug," Katie sighed, sadly.

"Screw it, we'll just buy a new one. Jack's loaded."

Katie's eyes widened, but when her tipsy brain caught up, she let out a nervous giggle that quickly escalated into a full-on laugh. Within seconds, both of them were sprawled on the floor, laughing hysterically.

"It's not going to wash out," Alicia said, pulling off her stained tank top and tossing it toward the trash bin.

"You got a new bra? It's nice," Katie remarked.

"Jackie bought it from La Perla's latest collection."

Katie gave a thin smile.

"You two doing okay?"

"No complaints." Alicia wasn't ready to bring up the move. "What about you? When are you going to find someone more serious than just a one-night stand?"

"Who says I need more than one night?"

They both burst into laughter again.

"Any more wine?" Katie asked, scanning the kitchen hungrily.

"Nope."

"Beer?"

"None."

"What about that whiskey left over?"

Alicia shrugged. Most of the alcohol in their house was for parties, and it had been nearly a month since the last. The whiskey had already been used up for Irish coffee.

"Oh well, let's just watch a movie then," Katie suggested. "There's a new thriller with some horror elements."

"Katie, I'm not supposed to watch scary stuff, you know that."

"Yeah, yeah, your therapist doesn't want you living your life to the fullest. But it's just a thriller with horror *elements*, not an actual horror *movie*," Katie said.

"I don't want to," Alicia replied firmly.

A crow's caw echoed from outside, immediately answered by the neighbor's dogs. The room grew stuffier, the smell of spilled wine spreading throughout. Alicia cracked open the terrace door to let in some air, carefully locking the insect screen. An unwanted thought crossed her mind, wondering how easily someone could slice through the screen with a knife.

A cracked-screen iPhone beeped and lit up. The lock screen displayed a full-length photo of Katie holding a bouquet of pink tulips. A notification about a new Tinder match covered her face, courtesy of the app's algorithm.

"Mmm, let's see who we've got here." Katie called Alicia over and unlocked her phone. With a satisfied smirk, she tapped the notification. Alicia, slightly swaying, sat down next to her and rested her head on Katie's shoulder.

Tinder profiles of guys flashed across the screen as Katie swiped through them rapidly: Andrew, a bearded freelancer with a shaggy dog; Joe, a programmer with his laptop in an Instagrammable coffee shop; an unemployed Felix in a messy bathroom mirror; and Alex, a delivery guy wearing a ushanka in the snow.

Most of the profiles were swiped left, rejected, until one

caught Ali's attention.

"Wait, was that a girl?" Alicia asked in surprise.

"Yeah…but I'm mostly looking for someone to hang out with at a bar." Katie licked her dry lips. "You know, people often find friends — even best friends — on Tinder."

"Why would you need best friends when you've got me?" Alicia teased, her voice slurring as she leaned in close to Katie's ear.

Katie's shoulders rose with a deep breath, but Alicia didn't notice.

"I'll limit the search to within one mile. Let's see who lives around here."

Alicia's eyelids started to droop from the endless parade of faces on the screen, but she tried to focus on the names: James, Ben, Nancy, Mike…

The sound of the doorbell — a single, drawn-out note — reached the living room.

"Who's that?" Alicia whispered, her eyes flying open. Her neck ached from the awkward angle in which she had been dozing.

Katie didn't answer, her fingers flying across the screen.

"Did you order something?" Alicia asked quietly, standing up on shaky legs.

"Mmm?"

Alicia bit down on her knuckles, shifting nervously from foot to foot. Who could be ringing the bell at this hour? Who would know that two drunk girls were alone in a big house? Just like the horror movies Ms. Dancy strictly forbade her from watching. *They mess with your mind, Ms. Brooks. They make you even more afraid. They keep you from living your real life.*

"I'll check," Alicia murmured.

She took off her slippers to avoid creaking the floorboards and tiptoed to the front door. *Not a big deal to check by myself. I can handle it.* Wasn't this the kind of progress her therapist always talked about — the kind she could brag about at her next session?

Behind the frosted glass pane, there was indeed a shadow. An unexpected guest. Tall, probably a man. *Not likely a burglar.*

"Ali..." Katie called softly.

"Shh!" Alicia pressed her finger to her lips. The last trace of alcohol disappeared from her system.

When the bell rang again, she reached for the lock and turned it to the left. Locked. Stretching her hand toward the chain, a remnant from the previous Peruvian tenants, she slid the loop onto the latch. Jack had never seen the point in installing an alarm, but when he came back, she'd bring it up again. No, she'd insist. After all, it was her house too.

The floor creaked behind her. Katie stood up from the couch and shuffled toward the door. Alicia frantically waved her hands, but Katie just twirled her finger at her temple.

"What are you doing?" she asked, irritated.

"We don't know who it is," Alicia whispered back.

Katie furrowed her brow and pressed her hand to the frosted window, wiping it clean with her palm. Alicia grabbed her shoulders, trying to pull her back from the door, but Katie's hands were already on the lock. A click, and the lock turned right. A clang, and the chain slipped off the latch. A creak, and the front door opened.

"Katie, right?" came a male voice from outside. "I'm Matthew."

Alicia peeked out from behind her friend, wearing only a bra on top. The guy wore a warm jacket with the sleeves rolled up. He held a bag from a liquor store. Not an athlete, but he looked like he could take them both. He reeked of freshly smoked weed.

"I'm sorry, we need to talk," Alicia said with a forced smile before quickly slamming the door in his face. She locked it and reattached the chain before turning back to Katie.

"What the hell are you doing?" Katie yelled.

"Who was that?" Alicia hissed.

"That was Matthew," Katie replied uncertainly.

"Who the hell is Matthew, and how does he know my address?"

"He's a match from Tinder. We were chatting, and he asked for the address to come hang out."

"A stranger?"

"Matthew."

"Are you crazy, giving my address to strangers?"

"Seems like I came at a bad time," came Matthew's muffled voice from outside. "I don't want any trouble, I'll just go."

There was the sound of a rustling bag and retreating footsteps.

"You're an idiot, Alicia," Katie yelled. "I invited some guys over to dance, have fun, and what do you do? You chased Matthew away, and now he'll never text me again. And he even had weed with him."

"Guys? You invited more people?" Alicia asked quietly.

"Maybe!"

"So, I invited you over to relax, to not be alone in this big house, and you just give my address...to random creeps?" Alicia grimaced.

Katie scoffed. "I thought you invited me over to hang out with *the* best friend, not babysit you," she snapped, poking Alicia hard in the chest. "Next time, post a job opening on Facebook."

"Chicago's not a safe city."

"YOU'RE ALMOST THIRTY, ALICIA!" Katie screamed.

Katie stood there, panting, her face flushed wine-red, beads of sweat forming under her nose. Alicia wrapped her arms around herself and bit her bottom lip. She hadn't had time to put on a clean shirt and was now shivering in just her bra as the cold, gnawing wave of dread washed over her. The alcohol was gone, taking with it any trace of laughter, leaving behind the slow-burning fuse of a hangover that would explode into a splitting headache if she didn't get to bed soon.

Alicia glanced around at the pink stain on the beige carpet, the empty bottle on the floor, and the dark staircase.

"Fine, fine," she muttered. "Let's just leave this for a sober conversation. Please stay the night. I've already made up the guest room for you. Don't leave. Please."

"I can't stay here with you any longer."

Alicia said nothing, hugging herself tighter, trying to stop the tears welling up in her eyes.

"You're crazy. You need help," Katie spat, seeing the scared little girl in front of her, nothing like the fierce woman from work. A poisonous smile crept across her lips. "I'm not staying. I'll see you at the office the day after tomorrow."

"Katie, please."

"Goodbye, Alicia."

Katie threw on her thin jacket and yanked the zipper up, but it caught and slipped out of the teeth again — she'd had it repaired twice just that month. She cursed and shoved the broken zipper into her bag. The lock clicked, the chain rattled, and the cold Chicago air hit her as she flung open the door.

Alicia watched Katie's retreating heels. The lock clicked, the chain rattled, and she slid down the wall to the floor and sobbed.

CHAPTER 11

She hadn't had such an awful night in a long time.

After downing (she couldn't remember how many) bottles of wine and the tearful meltdown near the front door, her face was swollen and looked like a puffy balloon. Clear snot still dripped from her nose as she finally crawled into bed. Every single light in the house was on, greedily adding to the three-digit number on the monthly electricity bill. The blinding brightness defined the loneliness. If anything could hide in the dark, full illumination guaranteed the opposite — no one was there to help.

Alicia lay in the middle of the bed, facing the door. Her left side was already aching, begging for relief, but to no avail — she wasn't about to let the bedroom entrance out of sight. She sat up, punched her feather pillow into shape with her fist, and lay back down again. It had been over an hour since Katie left; she was probably home by now. Her online status blinked with a blue light, but Alicia's messages remained unread.

From time to time, the dogs outside exchanged barks, but by three in the morning, they had fallen silent. Alicia compromised with her aching side — she didn't risk turning her back on the door, but she managed to switch positions, placing her pillow at the foot of the bed and her feet at the headboard. A couple of times, she managed to doze off for five minutes, maybe more, but the bright lamp on its three wooden legs repeatedly yanked her out of sleep. Turning it off wasn't an option — it would be even worse than lying with her back to the door.

Once, she went to the bathroom. She had a familiar routine for that: grab the phone (always grab the phone) and rush to the bathroom. Listen. Of course, close the door. Do your business. Listen. Flush. Wait for the tank to refill. Listen. Dash back to bed.

By four in the morning, she had already identified the "template" of each episode in the new Netflix legal drama — an intriguing start, the same ridiculous middle with a "shocking" twist, and a happy ending. The writers were as short on ideas as the set designers. She apathetically fast-forwarded through half the episode while her brain stubbornly erased the previous plotline from memory. Instead, unwanted thoughts began creeping in with small but certain steps. The creak of the bed — the first step. The shadow of the robe on the chair — the second. Her own reflection in the full-length mirror — and now fear stood tall, waving a hand. *Did you miss me, Alicia?*

She jolted awake, not recognizing the actors on screen. Had she dozed off again, or did she not notice the start of another episode? She glanced at her phone — less than an hour until dawn. And then five more nights. Could anything be worse?

Falling asleep with the first rays of light, she slept until afternoon. With the sunlight, her self-assurance returned, like a school friend — the kind who shows up after a couple of decades to ask for money. Without getting out of bed, she grabbed her phone. Several unread messages from Jack — photos of the luxury hotel he'd been put up in, and the night-time skyline of Los Angeles. Nothing from Katie.

Alicia snorted and tossed the phone. With sleep came another friend: pride — that old companion from university days. Never be the first to write. When Katie felt like going out on someone else's tab, she'd come around. And then Alicia would let her have it. They usually avoided the financial gap between them, but in very rare cases, Alicia could trip her friend up just enough to make Katie ask for help herself.

Her head was pounding, and a wave of nausea was creeping in. Groaning, Alicia slid off the bed, slipped on her fluffy slippers, now stuck together from the spilled wine, and began switching off the lamps around the house. The living room reeked of stale alcohol. The rug stared back at her with its sad, pink stain. She didn't feel like cleaning. She didn't want to be home. She wanted to leave it all behind.

Decision made. Time to go shopping.

An hour later, Alicia walked into the corner café on the ground floor of the shopping center. She didn't have the stomach for a proper breakfast, so she settled for a warm ham croissant and a soy latte. Sitting at a small table, she twirled the metal number eight stand between her fingers.

The central plaza was swarming with screaming kids, all hungry around lunchtime. A boy, not yet old enough for school, lay sprawled on the tiled floor, wailing. His mother circled around him, clapping her hands like a wind-up monkey:

"That bike is expensive, sweetheart. Let's buy it next month, sweetheart. Have a donut, sweetheart."

Alicia pressed the cold water glass against her flushed cheeks. Whenever people said children were the flowers of life, all she could think of was the Venus flytrap she saw during a school trip to the botanical gardens. A bloody, prickly trap.

When her order arrived, the little boy had moved from the floor to a chair, clutching a glazed donut. His chubby cheeks were dusted with powdered sugar. He had stopped crying but now chomped loudly and swung his leg. His little sneaker kept tapping the table leg, each thud sending a stab of pain through Alicia's temples. Thud-thud. Thud.

She threw the croissant onto her plate so hard that the ham flew out of the pastry and landed on the floor. The kid stopped kicking and looked up from his donut, wide-eyed. His mother seized the moment, quickly grabbing a napkin to wipe the powdered sugar off his glazed face.

Alicia stood up abruptly. She placed her half-finished coffee down and walked out, leaving the slice of ham behind on the floor.

***

Black boots, white shoes. Boxes floated before her like prizes on a wheel of fortune. Pinching her heel. Tight in the toe. Too long. Too narrow.

She had been sitting on the bench for over an hour and couldn't find the right pair. Even though several models fit her well, her mood was foul. And with a mood like that, no shoe felt right. She was lying to herself, but with each notification, her hands would automatically reach for her phone. Katie wasn't online anywhere — not on any of the three social networks. Her avatar hadn't even appeared as a viewer of Alicia's coffee story. Where could she be on a weekend?

Finally, more out of pity for the salespeople than joy for the boots, Alicia left the store, clutching a large fabric bag with a shoebox inside. The crowd thinned, as families with bulky, colorful shopping bags were heading toward the parking lot. She noticed a seasonal sports store ad — a tall, polished athlete with an airbrushed face tossing tennis balls to kids, and for the first time that day, she laughed. Her imagination painted a different picture — a small, dirty pig under croissant-shaped clouds, catching falling ham.

Her stomach didn't let her laugh for long. Alicia froze for a moment as a hunger cramp hit. When it passed, she hurried down the escalator to the underground level, searching for a healthy lunch. Surrounding the tables like defensive walls were McDonald's, Burger King, KFC. No chicken soup in sight. The food court smelled of fried chicken and wet rags. French fries were scattered like wedding rice. A girl in a blue vest, with empty, darting eyes, swept the floor. She swiped her brush quickly, unaware that a tangle of black, knotted hair had flown out of the dustpan, landing on a table, carried by the gust from her sweeping...Alicia bolted for fresh air, pressed her hands to her mouth, ignoring her growling stomach.

Never again to the food court level. Slowly, her eyes darted over the signs outside the shopping center, looking for a proper meal. The bars weren't open yet, and the cafés had already closed. She pulled out her phone to ask Google for advice, but her fingers instinctively checked Katie's status. Still offline. Alicia sighed, locked the phone, and immediately unlocked it again. She opened Google Maps. Just about a thousand feet away was an orange marker with a fork and knife — *Yuzu*, an authentic sushi bar. Plenty of reviews, an overall rating of over four stars.

Google didn't lie, and she reached it in six minutes. Thanks to the wall of panoramic windows, the room was bathed in daylight, and round mirrors the size of small plates hung from the ceiling. It felt as though the light was passing right through them. Inside, it was even brighter than outside.

There was no counter with an authoritative Japanese chef wearing a cotton headband. No traditional noren curtains hanging over the doorways or windows. No one shouted "Irasshaimase" and bowed as she entered. No promised authenticity.

Like an equator, a thin, gray carpet split the enormous hall in two, as if designed by architects from two different decades. People dined on both sides.

To the left, it smelled of wood. Hexagonal tiles hung from the ceiling like honeycombs, stopping abruptly at the carpet's border. The parquet floor was scuffed from the dragging of rattan chairs. Booths with high backs matched the floor, with cushions glued in place. Clean windows looked out onto the street, with single wooden benches facing out — each one equipped with a suctioned phone holder on the glass. Black table legs disrupted the two-tone balance like misplaced orphans.

The tables were the only thing shared by both sides. Alicia squinted and looked closer. On the right side of the "equator," what looked like an unfinished renovation turned out to be a loft. Everywhere there was concrete — above, beside, below. Cement blocks, from which live flowers sprouted, separated the long tables. A monstera, as tall as Jack's beanstalk, grew right out of a monolithic white block by the wall. The ceiling was a vast expanse of white, as if painted by an astronaut in space, where gravity didn't apply.

Alicia stood on the carpet, feeling like she was waiting at customs. A hostess in a lavender blazer hurried over. The woman, with spider-leg lashes and lips plumped by hyaluronic acid, smiled, her mouth a taut bow, and asked in a strong Slavic accent:

"Hello. You have table reserved?"

"No. Is this all the same restaurant?"

"Of course, this is very popular now, don't you know?" the woman's eyes mocked. "Table for two?"

"For one," Alicia said quietly.

"Please follow me."

With hips as large as two watermelons, the hostess led Alicia to the "living" side, to the benches by the window. A spot for loners. Alicia's hand reached for her phone, but she pulled back quickly. Food first, jealousy later.

For dessert, she ordered a raspberry cheesecake on a ginger cookie crust — it tasted like Christmas. Delicious, but it could be even better. Phone. Instagram. Tulip filter, spring vibes, tagged Yuzu sushi bar, and a tiny selfie. In the photo, a happy girl with faint circles under her eyes licked a spoon coated in pink cream. *See how happy I am without you, Katie?*

Before paying the bill, Alicia couldn't resist checking again.

Still offline.

CHAPTER 12

By the evening, Perry Avenue had become crowded. Neighbor Holly was walking her shaggy shepherd dog, muzzled for the outing. The dog barked when the elderly Harris couple stepped outside to put their outdoor lounge chairs back into the garage.

"Shh, quiet, I said," Holly said, tugging at the leash.

"It's fine," Mrs. Harris said, waving at the growling dog.

Old Bill was jogging by, having recovered from a heart attack in the fall. His hair had gone gray at forty, earning him his nickname back then. Wired headphones protruded from his ears, along with tufts of white hair, attached to a chest-worn player; the last person on the street who hadn't discovered AirPods.

Occasionally, someone would pause for a moment to glance at the two-story brick house, where light spilled from every window, tiny bulbs from outdoor string lights twinkled, and the television's voice tried to out-shout Holly's dog. It seemed like a big family had gathered for a celebratory barbecue, but the young woman, wrapped in a false sense of safety, dined alone while mindlessly watching the news.

When Alicia and Jack had moved in, they envisioned a

rental with spacious rooms, designed specifically for hosting guests and throwing parties. But as happens, work — mixed with routine and sprinkled with household issues — swallowed their plans. Even the joke about their postponed housewarming party had gathered dust.

Alicia both loved and loathed their current home. Vast and sprawling, it gave no sense of security, no matter where she was, except in the upstairs bathroom. Three large rooms — bedroom, office, and someday, a nursery — typical of a perfect American family listing. They had turned the nursery into a guest room, where Katie often stayed, while the office was used by Jack when he brought work home. The summer terrace in the backyard, built for children's laughter and a doghouse, stood almost empty. The outdoor furniture consisted of two wicker chairs, the kind no one would miss if stolen, and a heavy round table with a layer of dust instead of a tablecloth. Jars of snacks sat on it, their contents warning all snackers to abandon all hope, ye who dared to try them.

Jack called just as Alicia was throwing a tasteless burrito into the trash.

"Hey, babe, how's your day?"

"Oh, Jackie, I'm exhausted. Bought myself new boots. How's Santa Monica? How's the Walk of Fame?"

He chuckled wearily. "I know we haven't finalized the whole move thing yet, but Los Angeles is a total dump."

"Dirtier than last time?"

"Dirtier. And there are more homeless people. And I haven't even been downtown yet. So far, the client's only shown us the safe neighborhoods." Jack yawned into the phone.

"You must be tired."

"Yeah, I didn't sleep on the plane. And last night we went to a ca-a-sino," he yawned the last word.

"Get some rest. Call me tomorrow, I miss you."

"Of course. Are you okay being home alone?"

Her voice didn't waver, and as cheerfully as if she'd gotten plenty of sleep the night before, Alicia lied. "I'm fine."

After hanging up, she tossed her phone onto the pillows. If only she had gone with him...And who cares about the company not allowing partners on this specific business trip? But Jack had played by the rules, and now, instead of having a warm body beside her on the big couch, she had to settle for a square pillow. Shivering, she stood up and began her nightly round. Front door — locked. Terrace — locked. Garage — locked again.

Alicia climbed onto the couch, tucked her feet under herself, and turned on *Bad Boys*, raising the volume. Naively, she hoped that the Netflix comedy might change her mood, though it was still better than the monotony of silence. Pulling the bowl of cheesy chips closer, she slid under the blanket and stuffed her right hand under the pillows for her phone. Just in case.

When the credits rolled and the streaming service automatically started the second movie, Alicia hit pause to take the dishes to the kitchen. Out of the corner of her eye, she noticed the sheer curtain by the terrace door. *Not where I left you.* The translucent fabric, the color of watered-down coffee, usually hung straight to the floor, covering the door. Now, one delicate corner had hooked onto a branch of the bonsai in its pot. Alicia gripped the empty plate like a lifeline. Inhale. Exhale. She shook her head, much like one of those inflatable promotional figures flapping outside car dealerships. Maybe a gust of wind had caught the curtain through an open window. She turned toward the large panoramic window. Sure enough, it was open — the same window through which she had thought she'd seen a dog (probably a dog) a few days ago.

Beyond the hastily opened frame lay darkness, broken only by a single streetlamp on its tall post, illuminating the familiar boxwood bush — like an anglerfish luring curious prey with its glowing bait.

"Nightmares exist outside of logic," a great man once said — and he was right. On legs heavy as granite statues, Alicia moved toward the window to shut it. *Damn it, what a fool!* Why didn't she check the latch earlier? Comfort was no excuse, time couldn't be turned back, and the wind couldn't be stopped. She wouldn't have heard anything with the TV blaring so loud it drowned out even her own thoughts...

Alicia grabbed the cold metal handle and slammed the window shut so hard the panes rattled, but miraculously they didn't shatter. She slid the latch into place, gave it a tug, and sighed loudly, half-sobbing. She buried her face in her clammy hands, trying to stop the chaotic carousel in her mind. She forced herself to breathe evenly. A few deep inhales and loud exhales through her mouth. She imagined a beautiful, glowing light emanating from her chest. Imaginary, it expanded and traveled through every part of her body. With each breath, the light helped to chase the bad thoughts from her mind. Her shoulders relaxed, and the pulsing in her head slowly subsided.

Carefully, she opened her eyes and took a deep breath. The light-breathing exercise really had helped. Alicia turned away from the window.

Someone stood in the middle of the room.

It felt like a dream. Or she was dead, because being alive just didn't seem possible.

There was no face. It was hidden behind a mask the color of wet dirt, with two crooked, small holes for eyes. Through the slits, mud-colored eyes peered at her. The fabric ended abruptly at the neck and barely moved where the mouth should be. A tattered, dusty cloak covered in dried stains flowed in waves at his knees. His hands were tucked inside the wide folds.

"Who are you?" Alicia croaked, exhaling.

He didn't respond, but the mask shifted, as if he were silently mouthing something. A faint, elusive smell lingered in the air — subtle, yet disturbingly familiar. The scent nudged her subconscious, searching for recognition, but the answer slipped away before it could surface. Her heart leapt like a grasshopper caught in a jar. Alicia couldn't breathe, choking on her fear — gasping and wheezing, like a cat coughing up a hairball. The man in the mask slowly pulled his right hand out of his pocket, without unclenching his fist. He raised it to chest level, as if teasing her.

"Go away," she whispered, staring at her own upside-down reflection in the blade of his knife.

He took the first step toward her.

Scream — her brain sent the final signal before everything short-circuited.

Old Bill was passing their house on his way home when a

muffled sound, like a person crushed under a heavy slab, came from inside. But Old Bill didn't hear it. At sixty-five, hearing loss had already made itself at home in his head, even if it hadn't moved all its belongings in yet. He might have heard it if Jon Bon Jovi wasn't singing about Gina at full blast. He might have heard it if he'd taken care of that ear infection back in the day. But those free wired headphones from American Airlines did their job well, keeping out the female voice.

For the first time in her life, Alicia's mind went completely blank. The man in the mask was approaching slowly, stepping carefully with his foot. The long table separated them. Her jaw dropped and rose, as if she were cracking invisible nuts. The masked man was rounding the table, getting closer, close enough to reach out and grab her, knife in hand. A flash of light from the blade blinded her, and it was as if the gleam pressed the reset button in her brain. With a buzz, her mental machinery hummed back to life. A warning light flashed red inside her head: *Danger! Danger!*

Alicia backed away and then darted to the side. The distance between them grew again, but the man seemed to enjoy it. His lips moved in a silent whisper. Was he smiling? There was a playful look in his predatory eyes. The kind of look a hyena gives when it's about to mark its territory, showing its dominance. Giving a false sense of escape before closing in with a couple of leaps, killing, and leaving its prey to die.

Run — and she ran. Alicia turned away, too terrified to keep looking at him. Like a frightened ferret, she needed one last sprint to escape the stinking hyena. She didn't want to die.

Heavy footsteps behind her. He was running after her.

Alicia dashed past the front door, cursing herself for every lock she had secured earlier. Why did she bother locking every single one of them? Grabbing the banister, she leapt up the stairs and bolted toward the only room with a lock on the inside: the bathroom. The man in the mask had stopped running. Why chase her when the prey had cornered itself?

Alicia threw herself into the bathroom and glanced back. The masked figure was climbing the stairs, each step louder than the last. His cloak flapped with every footfall. *Please let him trip and fall.*

He didn't trip. He placed his foot on the last step. His black eyes locked with hers, level to level. Alicia let out a sob as she slammed the bathroom door shut and turned the lock. With shaking hands, she grabbed a mop and wedged it against the door handle.

Her legs couldn't support her anymore. She collapsed onto the cold tile floor, wincing as her tailbone hit hard. Her jaw continued to tremble uncontrollably — she pressed her hands against her chin to stop it. The door handle barely moved, held in place by the mop. He tried to open the door.

Bang! The door rattled as he slammed into it with full force.

Bang! Alicia let out a choked wail, scratching her face with her nails.

Bang! The doorframe shook, and the mop fell onto her.

"Go away, GO AWAY!" Alicia screamed.

She crawled to the mop on her knees and propped it back up against the handle. Then she lay down on the floor, bracing the door with her legs. Her tailbone throbbed; her core ached.

Bang! The man hit the door again, but it barely moved.

Her legs pressed hard against it, giving the door extra strength. That's when Alicia noticed the flashing circle on her watch.

S.O.S. DETECTED HARD FALL. DETECTED HIGH HEART RATE.

The one-minute timer was ticking down: 4, 3, 2, 1...

Suddenly, her watch blared an emergency alarm. At first quietly, then louder, and then unbearably loud. The echo in the bathroom made it deafening — loud enough that even Old Bill could have heard it through his headphones, had he still been on his jog.

And then, just as suddenly, the siren cut off, and a calm, female voice announced: "Stay where you are. Help is on the way." The watch screen went dark.

Stay where you are, as if there was any chance of surviving in this damn bathroom, Alicia thought bitterly, and then burst into tears, laughing hysterically through her sobs. Since the alarm had gone off, the door hadn't budged, but she still pressed her body against it — like a single curled finger clinging to the edge, refusing to let go into the endless abyss below. In her mind, the remnants of the siren echoed, bouncing back and forth between her temples like a tennis ball. The back of her head felt cold from lying on the tiled floor. Alicia tried to lift it, but her neck gave out, and her head thudded back down onto the tiles.

"Go away..." she murmured, and then everything went black.

CHAPTER 13

"Mom, look — it's the police!" Sam squealed. "This is the best day of my life!"

Seeing his favorite toy cars in real life for the first time — what a gift! And two of them, no less! Sam's best friend from school always bragged about how he'd already seen hundreds of real emergency vehicles: red fire trucks with huge water tanks, doctor's vans with the snake symbol, packed with giant syringes, and of course the white-and-blue cars with the big "Chicago Police Department" star.

"Mom, Mom, look at all the men and women in uniforms. So cool!"

"Samuel, we need to find out what happened. It's not right to celebrate someone else's misfortune."

"I can't wait to tell Nathan tomorrow," the boy went on, ignoring his mother. "He's gonna be so jealous."

Sam's mom, along with the rest of the onlookers, stood on the other side of the road, kept back by a cordon. People, like moths, were drawn to the flashing red-and-blue lights, waiting for something to happen. They whispered, stood on tiptoe, and lifted their phones, flashes on.

"Will someone explain what's going on?"

"Shooting?"

"Who got shot?"

"Who was shooting?"

The lights on the squad cars turned off. A police officer in a bulletproof vest stepped out of the car and approached the crowd. He lifted the brim of his checkered cap, revealing a broad forehead with a red line across it.

"Everything's fine, folks, go home."

"So, who's dead?" Mrs. Harris shouted.

"No one's dead. It's a routine call. Put your phones away unless you want to be called as the first witnesses and go home. We'll get in touch with the neighbors when it's time. Nothing to see here."

Grumbling under their breath, people began lowering their phones. Realizing they wouldn't get any gossip out of the police, they started heading home. Sam wasn't ready to leave just yet. And as soon as his mother's grip loosened, he broke free and ran up to the officer. The boy raised his hand like the grown-ups did in his favorite cartoon, though he didn't stretch it out too far, careful not to cross the "Police. Do Not Cross" tape. What if they arrested him?

The officer chuckled and shook his hand.

"Now off to bed with you, kid."

"Oh, Nathan's gonna be so jealous." Sam grinned, raising a triumphant fist. "Goodbye, Mr. Policeman."

The officer waved and headed toward the brick house.

***

REPORT

Based on the submitted documents, on April 28, 2023, at 10:02 p.m., a report was filed by Mr. Jack Sylvan, (DOB: 1993), residing at 9436 Perry Avenue, Chicago, Illinois 60620. Mr. Sylvan contacted the Chicago Police Department via an out-of-state phone call from Los Angeles, reporting a suspected threat to the life of his partner, who also resides at the aforementioned address. The information was relayed to him via a distress signal triggered by an Apple Watch Series 4 device, registered to the victim.

In response, a patrol unit was dispatched and arrived at the scene fourteen minutes after receiving the signal. Upon arrival, responding officers found the front door locked from the inside. After obtaining verbal authorization from the tenant, Mr. Sylvan, the obstacle posed by the door was removed. During the official inspection of the two-story house, a female occupant was found. The victim was identified as Ms. Alicia Brooks, (DOB: 1994), the cohabitant of the reporting party.

During preliminary questioning, the victim provided an incoherent account of an unknown subject entering the residence. Considering the possibility of a potential intruder still being present, the victim was relocated to a secure area on the first floor while the officers conducted a full sweep of the house. No intruder was located during the search. The victim declined medical assistance. Detective Gibbons was notified and responded to the scene to conduct a further in-depth investigation. Upon further examination, it was observed that Ms. Brooks had sustained a minor head injury. This information was documented in the report, and monitoring of the victim's condition over the coming days was advised.

The report has been completed and submitted for supervisory review.

Officer's Signature: _____

Civilian's Signature: _____

Date: April 28, 2023

Alicia drew a straight line with a flourish. This felt like some absurd movie. A forensic specialist in a pristine white suit was crawling on his knees by the dining table. An officer in a bulletproof vest was signing off on a report.

A young man seated across from her, so close she could see the fine stubble on his face. Before this damn day, she had no idea that police officers could wear casual clothes on assignment. The officer across from her was in plainclothes, wearing only a fall jacket, a scarf wrapped snugly around his neck, and a circular detective badge about the size of a saucer.

A female officer in uniform handed Alicia a hot cup. Little waves rippled on the surface of the water from her trembling hands, keeping the chamomile petals afloat.

Alicia obediently took a sip and almost choked on the boiling liquid. The gulp burned her throat, but the waves in her hands began to settle. The detective adjusted his badge.

"Ms. Brooks, I'm Detective Gibbons, lead investigator."

"Just Alicia is fine," she corrected.

"Sergio," he introduced himself and handed her a paper bag with a green mermaid logo.

Alicia smiled. Her fingers stopped shaking, and she expertly squeezed the bag like an accordion, retrieving the cold but delicious-smelling pastry — a cinnamon roll. She took a bite and almost rolled her eyes with pleasure — how good it tasted!

The detective pulled out a small notebook, the size of a waiter's pad, and a rectangular device that looked like a flash drive.

"First of all, I want to assure you that you are now completely safe. The house has been searched and is being secured by our

91

team. Your safety is our top priority."

The device beeped, and a small orange light turned on.

He continued, "I'm sorry you have to relive this moment, but I need you to tell me everything that happened, from the beginning to the end. Perhaps you'll feel some relief after talking about it. Could you tell me how you first noticed the intruder — the Man in the Mask?"

Alicia licked her sticky lips and peeked into the bag, looking for a napkin. There wasn't one. She scanned the coffee table, her eyes landing on the pink stain on the rug. It was hard to believe that just yesterday, she and Katie had spilled wine and laughed...*What were they even laughing about?*

"Ahem."

Sergio raised an eyebrow expectantly. Alicia wiped the corner of her mouth with her knuckle, leaving a streak of cinnamon on her hand. She wiped it away with her thumb, smearing it further, and started telling her story. The first few sentences came out jumbled, as if a solid stone was blocking their way, but soon the words began to flow freely. She spoke at length. The detective wrote very little.

"I think I blacked out because I don't remember how the Apple Watch sent the SOS. When I came to, the police were already in the house."

Detective Gibbons twirled his pen.

"That's everything," she said with a shrug. "I'm really tired. I'd like to call my boyfriend. He's the one who called you."

"I'm sorry, but I have a few more questions."

Alicia glanced at the small notebook in his hands. He hadn't turned a single page during her entire story. She nodded.

"Ms. Brooks, is there a chance you might have missed any details? Not intentionally, but maybe something slipped your mind?" He waved his hand, gesturing for her to think.

"What?" She stared at the notebook. "No, I don't think so...probably not."

The front door clicked open, and they were left alone. The detective didn't turn around. Alicia was hit by a wave of cold air, as if a glacier stood outside the door rather than the spring air of Chicago.

"My boyfriend, Jack, I want to call him. I want him to buy me a ticket to Los Angeles. For today."

Gibbons finally set down his pen, tucked the notebook into his breast pocket, and touched the gray device. The light went out.

"I'm afraid you'll need to stay until we've gathered sufficient information."

"But I've told you everything!"

"I'm sorry." He squinted at her. "But unfortunately, certain details need to be clarified right now."

"Can't we do this online?"

"We cannot."

"Alright, fine."

Alicia picked up the now-lukewarm tea and inhaled its chamomile aroma. The sweet taste of the pastry lingered in her mouth. Gibbons pressed the device again — the orange light blinked back on. He retrieved his notebook, adjusted his badge.

"Ms. Brooks, what kind of insurance do you have?"

"Insurance?"

"Your medical insurance company. Client number, personal

policy."

"Well, EMI, full coverage."

"Can you provide us with your policy? Most people keep it handy."

"I'd have to look for it," Alicia replied, confused. "My client number is on the fridge, but Jack has the policy. I can call him to —"

"No need," Gibbons interrupted. "We can obtain the necessary information through the proper channels."

"Why do you need that? I told you, the head injury is nothing."

"Have you or your family ever filed a claim for non-physical reasons?"

"No."

"Any history of anxiety or mental health disorders of any kind?"

"Well...no."

"Any stays in medical facilities for symptoms of psychological illness, disorders, or substance abuse?"

"What kind of questions are these?" Alicia shook her hands, and the teacup jumped, spilling the remaining tea onto the unlucky carpet.

"Ms. Brooks, we have to consider all possible versions of events."

"I don't know!"

"All right, we'll figure it out. Have you ever intentionally sent an SOS signal using your Apple Watch?"

"You think I staged this? Sent a damn SOS and then slammed myself against the floor?" She jumped up from the couch.

"We're simply following protocol, Ms. Brooks."

Alicia was breathing heavily, her cheeks burning like ripe red apples. What an evening — a full migration of emotions. Detective Sergio Gibbons looked up at her calmly. She tried to read the scribbles in his open notebook, but he caught her gaze and covered the page with his hand.

"I didn't do anything wrong!"

"Alicia, no one is accusing you."

"Then let me go!"

"No one is holding you," Sergio said calmly. "I apologize if you've gotten the wrong impression. We all make mistakes. Your safety is our top priority, and I just want to help you get through this awful nightmare."

Tears shimmered in her eyes. Her legs gave way, and her heavy, almost cement-like body sank back onto the couch. The detective handed her a packet of tissues. Alicia pulled one out and dabbed at her eyes.

"So, how many SOS signals have been sent from any of your devices before tonight?"

Chapter 14

Alicia bounced as the plane hit another patch of turbulence. *Damn it.* She tugged on her seatbelt for the hundredth time. Still fastened. The turbulence was tossing her around like everyone else, no matter if it was premium, business, or even presidential class — they all shook the same.

The little animated airplane on the rectangular screen in front of her was flying over a 3D-rendered Nevada. The screens in business class were bigger than those on Apple Airs. Alicia wrapped her legs in the JetBlue blanket and curled up on her side, pulling her knees close. Only an hour left until she'd be with Jack.

In the dark reflection of the screen, she saw a woman staring back at her, a woman who had aged in a single night, with a swollen face and dark circles under her eyes. No wonder the flight attendant had looked at her suspiciously earlier when she, late for the flight, had shoved her gray bag into the overhead bin of the business class section. His eyes seemed to say, "Miss, are you sure you're in the right place? How did they even let you into the airport looking like that?"

"More red wine, miss?" the flight attendant asked, his

figure slender in a tailored black uniform, a silky tie tucked neatly beneath his collar.

"Mm...do you have white?" Alicia asked.

The flight attendant pulled out an open bottle of Sauvignon Blanc from the cart and poured it into a plastic glass. He placed it on a napkin on the tray table and took away the two other empty glasses.

Alicia took a sip. The white wine was good, too, though the taste blurred as the alcohol began to take effect. Her thoughts raced faster than the seconds ticking by. Who was that masked man? What did he want? A burglar? Detective Gibbons had mentioned that crime rates were rising every year, with more and more homes being broken into. But who in their right mind would break into a house full of lights? It didn't make sense. It was stupid. But then again, could someone smart enough to erase all traces and fingerprints be that reckless? The police hadn't found anything right away...

Unless his target had been Alicia herself. She shuddered and drained the rest of the wine. She grimaced, tossing the plastic cup toward the tray table — but missed and it fell somewhere down. Ali turned toward the window, pulling the blanket up to her ears, and drifted off into a restless sleep. Her eyelids twitched.

"Excuse me, miss, we're preparing to land. Please return your seat to the upright position," the polite voice of the flight attendant interrupted her dark, endless corridor of thoughts.

Alicia rubbed her eyes. The little airplane icon on the screen was already circling over Los Angeles. She pressed the button on her armrest, folded up the tray table, and checked her seatbelt.

Her phone had finished charging, so she disconnected it along with the white cable attached to the screen. Less than twenty minutes until she'd be with Jack.

It was Jack who had first introduced her to Los Angeles. Back then, they had been dating for a year or so — he was already a project manager, while she was just an intern consultant. He'd invited her on a business trip, hoping to immerse her in the work world, teach her how to "show face" — meet important clients, listen to successful directors' stories, and collect a stack of expensive business cards.

What excitement! To rub elbows with such bigwigs at the start of her career. But it was only months later that Alicia realized why people at the office still referred to her without using her name. "Jack and his partner," "that girl," "Mr. Sylvan's girlfriend." No one bothered to learn her name until she had earned her own experience through hard work. Until then, she was just the girlfriend of the cool guy. And Jack wasn't to blame, either. As an employee, he had brought his personal assistant for training; as a boyfriend, he had invited her on a great trip, all expenses paid. A win-win for him.

On their first free evening after meetings, Jack took her to Malibu. A small town for the wealthy. They parked by someone's glass mansion with floor-to-ceiling windows, didn't even bother to take their laptops from the car — there were no thieves in Malibu. Hand in hand, they found a sandy path hidden between the luxurious homes and followed it, walking beneath towering palm trees until they reached the beach.

And there it was — the ocean.

Loud. Dark. Salty.

The first touch of bare feet on wet sand, the first salty kiss of the spray, the first whisper of crashing waves.

The ocean intoxicated more than the Prosecco they'd had at dinner.

Powerful. Blue. Endless.

"What do you think?" Jack had asked, gently wrapping his arms around her waist.

"Wow," she breathed.

Alicia wrapped her arms around his. The wind played with them, blowing from all directions. She pressed herself tighter against him. It felt warmer. Slowly, afraid of being swept away in the intoxication, she inhaled the scent of the ocean. A true wow.

Jack leaned in, towering over her like a lion. He pressed his dry, wind-chapped lips against her earlobe. She giggled at the tickling sensation but didn't pull away. Jack began softly humming the song from their first dance together. He swayed to the right. Swayed to the left.

"The sea washes our footprints from the sand..."

Alicia closed her eyes. A timid smile and a wildly beating heart — she remembered, too. Jack took her hands in his and swayed them right and left.

"But it doesn't erase this night from who we are..."

The salty spray settled on her slightly parted lips, and she licked it off. No longer cold.

Alicia opened her eyes and turned to Jack. Bright, bright stars sparkled in his eyes, and the orange evening sky reflected back. Somewhere deep in his gaze, she saw the outline of the ocean.

"The morning rises and swallows the dark..."

She touched his shaved face with both hands. Joined in the hidden dance, invisible to anyone but them. The wind wrapped around them, tossing blonde hair into her face. Jack brushed the stray strand of hair behind her ear. His fingers dove into unruly hair, sending sweet shivers down her tender skin. Alicia closed her eyes and rested her left cheek against his calloused palm, whispering in unison: "Part of me still wishes time could stop."

The majestic ocean didn't like being second to anything.

A powerful wave crashed against them, soaking them up to their waists, and their feet sank into the wet sand. They laughed, grabbed each other's hands, and ran away from the water. Wet, but happy.

The plane's wheels thudded hard against the runway. The rumble grew louder and louder until it quieted down. The seatbelt sign turned off.

"Ladies and gentlemen, welcome to Los Angeles. The weather outside..."

Such a vivid memory. Alicia licked the salty drops from her lips. No, it wasn't the ocean. It was her tears. Finally, she would be with the person who could help. Who would protect her.

Alicia grabbed her carry-on and was the first to head for the exit. When you fly business class, there's no need to wait for the people in front of you to move. You're the first to leave, and they'll even bring your luggage straight to the door.

Luckily, LiveSafe had also paid for a rental car and parking. Complaints echoed throughout the airport as tourists grumbled about having to wait half an hour or more for a shuttle. And the shuttle, though free, didn't take you to the city but only to the airport's designated rideshare zone: Uber, Lyft, or the ridiculously overpriced city taxis. Those who were local left their cars in the paid airport parking lots instead of bothering with taxis — more expensive, but less stressful.

The glass door to the inner terminal only opened one way. Security guards stood on either side, and beyond the doors was the chatter of people waiting for their loved ones: a large Chinese family with a frail grandmother in a wheelchair; a blond father with ginger twins and a miniature dachshund in his arms; teenagers holding a balloon with someone's poorly printed face on it.

And there was Jack. Although he hadn't slept much either, he still looked remarkably fresh — dressed in a crisp white shirt, his dark hair styled with pomade. He held a bouquet of peach-colored dahlias.

Alicia raced toward him, tears welling up in her eyes. She dropped her bag at his feet and wrapped her arms around him. Jack did a double take, and she realized he didn't recognize her at first. Was it possible she had really changed so much in just a few days?

"Sweetheart," he murmured, pulling her closer.

Jack stroked her tangled hair as she sobbed into his chest. The smells swirled around her like a personal calming elixir — his familiar cologne, a new masculine shampoo, her favorite flowers.

"Shh, baby, shh, I'm here. No one will hurt you," he whispered in her ear.

The tears stopped as if someone had turned off an emotional

faucet. Alicia pulled back from Jack. A damp spot had formed on his shirt where her head had rested. She bit her lip and, pulling the sleeve of her cardigan over her thumb, tried to wipe the stain. It was useless. Jack took her hand in his and shook his head.

A group of teenagers erupted in cheers — a skinny, curly-haired boy had just walked out of the doors. He waved at them, and the kids rushed over, lifted him up, and placed him on the shoulders of the biggest boy. Everyone in the room turned to look at the laughing kids. Someone tied the ribbon from the helium balloon around his wrist, and when the balloon turned, people started smiling. The balloon had a stretched, poorly printed version of the curly-haired boy's face on it.

Alicia laughed, too. Life kept going.

"How was your flight, baby?" Jack asked, smiling.

"I drank the whole way."

"Wine?"

"Wine." She nodded, looking down.

"No one's judging," he said as he kissed the top of her head. "Let's go to the hotel, I'll order breakfast in the room."

Jack picked up her bag from the floor and pulled a parking ticket from his pocket. Together they headed toward the sign "Parking 3," hanging from the airport ceiling. The curly-haired boy was already back on the ground, and his friends were taking turns posing with him and the ridiculous balloon.

"Did you eat?"

"No, I was waiting for you."

"I'm sorry."

"Don't apologize, I just wanted to be on time. The plane

was late."

"I'm sorry."

He turned so abruptly that Alicia bumped into him.

"Stop apologizing, baby, please."

Alicia nodded, stood on her tiptoes, and kissed him on his freshly shaved cheek.

"Today, you're going to rest," he continued. "You'll get a massage, sleep, and tomorrow we'll talk about what we're going to do. Agreed?"

"Agreed."

She took his arm, and together they headed to find the car in the multi-level parking structure.

Chapter 15

Alicia didn't go to any massage. She fell asleep in the car before Jack even left the airport grounds. She didn't wake up when they arrived at the hotel's underground parking.

Jack parked in the reserved spot 394 and turned off the engine. The shift in movement stirred Alicia slightly, but she didn't wake. Her jaw was clenched, her posture awkward.

"Babe, wake up." Jack gently shook her shoulder.

Her cheek twitched involuntarily, but her eyes remained closed. Jack shook her again — this time with a little more force.

Alicia cracked her eyelids open, squinted, and jerked upright in her seat. Where was she? One hand clutched her chest, and the other shot forward. Her head darted around the parking lot, the car, Jack...phew. She sank back against the leather seat, which bore a damp mark from her right shoulder.

"You scared me."

"Sorry. We're here. Let's go upstairs, and you can sleep again."

Jack exited the car. The underground parking lot stretched out into the distance, but their spot was conveniently close to the elevator. While Jack retrieved their items from the trunk (a duffel and the flowers), Alicia slowly got out and slammed the passenger door. The door closed with a loud, disgruntled thud. She wrapped her arms around herself and dug nails into her skin as she squinted, trying not to lose the remnants of sleep. She followed her boyfriend to the elevator, where Jack swiped the glossy hotel key card and pressed the "up" arrow.

In silence, Alicia trailed behind Jack down the carpeted hallway on the third floor. The door with the engraved number 394 was at the very end.

Jack swiped the card again, and they entered the room. The curtains were still drawn, keeping the previous night's twilight intact, and the bed was unmade from his early-morning departure. Papers were strewn messily across the desk — evidence of a chaotic workday punctuated by a police call.

"No housekeeping today," Jack said, hanging the "Do Not Disturb" sign before closing the door.

Alicia stepped on the heels of her sneakers one by one, kicked them off near the entrance, and trudged to the bed. She collapsed.

While Jack put the flowers in the vase, washed his hands, tidied the shoes, and adjusted the air conditioning, Alicia was already asleep. She didn't feel him remove her jacket and tuck her in with the down blanket. She didn't hear him call the Chicago Police Department and ask to speak with Detective Gibbons.

She slept the rest of the day and through the night while Jack worked, ate lunch, worked again, ate dinner, and watched YouTube, simultaneously responding to work emails.

The smell of strong coffee finally woke her up the next morning. Alicia rubbed her groggy eyes and yawned widely. Her head was aching from oversleeping. How long had she been out?

"Jackie," she croaked. "Jackie, where are you?"

The sound of running water came from the bathroom. On the nightstand sat a paper cup from Blue Bottle and a small Lindt chocolate. Behind the cup, an open card depicted a bear hugging a soft pink heart.

Hunger gnawed at her stomach, tightening its grip. The last meal she'd eaten was in another state, and the mental bitterness from the cinnamon roll at Starbucks still lingered, tainted by memories of the bothersome detective.

The bathroom door opened, and out walked her half-naked boyfriend. His wet hair stuck up messily, and the waistband of his boxers sat low on his toned hips. Droplets of water still clung to his shoulders. Jack grabbed a dry-cleaning garment bag from the chair — laundry delivered right to their room.

"I was just about to wake you," he said, removing the plastic covering from the freshly laundered shirt.

"Good morning."

"Are you feeling alright, Ali?"

Alicia reached for the coffee and motioned toward the card.

"Thank you, Jackie. And thanks for the coffee too. I'm so hungry I could eat the cup."

"Well, well," Jack chuckled. "I'll order breakfast. Pick whatever you want. And get a double portion if you want."

He took the room service menu out of the drawer. The desk was now neatly organized — his work papers stacked on the left, the closed laptop in the center, and a large envelope from Chicago on the right.

"I want a big American breakfast," Alicia said, leaning back on the bed.

"Not going to look at the menu?"

"They can make it even if it's not listed."

Jack smirked and reached for the hotel phone.

Fifteen minutes later, the waiter delivered breakfast. A three-tiered cart with metal rails for trays rolled into the room, followed by an elderly man. On the top tier sat a small cup and a large white plate covered by a metal cloche. The gray-haired waiter locked the front wheels, unfolded a portable table, and placed the dish on it. He set down the cutlery, wrapped in an ironed napkin, and lifted the cloche. Two thin sausages, an omelet with herbs, three crispy bacon strips, and hash browns — for Alicia. Espresso — for Jack.

Alicia devoured the meal, balancing the large plate on the folding table perched on her lap in bed. On the TV, a travel show host explored Vietnam's street food scene, chewing skewered meat at a bustling market. Alicia chewed in sync with him.

Jack sat on the edge of the bed with his tablet. "Ali, we need to talk."

"About what?" she asked, still focused on the show.

"Turn off the TV, please."

She clicked her tongue but turned it off.

"Tell me everything that happened in Chicago. Everything you remember."

Alicia looked at her boyfriend with disinterest. Half of her breakfast was on its way to her stomach, but the hunger still lingered. She pressed her lips together and glanced at the empty nightstand.

"Where's my coffee?"

"You drank it already," Jack said, raising an eyebrow.

"I want more."

"Okay."

He picked up the hotel phone again and dialed reception.

"Could we have more coffee, please — with soy milk."

Alicia turned the TV back on. The sound of sizzling meat and the show host's satisfied groans filled the room once more. Jack silently waited for the coffee, tapping his knuckles on the wooden table. Alicia turned up the volume.

A few minutes later, there was a knock at the door. Jack opened it for the gray-haired waiter, who wheeled in the now-familiar cart. The top tier was nearly empty, except for a tall cup on a saucer and a small pitcher of milk.

The waiter parked the cart by the nightstand, spread out a fabric napkin embroidered with the letter "R," and placed the coffee and pitcher on top.

"The milk is warm but not hot — you can pour it right away," he said.

"I wanted it foamed." Alicia rolled her eyes.

"We did inform you that the coffee machine was broken," the older man replied, adjusting his starched towel.

"So what?"

"The soy milk in the pitcher is warmed," he repeated.

"But I want a barista coffee! Can I have it delivered from the nearest café? Jack, where did you get that coffee?" she asked, looking past the waiter.

Jack wasn't there. He had disappeared.

She was alone in the room with a tall, unfamiliar man. The scent of artificial pine trailed in with him. His gray eyebrows furrowed, creating deep lines across his forehead. The corners of his lips, tinged with blue, sagged downward.

His murky old eyes stared at her with malice.

A cold sweat ran down her back, and her fingers let go of the fork.

"Jackie..." she whimpered in a trembling voice.

"Is something wrong, ma'am?" The waiter stepped closer, extending his wrinkled hand.

A long arm toward her fragile neck.

"JACKIE!" she screamed at the top of her lungs.

The waiter stepped back, clutching his towel.

A towel in the throat — to stop her from screaming.

Alicia curled her knees up to her chest and began kicking wildly, as if trying to push both herself and the bed away from the wall. The folding table wobbled, and the last sausage rolled around the plate. Tears streamed down her face, accompanied by hysterical sobs.

The waiter gripped the edges of the table, lifting it.

"DON'T TOUCH ME!" she screamed at the top of her voice.

The door slammed open — Jack rushed into the room. He took in the scene: the terrified elderly man clutching the table, and Alicia thrashing on the bed. Jack tossed his phone onto the bed and wrapped his arms around Alicia.

"What happened, what happened?"

He pressed his hand on her knees, gently forcing them to stop kicking. Her legs fought back for a moment but gave in. The thrashing ceased, and tears and snot mixed as they smeared across her face, wiping onto Jack's freshly laundered shirt.

"Shh," he soothed her, rocking gently.

"I can call for a medic," the waiter said loudly.

He placed the table back on the cart and pulled a walkie-talkie from his pocket.

Alicia peered out from the safety of Jack's arms and shook her head. Her tears were drying, and the sobs were subsiding. The man no longer felt like a threat. She no longer smelled his scent.

"It's okay. She's been through a lot of trauma and still hasn't recovered," Jack explained, rubbing her damp back.

"I didn't understand what happened," the waiter responded, confused.

"I was warned about this." Jack glanced at his laptop. "But I didn't expect the trigger to come so suddenly."

"If I'm no longer needed..."

Jack reached into his pocket, pulled out a crumpled twenty-dollar bill, and handed it over.

The waiter slipped it into his jacket pocket, bowed, and left with his cart. Once the door closed and they were alone again, Jack gently touched Alicia's cheek.

"What happened to you?"

"Where did you go?" she asked, still shaken.

Jack nodded toward the door. "Work call."

"You couldn't take the day off?"

"I was gone for five minutes."

Her eyes welled up with tears again, and she bit her lip. Instead of crying, she threw off the blanket and stood up from the bed.

"Ali, I can't imagine how hard this is for you."

"You can't."

"Are you mad at me?"

"You don't get it?"

"No, tell me what happened," Jack said calmly.

"That...that guy could have followed me here, tracked me down to finish what he started!" Alicia yelled, waving her hands in frustration.

"You thought that waiter was the masked man who attacked you?"

"The Silent Walker."

Jack furrowed his brow. "What?"

"The police call him the Man in the Mask. But I can't bear to hear that word...*mask*. Every time I hear it, I see him right in front of me. Closer than I see you! I don't want to hear that name anymore! He's called The Silent Walker."

Jack stood from the bed. He whispered to himself, almost like he was testing the words: "A walker..." The confident, beautiful graduate he had met at a party years ago was unrecognizable. Calling a criminal a "walker" was strange. Walkers are people on evening strolls, people going about their daily routines. Walkers are harmless. A maniac is not a walker.

But as Detective Gibbons had advised him, it was crucial to tread carefully with victims. The critical emotional breaking point came two or three days after an attack. Jack approached her and hugged her tightly.

"Why give him a name, babe?" he asked softly.

"It makes him seem less scary. Less real," she whispered.

CHAPTER 16

The workweek dragged on slowly, anxiously, and full of bumps. Jack was torn between demanding clients and his unstable girlfriend. He missed Chicago. Hotel rooms, food deliveries, and late-night work — it had all become tiresome.

Jack would leave Alicia alone in the hotel room for a few hours at a time, always hanging the "Do Not Disturb" sign on the door. He paid extra to the young concierge, Macy, to ensure she only informed Alicia of food deliveries after the server had left the floor. Three or four times, Jack called to check that everything was fine. A few times, his calls clashed with important client meetings, so he sent messages to the hotel instead. When Jack returned to the lobby, Macy would smile with her plump lips, giggle, flirt, and once even "accidentally" unbuttoned her top buttons. But Jack never took it any further than tips.

Alicia didn't mind the calls. She settled into a rhythm like an old cat: sleep, eat, sleep. She watched teen dramas on TV, envied the high school characters, and even found the sweet local star of a surfing series on Instagram. Alicia wasn't using her own social media accounts — she didn't want to think about life back in Chicago. She didn't check Katie's status or reply to her messages, even though her friend had finally written:

```
We're adults, Alicia. Let's meet?
```

Adults? *Yeah right*, Alicia thought bitterly, angrily swiping away the notification. Clear all.

Alicia had become reclusive: she hadn't seen the gray-haired waiter or the squeaky-voiced Macy. She hadn't seen anyone except Jack. And strangely, she liked it. She'd never felt so good before. So free. So clean. She was looking forward to the weekend — Jack had promised a surprise.

On Friday morning, she got bored — the last episode of the teen drama had ended, replaced by a news report about yet another hurricane in Asia. Alicia sighed sadly — had the fictional story ended, or had it been her inner journey to peace? Her clean outdoor clothes hadn't left the closet since they were washed and neatly ironed. No matter how long she lived in the world of plasma pixels, eventually, she would have to step outside.

Alicia scrolled through TikTok on a new account — dumb, funny videos, each one five seconds long. Fast dopamine. No end. No catching up.

Resolutely, she opened the map app on her phone and tapped on a coffee cup icon. The map zoomed out, clusters of orange icons forming numbers. Alicia spread two fingers across the screen, and the circles split into smaller orange bubbles. Starbucks was five minutes away. Blue Bottle was a seven-minute walk. What's this? Alicia tapped a nearby icon. A coffee truck. Only forty-one reviews, but five stars — a hidden gem.

Perfect. Added to favorites.

Alicia pulled herself out of the cocoon of blankets and looked in the mirror for the first time. Her once-shiny hair had clumped together. Small brown hairs formed an ant trail between her eyebrows. Her cuticles had overtaken her nails.

What have you done to yourself, girl? Somewhere in her bag was a professional hairbrush she'd never even unpacked. There should also be an emergency makeup kit — the bare essentials for every day.

Half an hour later, she nodded approvingly. A high ponytail, powdered face, matte lips. The skin between her brows was slightly red after the tweezers' work. Her clean clothes smelled pleasant, free from any body odor. She had almost forgotten the scent of crystal clarity and alpine freshness.

Alicia grabbed a spare plastic key card and stepped out of her comfort zone.

It was time. Time to return to life.

Despite the long line for coffee at the street kiosk, no one seemed to be in a rush. The barista — a tan guy with sun-kissed hair — chatted about the weather, the beautiful day, the warm sun, all while taking orders. He handed customers a tablet, where "20%" was already filled in for the tip, and a large "OK" button stretched across the screen. There was an option for "No Tip" — but it was off to the side, a button seemingly designed only for very skinny fingers.

Next up was the shiny red La Marzocco coffee machine. Two black handles on the sides, with the coffee filter in the middle — from the side, it looked like a toy robot.

The barista scooped out fresh coffee, wiped his hands on his jeans, dusting off ground coffee onto his white sneakers, and started humming a tune. Something about a señorita, something in Spanish.

The scent of jacaranda flowers overpowered even the smell of coffee. The first time Alicia had seen the clusters of lilac blossoms, she'd spent half an hour taking pictures — from above, from below, and plenty of selfies — you didn't see jacarandas growing in Chicago. But here in Los Angeles, several trees bloomed near their hotel. All giants.

Under one of the jacarandas sat a girl on a stone ledge. She wore a cotton beanie with a pom-pom on her head. A short puffer jacket hung loosely off her shoulders, revealing her silk camisole — pajama-like, very Californian fashion. A strand of purple hair escaped from under her hat, curling around her Apple earbuds. A violet-haired girl under a violet tree. She held a disposable bowl of poke and was explaining something into her earbuds.

Next to her sat a fluffy Shiba Inu. His reddish fur was almost plush. The dog's eyes were locked on her wooden fork, and his little black nose was at the ready. Every now and then, the girl gestured sharply, causing rice to scatter from the bowl, and the clever pup collected his rewards for patience.

"Hola, amiga! What can I get you on this lovely day?"

Alicia turned to the kiosk. Up close, the barista's hair almost blinded her.

"A soy milk latte, please."

"Si, señorita."

The coffee tasted more bitter than the sweet Mexican guy's smile, but the foamy soy milk smelled like vanilla. She sipped her mediocre coffee and headed toward the ledge.

The violet-haired girl was still talking. She had taken off her jacket and placed it under her legs. She absentmindedly scraped the remaining rice in the bowl with her fork, either searching for the last bits of fish or for answers in her head. She paid no attention to the drooling dog at her feet. His ears twitched like antennas, and he noticed the blonde girl approaching.

"Hi there, cutie," Alicia cooed.

The Shiba Inu wagged his tail, did a circle around the violet tree, and leaped off the ledge. He ran to Alicia, wagging his tail faster and faster, like a bobber caught in the wind.

"What a good boy." Alicia bent down to pet him.

The good boy placed his neatly trimmed paws on her jeans. Alicia laughed and scratched his white beard, brushing off the rice stuck in his fur.

"Milo! What a naughty dog!" The girl in the beanie rushed over. "Don't worry, he doesn't bite — he just loves people."

Milo jumped off Alicia, gave a displeased whimper, and stuck out his tongue. His owner pulled out a portable water bowl and wiped the rice from his muzzle while he drank.

"It's fine," Alicia said as she brushed the dusty paw prints from her jeans. "I love sweet dogs like him."

"He really is a good boy. It's a shame not everyone gets that. I'm sorry, but I have to run to work."

Milo perked up at the familiar sound of the word and let out a whine. He sat down between the two women, lifted one paw, and waved it a few times. Alicia bent down and took his white paw in her hand. Soft, rough paw pads. She shook it like she was greeting a new boss, then let go. Milo barked his approval.

"He really likes you. Do you live around here?"

"Just temporarily," Alicia answered lightly.

"I walk Milo here every day at noon. If you want to play with him again, stop by tomorrow."

Alicia watched the furry pup trot away and set a reminder for tomorrow. Maybe she should really agree to the move to Los Angeles?

She practically floated back to the hotel lobby on coffee-induced wings. There was a paw print left on her jeans, but she didn't rush to wash them. She'd need them again tomorrow for her walk with Milo. Alicia put away her summer sandals in the closet and hung her long-sleeve shirt back on the hanger. She placed her still-warm coffee on the table and dug into her bag for sweets. Found them.

Alicia spread out the colorful squares. Chocolate squares. There were only three left — milk, dark, and white, the least tasty one. The rule from childhood: save the worst for last. The last cold cutlet with a greasy, congealed crust in the pan. The last half-wrapped candy, like a butterfly emerging from its cocoon, in Grandma's glass dish. The last rotten apple in the wooden bowl.

Her fingers grabbed the matte red square. With one long nail, she tore open the seal. She popped the chocolate into her mouth, savoring it greedily. A hard square of pleasure. She leaned back against the hotel bed's headboard. The chocolate began to melt, spreading from the center to the tip of her tongue. Her eyes closed on their own. Her thoughts soared into the sky.

How could anyone not love chocolate? It was so delicious, so fragrant. And those chocolate factories — weren't they magical? Crackling cocoa beans in fiery ovens, swirling chocolate whirlpools, gleaming metal molds filled with creamy goodness. There wasn't a single popular factory open to guests that she hadn't visited in Illinois. Even small-town cafés or tiny shops that melted chocolate into delicate, thin, exquisite chocolate figurines had their place in her heart. Like the café *Two Sweet Cats* — a family-run business on Burke Street, just a block from her home in Chicago...

The taste of the city soured on her tongue, with no connection to the square of chocolate.

Chicago — it made her sick, like a hangover.

Chicago — a rotten plank in a fishing pier.

Chicago — red circled "No Guns" signs.

Alicia swallowed the melted chocolate and chased it down with a gulp of fizzy water straight from the bottle. Ignore it or not, Jack's business trip was coming to an end, and soon they'd be checking in online for their flight back to Chicago.

But she had already decided — they should move to LA! Funny how sometimes the solution to a big problem comes into focus through an unexpected lens.

Alicia hadn't told Jack her decision yet. She didn't want to jinx it. She just needed the perfect moment. To pitch the idea, she had to look her best. The setting mattered too. A date at *Morté Restaurant* would do.

There were other hurdles to clear first — investor approval, then the company owner, then the department director.

Only after that bureaucratic chain would their move to sunny California become real.

CHAPTER 17

Tears had dried. Anger was boiling.

Her frozen toes curled into the wet sand. The ocean pulled back its salty blanket, foamed, and embraced her knees again. Droplets sprayed onto her dress, forming into larger beads — like a sea giant shaking off its hands.

In her clenched fist, a crumpled napkin from *Morté Restaurant* — a leftover from the failed date.

Half an hour earlier, Alicia had stepped out of the taxi at the pier. The Ferris wheel was sparkling, glowing with Barbie-and-Ken-colored lights. Couples everywhere — hugging, holding hands, tossing coins over their shoulders. Tourists grinned into cameras, ready to flood Instagram with photos tagged "Santa Monica Pier."

Alicia headed toward the restaurant. A valet had opened the doors with a bow, ushering her into a royal palace. Floating chandeliers cast shadows on stone walls; two statues of maidens sipped wine beside a marble vineyard at the entrance; a bright red carpet woven with silver threads led to a staircase with gilded rails. In the center of the hall, a grand piano stood. A dark-skinned girl in a backless dress sat at the bench, pearls draped like a necklace down her bare spine. The slender fingers of her right hand danced across the keys while her left squeezed out chords.

"Allow me to show you to your table," the valet offered, extending his hand.

Alicia followed him. Shoulders straightened, posture poised. Guests turned as she floated past, holding the hem of her scarlet dress. Two loose strands fell from her neatly pinned-up hair, brushing against her collarbones. Her eyes, accentuated with sharp eyeliner. No sign of the recent breakdowns on her face.

Jack was on the phone, wearing a dark gray suit buttoned at the waist and a crisp white shirt. Seeing Alicia, he stood from the table, kissed her hand, and whispered while pulling the phone's speaker away: "I'll be back in a moment."

The valet pulled out her chair and bowed. The room felt crowded, though the guests were spread out. Every table was taken. Alicia bit her lip, then stopped at once — she'd remembered her lipstick. Nervously, she grabbed a soft napkin from the empty plate and squeezed it.

She had made up her mind. As an aperitif, she would present her decision to move to LA.

Jack's tablet lit up. Alicia's eyes instinctively darted toward it. A notification. An email. Her hands trembled before she even touched the tablet. It took her three attempts to enter the four-digit code, and then she opened "Mail."

In an instant, the palace vanished. She was back in Chicago. Above the work emails, there was a new message.

The ever-clear California sky darkened. Thunder. Lightning.

A storm.

A bid for the purchase of the property at 9436 Perry Avenue in Chicago.

The house where she was almost killed.

A minute — or maybe twenty — later, she was standing on the shore of Santa Monica's beach. The napkin crumpled in her hand.

"Ali?" Jack's voice came from a distance.

She didn't turn.

"Alicia, what's wrong? Are you having an attack?"

He was running toward her, his Jimmy Choo shoes sinking into the sand.

The faintly glimmering stars gazed down at her while her personal dream stars fell. Trust in their relationship? Shattered. Farewell to wretched Chicago? Crumbled. Eternal summer? Broken into pieces.

Naive fool — she thought he needed her approval to move. He had already made the decision himself.

"What's wrong with you?" He grabbed her by the shoulders and turned her to face him.

The familiar swollen eyes and smeared eyeliner streaked down her cheeks.

"I know everything."

"What are you talking about? Let's get out of the water."

He pulled her, his shoes sinking into the sticky sand, but she yanked her arm away. Jack stumbled and jumped back — just in time. The wave nearly reached him.

"Ali, what happened to you?"

She exhaled slowly. Shaking off the chill. Anger warmed

her from the inside.

"I saw your email. The bid on the house. The one where they almost killed me."

Jack frowned.

"You're reading my emails?"

"You! Bought! The house!"

"I didn't buy anything."

"You're bidding on it! You lied to me!"

"How did I lie to you?"

"We were supposed to move to Los Angeles."

"They just offered me the position."

"I already agreed to move, and you ruined everything!" she shouted, but the ocean's roar muffled her scream.

Another wave splashed against her back, foam swirling around her. Alicia wobbled, flailing her arms for balance as the retreating water pulled at her.

"Get out of the water!"

"Screw you!"

"Get a grip already!" Jack snarled. He stepped into the water, grabbed her by the elbow, and dragged her out of the ocean. "I've been running around taking care of you all week — feeding you, looking after you — while you're snooping through my documents and embarrassing me. You went into the ocean? Planning to drown yourself?"

She wrenched herself free and pushed him away. "You're hurting me!"

"You didn't even want to move in the first place. You haven't seen my new work contract, and you don't even have one of your own. You're not a child for me to support and cart around.

And now you're yelling at me? You — so smart — didn't even try to figure out what's going on? The owner wants to sell the house because of issues with the police, and at the price he's asking, it'll be sold fast. Either we buy it, or someone else does, and we get kicked out."

"But I don't want to live there!"

"We can rent it out."

"I don't want to live in Chicago anymore! There are bad people there! I want to live here! Without you!"

Jack closed his eyes. "I'm exhausted, Alicia. I can't deal with this right now. I'll see you at the hotel."

He turned and walked away.

The wet, dark red dress clung to her skin. The salty water stung her freshly shaved legs. Sand stuck to her skin, coating her from feet to thighs.

The anger no longer warmed her. Nothing did.

***

Ali entered the dark hotel room. Jack's shoes were by the door, sand scattered from the toes onto the carpet. He was asleep. Or pretending to be.

She quietly closed the door behind her. Kicked off her shoes, using her nearly dead phone for light. She let the dress fall down her hips like a red ribbon, stepped out of it, and untied her hair. A wet wipe took care of the smudged makeup on her cheeks, forehead, and eyelids before she slid under the blanket. Sleep revved down the racetrack. Her phone blinked with its final percentage and died. Ali groped for the dangling charger cord in the dark. *I need to set an alarm,* she thought. And she fell asleep.

The rumble of an exhaust pipe. An annoyed taxi horn. The roar of a revving motorbike. Monday arrived from outside. Ali turned on her side and opened her eyes, propping herself up on her elbow with a squint of displeasure. Her phone was completely dead, lying inches from the charger. Her dress lay crumpled on the floor. Jack's presence had vanished from the room — no trace of him on the table, the nightstand, or in the closets. Other than her scattered belongings, the only thing left was his packed suitcase in the corner. The zipper was already locked.

She glanced at the round wall clock — four hours until the flight. She felt hunger gnawing at her stomach, but there was no sign of breakfast — not even the smell of coffee. For the first time during her stay in Los Angeles, it dawned on her that Jack had been the one ordering all the food. Every time.

Ali picked up the dress from the floor and brushed off the sand. The ocean water had dried, leaving salty white stains on the fabric. The last hope for a dry cleaner.

The bathroom door opened, and Jack emerged. Brown eyes met blue ones. Hair slicked with pomade and the perfectly ironed blue shirt made him look composed. His mouth twitched as if he wanted to say something, but they just stared at each other for longer than was comfortable, until Jack was the first to break eye contact and turned toward the mirror.

Ali pulled her suitcase from the closet and began stuffing clothes into it. The crumpled red dress went in first. A pajama set scented with lotion, cotton blouses, a brown skirt — all tossed into one large compartment. Next was her travel makeup bag: a round hairbrush, red lipstick to match the dress, a palette of cool-toned eyeshadows, day and night creams. Ali added her perfume bottle last, but when she tried to zip the bag, it jammed. The bristles of her large makeup brush had gotten caught in the zipper. She tried pulling it back, but it wouldn't budge. She tugged harder, and the zipper slider came off. The makeup scattered across the floor. Ali exhaled and sank to her knees.

"Do you want to talk?" she asked without lifting her head.

"No," Jack answered curtly.

They ate breakfast in the business lounge at the airport. Jack opened his work laptop and didn't close it until they were boarding. His focused gaze, fingers gliding over the trackpad, and constant typing hinted that he wasn't just avoiding her — he was genuinely busy. That thought made her feel somewhat relieved.

After takeoff, the in-flight Wi-Fi became available for business class. Ali unlocked her phone and glanced out the window at the sprawling city of Los Angeles. She sighed heavily and switched back to her main social media account. Red notification bubbles from unread messages were scattered across her screen. Pictures, reactions, TikTok videos. Her fake friends hadn't even noticed she'd been offline for over a week. But what about real friends?

Just two messages from Katie — one from a week ago:

```
When are you coming back to work?
```

And another, more recent:

Any news about C.?

That's it? After their argument the day before the attack? It wasn't exactly a small fight, but still...*So, what has she even been doing without me?*

Ali closed Katie's profile after watching her third muted video of club dancing. Her friend hadn't missed her. Katie didn't need her. Ali glanced at Jack. The business class seats weren't too close, but she could still reach out and touch him if she wanted. He didn't return her gaze. Maybe he didn't notice. In this big plane, Ali felt like she was flying alone.

The captain announced some mild turbulence. Ali fastened her seatbelt and looked down. If the plane crashed, there would be no return to Illinois. She could stay in California forever and not suffer anymore.

The plane jolted violently. Ali pressed her head into the seat. *Stupid! Thinking about a plane crash?* The plane shook again. *Jinxed it.* She gripped the armrests, sharp pain shooting through her ribs on the left side. *I don't want to crash. I don't want to die. Oh God, please let everything be okay. Let this plane land safely. I can handle it. I can handle Chicago. I can handle going back home.*

She squeezed her eyes shut. Bit her lip. Inhaled, flaring her nostrils. Pursed her lips. Exhaled through her mouth. Breathed in through her nose. Out through her mouth. In through her nose. Out. In. Out.

The turbulence stopped.

The seatbelt sign turned off.

Home.

CHAPTER 18

The low ceiling fan sliced through the stagnant air, its metal blades spinning so fast that they blurred into a large, single eye. It whirred with such speed that the base creaked, as if threatening to detach, flying downward with enough momentum to decapitate everyone in the room, splattering blood across the swamp-colored walls of the windowless space.

"Ms. Brooks," a voice pulled her out of her dark thoughts. "If you don't mind, could you describe the intruder's appearance once more?"

Detective Sergio Gibbons turned on his recording device.

Ali sat in a chair, anything but cozy. Her shoulders slumped, weighed down. Aside from the fan that felt like it could kill at any moment, Ali was distracted by the large, wall-sized mirror. How many people were watching from behind it? One? Ten? Maybe even a reporter with a tripod and camera. What could she say? What should she keep to herself?

After landing at O'Hare, without stopping at home, Ali and Jack had grabbed burgers at the terminal and then headed straight to the police station. Lead Detective Gibbons had scheduled this meeting last week. Ali, disconnected from the outside world, would've probably missed the email invitation, but Jack, despite their argument the night before, hadn't forgotten and had gotten them there on time. He sat on a stool, back to the mirror, one leg crossed over the other, fingers interlaced. He seemed completely unbothered by the fact that people were watching him from behind the glass.

"Ms. Brooks...?" Sergio Gibbons smirked slightly from the corner of his mouth.

A stylish man; his white knit sweater with sleeves rolled up to the elbows and a new, light navy scarf looked out of place for a detective. Yet the predatory gleam in his eyes and the five-pointed star dangling from a thick chain around his neck, engraved with "Chicago Police Department," reminded her who he really was.

"Who's watching us?" Ali asked, glancing back at the mirror, squinting, as if trying to peer through the thick glass.

"Ali, let's just get this over with," Jack said, shifting his legs.

"I'm just curious," she whispered back.

"We don't have time for curiosity," Jack snapped.

Ali pressed her lips into a crooked smile, placing her hands on the thick wooden table, which looked like it had been pulled straight out of a Soviet spy movie — a blinking recording device, witness statements, and black-and-white photos of the all-too-familiar house were scattered across the table. Above Detective Gibbons, an old clock hung, its faded numbers framed by a stained wooden circle. The ticking second hand marked the passage of time, counting down to either someone's dinner or someone's trial.

"You couldn't make out any distinguishing features?" the

detective pressed on.

"Black cloak, black mask, black eyes, and a knife," Ali recited, ticking them off on her fingers.

"And his movements? Quick? Slow? Did anything stand out?"

"I don't know," Alicia hesitated. "Both quick and slow at the same time. Fluid."

"Graceful?" the detective clarified.

"Graceful?" Jack scoffed, throwing a sharp glance at the officer. "Are we seriously discussing the gracefulness of a criminal?"

"Mr. Sylvan," Gibbons replied calmly. "It's incredibly difficult to create a profile based solely on Ms. Brooks's description. We can't rely on just a shadowy figure; we're trying to piece together the full picture." He turned back to Alicia. "And the voice? Rough, gentle, masculine, feminine?"

"He didn't speak. He just...rasped."

"Rasped how?"

"Like he was struggling to breathe."

"Hmm, maybe a medical condition?" The detective scribbled "med" in a circle. "But if we had to guess from the rasping, the voice..."

"Definitely a man," she said and nodded.

"Why do you think that?"

"Because I could feel it. A male energy...predatory energy," she replied, glancing at Jack, who remained fixated on his hands.

Silence settled in. The detective jotted down notes, this time in a much larger notebook than the tiny one he'd used earlier — something more like an A4 journal.

"Ms. Brooks, the lab has completed the analysis of the evidence, and unfortunately, we found nothing significant. There were no fingerprints, no fibers from the clothing."

Ali hugged herself. *This felt pointless*, she thought. No evidence…did she really have to wait for blood to be shed for them to find clues?

"By the way, we're still waiting for your list of potential suspects."

"I forgot," Ali mumbled. She really had forgotten about it while in Los Angeles.

"What about the security cameras?" Jack asked.

Ali gave him a thankful glance. *At least he still cared.*

"That's where things get tricky. The street doesn't have public surveillance, and the only cameras, as you mentioned, belong to your neighbor. However, on the night of April 28th, around one a.m., the footage cut off — the owner claims the wires were cut. We confirmed this ourselves — a clean, deliberate slice had severed the power. When we questioned your neighbor, he had no idea the camera was down. Unfortunately, the most recent image we recovered was taken nearly eighteen hours prior, which doesn't help us."

Gibbons spread three photos across the table in front of Alicia. She flinched and glanced at the clock again, avoiding the images. *Couldn't bear to look.*

"The quality is decent," Gibbons continued. "But as I mentioned, they don't offer us anything useful."

Jack scraped the legs of his stool against the floor as he leaned over the photos, running his finger over each one. The camera's wide lens captured the street and the house opposite.

All the shots were from the right corner of the neighbor's house. Jack couldn't recall the man's name — just some renter, a die-hard Trump supporter.

The first photo showed a closed front door, a bright white reflection from the glass — Alicia had, as usual, lit up every room in the house. The second photo was of the terrace doors, bathed in overexposed light. The house looked like a festival of lights. The third photo was a close-up of the severed wire — a surgical job.

"Was this before or after Katie left?" Jack asked Alicia, turning to her.

Alicia shrugged, her shoulders stiff. Her memory sluggishly rewound to the argument she didn't want to revisit. "She left right after Matthew showed up."

"Ms. Brooks, could you describe the events leading up to this in detail?"

"I'm trying," Alicia's voice wavered with frustration. "Katie and I were drinking wine, then I dozed off...and woke up when someone knocked on the door. Katie — she's the friend I was drinking with — invited some guy from Tinder over, but I wouldn't let him in. We argued. Me and Katie...fought."

Alicia flinched, nearly falling off her chair. The sound echoed in the room, followed by a steady beeping, like an annoying fridge door left open. Detective Gibbons coughed and signaled toward the mirror with his thumb. The beep stopped. The echo slowly faded.

"Why didn't you mention this before? Maybe that Tinder guy is the one in the mask!" Jack burst out.

"I don't know!"

"Mr. Sylvan, please remain calm," Gibbons said firmly. "Provide us with your friend Katie's details — we'll speak to her and track down this Matthew."

Alicia gasped, covering her mouth with both hands. Both men turned to her, but she shook her head frantically, her eyes wide. A horrible thought was forming.

"Did you interrogate that neighbor?" Jack asked, slumping back onto his stool. "Maybe it was him. Maybe he cut the wires himself."

"We questioned him on the first day. He has a solid alibi," Gibbons said. "And there's absolutely no motive."

Alicia still sat with her hands pressed to her mouth, her breath dampening her palms. Eyes fixated on the photograph on the table. The thought was nearly fully formed. She needed to ask, to know if anyone else was thinking the same thing. To know just how slim her chance of survival had been.

"The Silent Walker was prepared...he knew..." Alicia's voice turned into a panicked shriek. "That sick bastard knew about the cameras and cut the wires beforehand! He was waiting! He was watching! Watching me, Jack, even the neighbors. He was there a whole day earlier! I'm lucky to be alive!"

She looked at the men, tears brimming in her eyes. Both were silent.

CHAPTER 19

The clock hands made a full rotation for a second time.

"We need to establish the motive and type of crime," Gibbons concluded, pushing his squeaky chair back under the table. "This was either an intentional attack with the aim of causing serious harm or just a failed burglary."

"But he had a knife, and he...he wanted to kill me," Alicia stammered.

"That's not confirmed. It could have been just to scare you. The most important thing for you both right now is not to panic or fall into depression. You need to cooperate with us — the police — daily and as closely as possible so we can catch the perpetrator quickly."

"Is it safe for us to return home? Can you do something to ensure our safety?" Jack asked.

Gibbons rubbed his chin, glancing toward the mirror before answering.

"At the moment, it's difficult. For the police to assign resources, even one person, we need a pressing reason and one hundred percent confirmation that Ms. Brooks remains in danger. Unfortunately, our department is currently facing a clear shortage of staff."

"You're always short on staff," Alicia muttered.

Gibbons raised an eyebrow but didn't respond.

"What if we get a lawyer involved?" Jack asked, narrowing his eyes.

"Feel free to, but do such matters get resolved quickly? Instead of focusing on finding the culprit, the department chief will have to allocate resources to a legal case." The detective spread his hands. "I suggest you hire a private security company, install surveillance cameras, and an alarm system at home. It will be cheaper than a lawyer, and Ms. Brooks will always have an emergency button with her."

Alicia clasped her hands together. Rely on the police, but don't leave it all to them.

The detective walked them to the exit, handing Jack a business card for an agency called "Security and Reliability." The couple silently stepped out onto the wide street. Alicia took a deep breath of fresh air, feeling the coolness on her cheeks — there had been no air in the room.

"How are you?" Jack placed a hand on her shoulder and gently squeezed. The first moment of closeness since Los Angeles.

Alicia placed her hand over his. The world was tumbling downhill in a mess, and she hadn't managed to stop it, climb on top of it, or even catch up to it.

"I don't know," she answered honestly.

Jack put his other arm around her waist, pulling her close. She leaned into him, wrapping her arms around his back. A subtle hint of airplane air still clung to him.

"You'll get through this. The police will catch the scumbag. We'll put him in jail for a long time, and everything will go back to normal soon."

"Thank you for coming with me, Jack." Alicia rested her forehead against him. "I really appreciate it, and I'm sorry for saying those things last night."

"It's okay, I understand," he said, brushing a loose blond curl from her face. "You're still under a lot of stress. It'll pass; I'll help you. Let's set up daily sessions with Ms. Dancy? Until the police catch him, I think you need that."

"Okay, but..."

"Do you want me to call her for you?"

"Yes, just..."

"I'll cover everything, don't worry." Jack kissed her on the lips.

Alicia responded to the kiss — gentle and soft, holding back tears, she pulled his lips closer before letting go.

"Thank you," she whispered.

He took her hand, and they walked toward the car. The road was calling.

***

The blue Mercedes turned onto Perry Avenue.

The first corner house, the Hodges family's orange grove, the familiar pothole now patched with fresh asphalt — Jack instinctively turned the wheel right to avoid it.

Alicia glanced at the speedometer — the needle hovered near twenty, yet time dragged on, as if the car were being pulled by actual caterpillars.

Returning home had haunted her ever since the plane's wheels had lifted off the ground. Her attempts not to dwell on it had failed — images of the living room and its tall railings flashed before her eyes, like the face of a grotesque creature glimpsed through fingers during a horror movie. The neighbor's house appeared through the window, and then...

There it was — the brick monster staring back at her through the tinted glass. If objects didn't have souls, why did it feel like this one was reaching out with a gaping mouth? The garage, the balcony, the wide windows (*why were there so many?*) gleamed in the sunlight, beckoning her inside. She imagined prying them open with a crowbar and squeezing through.

Alicia didn't dare say any of this out loud. In her mind, a woman's voice whispered. "You're almost thirty," followed by a man's loud, tired voice: "I'm exhausted." She feared being left alone.

But there was no escaping. She couldn't sink into the car or vanish into the seat forever. Jack pulled into the garage, turned off the engine, and pressed the button to open the trunk. Alicia clenched her fingers, trying to stop the cold shiver crawling through her body. It didn't help. She opened the car door, and the smell of the house hit her like a punch to the nose. The smell of death.

Alicia put one foot on the slick garage floor, stepped out, and nearly twisted her ankle. She caught herself by grabbing the door and glanced at Jack — he was busy pulling out the first suitcase, oblivious. As he bent over to grab the second, she quietly slipped inside through the garage door.

The hallway greeted her like a slap in the face. Police boot prints stained the floor; yellow tape had almost peeled off the wall, curling on the ground. The pink stain on the carpet wasn't alone — another dark one had joined it, likely tea or coffee spilled by one of the officers. Chairs were scattered across the living room: one had been stood on, another kicked aside. The third still held the memory of the detective who had offered her a cinnamon roll.

Alicia kicked off her shoes and buried her feet in the carpet — soft, plush, untouched by a washing machine. She sat down and ran her hand over it, the fibers springing up like untrimmed grass. Her fingers reached the edge and stopped. Something stuck out from under the couch.

A clue? She reached in and pulled out a wine cork. Pressed, perfectly round, just like her old life before The Silent Walker came. The last bottle of wine shared in that previous life. The last party with her best friend, now only a memory lingering in this carpet. What now? Alicia threw the cork back under the couch and stood up.

Her hand rested on the cold dining table — one of the things that had saved her that night. If they had bought a smaller one, maybe she wouldn't have escaped, and he would've caught her right there. In this very room. Alicia circled the table until she stopped at the spot where she had first seen The Silent Walker. Her feet stuck. Couldn't recall what happened before that. She had probably finished watching a movie — a comedy, maybe? She might've wanted some chips. Had it been the draft that made her close the window, or was it something else? Her memory began right here, at this point. She had been standing — between the window and the table — and then…he appeared out of nowhere. He had been hiding.

Where? Where had he waited?

The garage door banged, and Alicia instinctively dropped to her knees, covering her head with her hands.

The Silent Walker had come back!

"Home sweet home," Jack said without a trace of sarcasm.

Alicia grabbed the edge of the table and peeked out.

"Why are you sitting on the floor?"

"Picking up some trash," she lied.

"The police really trashed the place," Jack said, glancing around the room before waving it off. "Don't worry, I'll order a cleaning service for tomorrow."

He picked up both suitcases by their side handles and headed upstairs. Alicia clung to the table, trying to stop her shaking. Her smartwatch pulsed red — heart racing. She pressed her weight onto her heels to steady trembling legs.

"Ali, help me unpack," Jack called down from upstairs.

"Coming, Jack," she answered in a false, chipper voice.

Almost thirty, she reminded herself. *Get a grip.* Her fingers let go of the table and pressed hard against her eyes to stop the tears from flowing. White spots danced in the darkness. The pain replaced the urge to cry. Alicia lightly slapped her cheeks and dragged herself toward the stairs.

During the house viewing, the realtor had hesitated to mention the stairs, which didn't meet code. Steps taller than ten inches were considered dangerous for small children, but Jack had reassured her they wouldn't be having kids anytime soon, and thankfully, they had no friends with kids.

The Silent Walker hadn't been slowed down by those tall steps. He had raced up them without stumbling, without getting tangled in the long folds of his black cloak. Alicia looked up at them now. How much she had to overcome.

Jack...No, she couldn't call Jack. *He was tired, Ali.* He wouldn't take care of a broken woman.

Alicia gripped the handrail with both hands and placed her foot on the first step. Her knee trembled again. The forensic team had dusted every inch of the staircase, used UV lights, but they hadn't found a single clue.

How? How could anyone move so quickly and leave no trace? Leaning on the rail, Alicia climbed. Third step, fourth... tenth...thirteenth. Thirteen steps. Thirteen steps, then seven more strides — just long enough for her to reach the bathroom and lock herself in. Thirteen steps, seven strides, and a sturdy lock had stood in The Silent Walker's way.

Alicia touched the bathroom door with her hand — another savior. She ran her fingers over the wood — no dents, no cracks, though it had felt like the door was about to be ripped off its hinges. And yet, the police had found nothing.

She pushed the door open and stepped inside. Sat on the dusty floor. Lay down on her back, using the bathmat as a pillow. She lifted her legs, bending her knees against the door. Stared at the ceiling. It was strange how some moments in life sped by like a rocket, while others stood still. And that feeling of eternity — like it would never, ever end. She wondered: When you die, does time slow down too, torturing and exhausting you?

Or the opposite?

"I can't go on like this," she whispered to herself. "But I can do this. I lost the battle, and I still have to live in this house. But I have to get through it."

She had to. Otherwise, she'd lose the war.

CHAPTER 20

For the next few days, she managed — or so Jack thought.

He took care of her just enough, but no more. Not like in Los Angeles. Mostly, it was because of his busy work schedule, and partly due to the lingering tension from their sea-salty argument. Jack had made it clear: he wouldn't tolerate being leaned on too heavily.

In the mornings (Ali would wake up an hour later), they had breakfast, usually delivered by Uber Eats. Once, a Mexican courier managed to deliver the pancakes to them while they were still warm, but most mornings, the heat evaporated by the time the food arrived, and they were left eating cold meals.

By nine a.m., Jack would drop Ali off at North Way Street and head to his office. Three hours of daily therapy sessions with Ms. Dancy were supposed to free her from panic attacks, potential depression, and prevent any form of post-traumatic stress disorder. Ali dutifully answered the questions and echoed Ms. Dancy's affirmations, but she never truly opened up.

"Everything good?" Ms. Dancy would ask with her morning smile.

Jack had covered the full cost, buying a month-long trauma-intensive program in advance. Ali suspected that the plan was an "all-inclusive" package: six sessions a week, no penalty for lateness, and a full progress report. What exactly the progress report contained or who received it, Ali had no idea.

"Better than yesterday. Thank you. Our last talk really helped," Ali would respond, sitting down in the chair, reciting the same lines each day.

She played her role. She had learned this skill back in her childhood, in the "Fairy Tale" theater group, where she was taught to cry and laugh at the snap of a director's fingers. Once, she had the role of Bluebeard's wife — acting curious and then hysterical at the sight of lifeless, doll-like corpses.

But her favorite role had always been Cinderella, the unlucky princess who believed in her dreams and waited for the fairy's rescue. Just like back then, Ali could convince others that she blindly believed in a bright future, where kindness and the help of those around her would put an end to the string of scary events. Now, she was acting again in the theater of real life, performing for Ms. Dancy and Jack, "improving" her mental state, day by day — anything to avoid being left alone.

Yes, I'm falling asleep faster. Yes, I don't wake up in the middle of the night. Yes, I hardly remember that evening. Yes. Yes.

Now, she only needed to believe it herself.

But what she really wanted most was to return to her beloved job. Ms. Dancy had recommended that Alicia limit her interactions and delay going back to her normal life until she was fully mentally recovered. The department head (who, of course, had spoken to Jack on Ali's behalf) required written confirmation of Alicia Brooks's stable mental condition before ending her forced leave of absence.

"I think I'm ready to return to work," Ali said hopefully. "I want to take the psychological test."

"Oh, dear Alicia, I would love to agree with you, but it seems you just need a little more time," Ms. Dancy said, opening a very small space between her thumb and forefinger.

That damn "little more time." Every day, the annoyingly sweet therapist wouldn't let those fingers move a single inch closer.

Ali tried to keep her frustration at bay, but Ms. Dancy caught the flicker of irritation in her eyes and scribbled something down in her thick notebook, the one with "A. B." on the cover.

"Let's focus on the here and now," the therapist said, flipping the page. "You've gotten closer to feeling the present moment, but we still have work to do. In difficult situations, you keep jumping between the future and the present, which is why the emotion of fear hasn't left your consciousness. I notice it in your body language: your eyelids twitching, your mouth slightly pulling during the last forest meditation. Tell me — were you afraid?"

That last meditation...no matter how hard Ali tried to close her eyes and mentally transport herself to a secluded field with a warm campfire (fueled by the scent of IKEA incense) and the sound of an owl hooting (on a loop from YouTube), it didn't work. The darkness crept in, tightening its grasp on her imaginary sanctuary. Then he came: The Silent Walker.

"I was fine," Ali whispered.

"Ms. Brooks, I suspect you aren't evaluating your condition

clearly. When we try to shift your focus solely to my words, you think of something else. What if someone attacks in that forest clearing? What if someone jumps out from behind the trees? What if a maniac —"

"The Silent Walker."

"The Silent Walker, fine," Ms. Dancy agreed. "But our goal is to help you eliminate those thoughts. You're afraid because you live in a future that's entirely built on fear, even though the chances of that future happening are almost zero. You're walking on thin ice, risking a deep plunge into stress, simply because you were unlucky enough that someone broke into your home."

What's the point in fighting it? Ali woke up every morning with her heart racing out of her chest.

"I guess I'm just that unlucky," she snapped, dropping her Cinderella act. "But maybe it wasn't just luck. Maybe The Silent Walker was stalking *me*. He was waiting for *me*!"

"Alicia, I'm only repeating what the police have said. Focusing on the idea that he targeted you specifically will only make your state worse," Ms. Dancy countered. "But regardless, you must not let this ruin your life. Instead of thinking about the dozens, hundreds, thousands of 'what-ifs,' you need to focus on the present moment. What is around you? What are you grateful for? The sunny weather, a cozy bed, good food. Focus on presence. What are you feeling right now?"

"Uh..." Ali hesitated. "Well, I'm here today."

"Good. What else?"

"Jack drove me."

"Anything else?"

"I have sessions with a professional."

"And?"

"I'm alive," Ali whispered.

Ms. Dancy clapped her hands silently. "Excellent, Ms. Brooks, very good! From the little things to the biggest: You're alive, you're here, and the police are looking for the criminals responsible for your home break-in. You're surrounded by people who care for you and provide safety. If you feel scared, just list at least three things you're grateful for."

A phone rang. Ali quickly pulled hers from her pocket and silenced it. A message popped up.

"Jack said he won't be able to pick me up soon," she said apologetically, noticing Ms. Dancy's reproachful look. "I have it set to silent for everyone except his calls."

"It's all right, our session is over anyway," Ms. Dancy said, putting away her notebook. "You can stay in the waiting room if you'd like, to wait for Mr. Sylvan."

"No, I'll head home."

"On your own?"

"Yes, of course. I'm feeling much better today. Thank you, see you tomorrow." Ali waved with a wide smile.

Ali left the building, unaware that this would be her last session with Ms. Dancy. The cool breeze carried the scent of freedom. If this act of resolve didn't speed up her return to work, then she'd have to ask Jack to talk to the therapist. After all, it was because of him that she was stuck without a job.

After sending Jack a voice message, saying everything was fine, her mood was great, and she was going to take a walk, Ali headed for the nearest train station.

It had been a while since she'd taken the train. Since her old life.

The metallic screech of the train arriving filled the platform. It wasn't rush hour, and only a few passengers were scattered throughout the car. The once-blue seats had grayed with age, and the walls had lost their sheen, dulled by countless attempts to scrub off graffiti.

Ali took a seat by the window, choosing one with fewer old chewing gum stains. She placed her bag on her lap and wound the strap tightly around her hand. Just in case. Therapy sessions were exhausting, no less than work.

She didn't notice the man when he boarded at the last station, but she first heard him when they entered the tunnel. He was sitting across from her, back to the window, with a round backpack resting on the seat beside him. The man was muttering to himself, barely audible.

"Fucking train...damn blue line..."

Ali shifted discreetly in her seat, positioning herself to get a better look without drawing attention.

"Standing there, waiting, always fucking late. Damn state can't even run trains on time," the man said, then spat onto the floor.

Apart from them, the only other passenger was a guy with his eyes closed. White earbuds dangled from his ears, standing out against his dark green T-shirt. His head rested against the side window, probably asleep.

"No one cares about transport. All these rich bastards driving around in their fancy cars, while we honest folks..."

The man's head suddenly jerked in her direction. Ali froze,

her gaze locked on her lap, but she kept him in her peripheral vision.

He reached into his pocket. "Fucking Democrats..."

Ali's grip on her bag's strap tightened. *What's in his pocket?*

He rummaged around inside, swearing under his breath, then reached for his backpack.

Please don't be a gun.

A wave of fear exploded in her stomach, radiating out to the rest of her body. Her hands jerked up like a marionette's, fingers twitching involuntarily. The fear surged up to her temples, pounding like a warning bell.

Don't make eye contact. Don't.

Get out. Now.

But where? Where could she run?

The train hurtled through the tunnel, lights flickering in a strobe-like rhythm.

What if he chases?

What if he shoots?

What if it's...him?

The terror coiled tighter, building into a roaring turbine, spinning faster and faster inside her. As the motor of panic revved louder, she felt herself unraveling, fragmenting into pieces. The train's rumble blurred into a dull hiss. Ali's lips moved silently: "I'm grateful...I'm grateful for...I...I..." She tried to grasp for a shred of calm. It was useless. The noise of the turbine drowned out her own thoughts.

Somewhere deep down, she had always known the truth. She knew how weak she was. She knew she couldn't be strong, couldn't hide her panicked, darting eyes behind sunglasses.

She was born to be weak. To hide inside her home behind steel locks, never again looking through the peephole, never responding to friends' calls, never talking to loved ones.

Forever shut away.

A cheerful melody filled the train. *Tru-ta-ta, tru-ta-ta.* The jingle of coins dropping into a slot machine. Ali jumped, startled out of her imaginary grave. The music was coming from the man.

He wasn't reaching for a gun. He'd been looking for his phone to play a game.

The train slowed to a halt, and Ali bolted off at the next station. She glanced back at the man, but he didn't even notice her. He was too engrossed in his game.

Something was wrong. She had never been this scared of something so trivial before. Or had she? Could this really be post-traumatic stress?

Her head swam, and she vomited right there on the station platform. Panicked, she glanced around, quickly wiped her mouth with a napkin, and rushed off before anyone noticed. She needed to get out. Think. Go back to Ms. Dancy and admit the therapy wasn't helping. To hell with work.

As she slumped onto a bench in the park, a message from Detective Gibbons appeared on her phone. A meeting. Today. Without Jack.

Ali called a taxi to the police station. Enough public transport for one day.

CHAPTER 21

The damp, murky walls, the large mirror, the oak table — everything was in its usual place. Even the musty air lingered — unchanged. But the stool was gone, as was Jack's reassuring presence from previous meetings.

"Ms. Brooks." Detective Sergio Gibbons rested his elbows on the table. "How's your day? I hope I didn't pull you away from anything too important?"

"Not really," Ali replied tersely, her eyes scanning the room, careful not to look at the empty space. "Is there any progress?"

Gibbons glanced at the mirror. "You might feel like the case is dragging, but we're working diligently, still trying to find the person responsible for the attack."

Ali shivered. The thought that the maniac with the knife was after her specifically had burrowed deep into her mind, gnawing at her from the inside out. The stale air made it hard to breathe fully, and she had no idea how to stay calm anymore. And why was she alone again?

Gibbons stood up, straightening the pile of folders and papers on the table before rolling up the sleeves of his checkered jacket. She had never seen him in the same outfit twice — not even his belt. Today it was chrome. *He must have his own tailor*, Ali thought. Only the detective's badge, always polished to a shine, remained constant.

Gibbons retrieved a familiar small notebook from his inner pocket, spun it on one finger through the metal rings, and approached the large mirror. Through the reflection, Ali saw him frown, spinning the notebook slowly.

Was someone behind the glass? Was he communicating with someone? Why wasn't he speaking? Or was information being fed to him from the other side?

"Alicia," he said as he finally turned toward her, his voice carrying an odd tone. It was something between tenderness and sympathy — the kind of voice doctors use to deliver bad news. "We spoke with your friend Katie and got in touch with the uninvited guest, Matthew Ross, but we didn't find a clear motive for either of them. Right after his visit to your place, Mr. Ross went to see his friends — we have proof of that. I'm not saying this is a final conclusion," he raised his finger. "But so far, this version hasn't been confirmed. The neighbors' testimonies didn't give us the expected results, either."

Ali forced a tense smile and exhaled sharply through her nose.

"So, Detective, you're telling me this is all the progress you've made in nearly a month?"

"No, Alicia —"

"I prefer Ms. Brooks," she cut him off.

Gibbons carefully adjusted his badge chain without touching the shiny star on his chest and moved his chair to the other side of the table, directly in front of her. He sat down, his elbows resting on his knees, hands clasped together under his sharp chin. His head was now lower than hers, and for the first time, Ali saw it in his eyes: R-E-G-R-E-T.

Something wasn't right.

"Sometimes, Ms. Brooks, people do strange things for their own benefit. Even those close to us."

"Mm-hmm." Ali said, biting her lip.

"Despite already interviewing Mr. Sylvan, we've returned our focus to him. A few days ago, we received information about a finalized deal on the purchase of the house at 9436 Perry Avenue — the current crime scene. The deal was signed by the former owner, Gary Black, and Jack Sylvan. It's a record-low price for the area since 1992."

"Yes, Jack bought the house. We're no longer renting. So what?"

"Ms. Brooks." Gibbons leaned in, his dry, chapped lips forming words slowly. He was a lip-biter, too, it seemed. "We have to consider Jack a suspect. He has a motive."

"My Jack? You think my Jack —?" Ali gasped.

"Yes, your de facto partner."

"What kind of nonsense is this?" She grabbed the armrests of her chair, trying to stop the wild spinning sensation in her head. "He was in California!"

"I know this is hard to hear, but we have to explore every possibility. We can't rule him out."

It didn't make sense.

"You think Jack wants to kill me? Are you crazy?"

"Listen —"

"Jack isn't capable of something like that! He's not!"

She squeezed her eyes shut as her mind spun like a kaleidoscope of chaotic thoughts.

Gibbons straightened up, towering over her. His voice softened but remained steady. "Ms. Brooks, this is a standard procedure. Jack may have an alibi, and that does play a significant role, but it's not uncommon for perpetrators to outsource their dirty work. Motive is key. Crimes don't happen without motive. And right now, Jack has the strongest one. Besides...he knew about the neighbor's surveillance and could have prepared in advance."

The spinning in Ali's head sped up, distorting her vision. The swampy color of the room nauseated her.

"Why would he want to hurt me? He didn't even know if Black would even agree to sell the house."

"You're not aware?" Gibbons squinted. "The house was listed for sale a month and a half ago. Before the attack."

"What?" Ali couldn't believe it. Did she hear him right?

"The house went up for auction on April 2nd. We spoke to the owner earlier that week. None of the offers at the time appealed to him. Mr. Black admitted the initial price was inflated, but he didn't expect to lose money. After the attack, he had no choice but to cut the price when selling to Mr. Sylvan."

She wanted to run, but her legs wouldn't carry the weight of the truth.

"Sergio." Ali placed a trembling hand on the detective's knee. He glanced nervously at the mirror but didn't move her hand away. "Do you *really* think it was Jack? Tell me the truth."

"Alicia..."

"Tell me, Sergio!" Her grip tightened on his knee, eyes

locked on his troubled gaze. "I'm going back to that damn house tonight! To the man who...who might have attacked me. For God's sake, tell me!"

"I don't think it was Jack," the detective said quietly. "But understand, we have to follow protocol. Besides Jack, we're also questioning others who bid on the house, but right now, your boyfriend is our priority."

Ali released his knee. Gibbons stood immediately, as if freed from invisible chains. He walked over to the mirror, biting his lower lip. The chair creaked as Ali rose to her feet. As Gibbons turned back to her, Alicia caught the brief flicker of surprise in his eyes — the way he was taken aback by the shift in her. She sensed her own reflection in his gaze: a hollow resolve in her straight posture, head held high.

"Let me know when there's real progress," Ali said coldly, heading for the door. "Goodbye, Detective Gibbons."

"Until next time, Ms. Brooks."

Ali stepped out of the police station into the crowded streets of Chicago. The city buzzed with people rushing by, but her thoughts spun only around Jack. The idea that he was a suspect was absurd. Why would he do such a thing? What would he gain?

No. It was nonsense. Complete madness. The Silent Walker wasn't Jack.

Yet, despite all her reasoning, a tiny shadow of doubt crept into the darkest corners of her mind. Among her memories and experiences, a sinister thought waited, barely perceptible — but there.

They still hadn't caught him.

The Silent Walker was out there.

Ali kept walking forward until she realized no one was brushing past her anymore. She had left behind the office and tourist streets with their multi-story parking lots and loud shopping centers. There were no more people around.

A quiet, sleeping neighborhood. Evening had settled in, yet the houses remained dark. Ali turned her head, searching for familiar signs — nothing. The suburb was completely unfamiliar and not particularly affluent — much poorer than Hunter. On the sidewalk, the wind played football with a plastic bag from a supermarket. A rat could easily fall into the cracks in the asphalt. An overgrown vine had wrapped itself around the façade of a single-story house on the corner. Ali stood on her tiptoes, peeking through the dark window.

No one was there.

She unlocked her phone and opened the map. The blue dot floated in the center of the screen. Ali rotated the map, trying to orient herself. There was the house with the ivy she'd just passed, but where was the police station? After circling her location on the screen a few more times, she exhaled sharply and typed the address in.

Her phone calculated the route: an hour and a half on foot or twenty-four minutes by car. She brushed a stray lock of hair from her forehead and looked around again. How had she gotten so lost?

That's when she felt it. First, her nose caught it — a chill ran like a blade along her legs, making her hands tremble. Only after her brain finally processed the alarm triggered by the scent did she look up.

He stood in the middle of the street.

His raspy breath carried on the wind beneath the mask.

The Silent Walker had found her.

CHAPTER 22

Same coat. Same mask.

The eyes were different. Hungry.

Ali took two steps back, gasping for air. The Silent Walker remained still, yet the smell — the unmistakable scent of him — grew closer. This time, it broke through and resonated deeply. Stale, sharp, dusty. It smelled like a forgotten attic in a crumbling house. Like an old wardrobe left unopened for years. Like her grandfather's polished table stored in the garage. It smelled like the imprint of time itself.

Sixty feet or so — that's all that separated life from death.

"Maybe you're imagining him?" whispered a voice in her head — Ms. Dancy, perhaps.

No, no. I'm not imagining him. No, dammit, he's real!

"Maybe if you don't look at him, he'll disappear?" suggested another voice — this time, Jack's.

Where would he go? He's here for me! He found me! He's hunting me! What should I do?

"Run," answered The Silent Walker.

And he rushed toward her.

Ali sprinted. Stopping wasn't an option. She couldn't hear

his boots hit the pavement, but the swish of his black coat tangling at his legs and his heavy breaths echoed in her ears. *Shouldn't the coat slow him down*, she wondered. *God, give me the strength to run.*

She stumbled and twisted her ankle but didn't fall — thank the baseball lessons at school, where she learned to balance. She stayed on her toes, but her Pedro sandals betrayed her — the heel snapped. Her legs kept running. With every step, the heel wobbled like a loose tooth, ready to pop off any second. Ali glanced over her shoulder: The Silent Walker wasn't falling behind; if anything, he was closer.

Damn, damn, damn.

Running on a broken heel was a countdown to being caught. Ali bent down and yanked the damaged shoe off her foot — it tumbled across the pavement, flipping. She wished, as if by magic, it would trip him, slow him down, stop him. But she didn't believe in magic. She ripped the other sandal off mid-run, gripping it tightly. She didn't throw it — it might still be useful.

The main street ended at a house with two dry bushes. A fence of wooden planks was broken, and a moldy bucket stood where a mailbox should be. The street forked: both ways empty. *Which way to run?* The road to the right twisted between dark houses. The left led to a dead end, with a lonely streetlight.

She turned right, catching a glimpse of the black coat flapping in the wind. The Silent Walker had no doubt. He knew where to run.

"HELP! SOMEONE HELP!" Ali screamed, only to start coughing.

Her breath was ragged, her head spinning. She tried to scream again, but her throat closed — the sound that came out was no more than a kitten's squeak.

Small stones scratched her bare feet, lodging between her toes, and cut into her filthy heels. One pinky toenail peeled halfway off, leaking fluid that turned sticky with dust.

Run, run, run.

A local homeless man named Gwyn was temporarily camped at the junction of two streets. He didn't care much for other drunks without a home, nor did he collect bottles. He thought himself too proud to drag clinking bags of glass and wait in line for a few crumpled bucks. Truth be told, he was just lazy. After his last sip, he released the bottle into freedom. Occasionally, he felt like smashing "roses" — grabbing the bottle by the neck and splitting it with one professional swing against a wall. Gwyn tossed both halves onto the road. Sometimes a car drove by, and if he was lucky, the bottom or neck would pierce a tire's sidewall. That's when drivers would stop, step out to inspect the damage, and Gwyn would shuffle over with a paper cup, asking for clean, crisp cash.

The bum was snoring softly in his makeshift tarp tent when Ali, blind to the road ahead, ran straight over his handiwork. Three broken bottles, set for tomorrow's hustle, waited patiently in the middle of the road. The sharp glass petals slid into her left bare foot like a knife into butter.

A scream tore through her throat. Sparks flared behind her eyes. Ali bent over, pulling her leg to her chest. Her filthy foot split open like a shell, blood, mixed with dirt, pulsing out in a steady stream. The rose bloomed red.

The footsteps were louder now. Ali glanced over her shoulder. Tears blurred his figure, but she still saw those sick, black eyes. The Silent Walker was almost on her. So close, he could probably smell her blood. He pulled a familiar long knife from his pocket. No longer shiny, and not as clean as before.

Oh God, were those dark round spots...dried blood?

Ali bent down to the mess of her foot and yanked out a long shard of glass. It had gone in deep, nearly an inch. The foot stung with an invisible blade, but for once, fear worked in her favor. Adrenaline drowned out the pain. Ali placed her bleeding foot on the ground and pressed down — tears flowed freely again. Pity could come later. If she survived.

Ali wiped her eyes with the back of her hand. With trembling fingers, she raised the sandal. She turned it heel-first. Took aim. *Like baseball.* Held her breath...and hurled it with all her might.

Just hit. Please, let it hit.

A dull thud — direct hit! The shoe struck right in the middle of the mask — maybe the nose, maybe even the eye. There was no time to waste. Ali clenched her fists and jumped to the side. She didn't need to look back — the plan worked, the throw slowed him down. But she knew it wouldn't last — a second, maybe five.

Don't waste the luck.

Run. Run faster.

The street split again, and Ali veered right. Her foot exploded with searing pain, blood still pouring, leaving behind a trail like a red carpet — one she never asked to walk.

A miracle! Salvation!

Between a brick house and another corner stood a small local shop with a glowing purple "Open" sign. Light poured from the barred window.

"Help! Open the door!" Ali groaned.

Her face turned pale. She didn't know how much blood she had lost or whether she had enough strength left to run. She felt drained — like her body was running on empty. Her healthy leg twitched at the knee, her cut foot pulsed and throbbed, as if something was crawling inside. Every step felt sharper. Ali groaned and hopped on her good leg. Pulled the other one. Squatted and leaped again. The doorstep was only several feet away.

One more jump.

She fell onto the platform. A new wave of pain shot through her body as her knee slammed into the concrete. Ali tried to stand, but her right leg cramped up. She leaned her elbows on the cold door, reached for the handle, and pulled.

A shock wave ran through her fingers. The glass door, painted with a drawing of green trees, didn't budge. Ali pulled again, but the handle dropped only a half an inch.

Closed.

"Let me...let me in," Ali whispered.

She raised her clenched fist and banged on the glass. Her knuckles turned red, her body shuddered with pain, but she bit her lip and hit again. Harder. Again. *Come on! COME ON!*

Her wrist bent, and unexpectedly, she lurched forward. Ali, still gripping the handle, felt the world collapse — the ground disappearing as she tumbled through the glass door and into a strange, silent void.

But she didn't fall into oblivion — she hit the cold, gray tile.

Darkness gave way to brightness. A yogurt ad broke through the pounding of her heart. Shelves filled with instant noodles, glossy bags of chips, soda bottles, and beer cans surrounded her.

A man's face loomed over her. Large ears stuck out from beneath dark, scruffy hair. His chin was sharp and clean-shaven. Round, brown eyes stared in shock.

Her fate now lay in the hands of a young boy.

Ali reached out to him. Fresh scratches streaked her palm, fingers stained with blood.

"Help me...please," she whispered and closed her eyes.

Chapter 23

Knuckles rapped on the door, just like his mother's frail ones had tapped eight years ago. She didn't break in looking for money for a bag of that coveted crystal like his father but politely asked.

"Hey, kid, still asleep?"

Jordy Evans jumped out of bed. It wasn't his mom knocking, and he wasn't fourteen anymore. While he untangled himself from the scratchy thin blanket, the last remnants of his dream lingered in his mind. Happy dreams only came after a day off — once a week, no more.

"Forgot about your schedule? Your time's running out, kid. Hurry up and get up," the old lady called from behind the door.

Auntie Chang, originally from China, had been living in this communal apartment since long before Jordy's parents ever tried meth. She disliked being reminded of her missed chance to become someone's American wife, and insisted on being called Auntie Chang, just like in her home province of Hebei. Since Jordy had become her neighbor, she'd taken care of him like family, though clumsily, with a roughness that in China was called care. Thanks to her, Jordy had never missed his turn in the bathroom.

"Thanks, Auntie Chang, I'm getting up."

He rubbed his sleepy eyes with long, skinny fingers, searching with his foot for the switch on the paper lampshade. The bulb flickered to life, illuminating his tiny room with a small rectangular window near the ceiling. The only remaining built-in shelf reminded him that this space used to be a closet. White walls were covered with taped-up medical notes and lecture handouts. Half the room was taken up by a single bed, a quarter by a plastic outdoor chair and a foldable table surface. The wooden sliding door with a makeshift lock led to the shared living room of the four-bedroom apartment, which had only one bathroom and a spacious kitchen. At least it was downtown.

In the dim light, Jordy found his dark green, worn T-shirt from last week. He sniffed it. A faint hint of deodorant and a little sweat — good enough. He pulled it over his smooth chest, hairless like that of a teenager. Then, he jumped into his second-year jeans, which he had rolled up and re-stitched when he'd started his master's. Grabbing the still-damp towel from the day before, he stepped over the pile of dirty clothes on the floor and ran out the door barefoot, nearly knocking over the tiny Auntie Chang.

"Aiya Huài xiaozi!" *Oh bad boy!* "I almost fell because of you."

The tenants shared a single bathroom: a tiny bathtub that could only comfortably fit Auntie Chang, a metal sink and a toilet. A schedule for morning and evening use hung on the door. Auntie Chang always went first, as the only woman in the apartment. After her, the men took their turns in order of age, from the youngest — Jordy — to the pensioner, David. Outside the scheduled times, the bathroom was free, but no one could use it for more than ten minutes at a time.

Jordy ducked down, wiped the foggy mirror with his hand, and smoothed his messy black hair with his wet hands. *Will get a haircut with the next paycheck*, he thought. He used to try hiding his awkward crescent-shaped ears, which stuck out like two wings, with longer hair. But longer hair needed more shampoo, and that meant more money. Better to be teased about his ears.

Carefully holding the sagging door of the cabinet to stop it from falling off, Jordy pulled out his disposable Bic razor from a Ziplock bag. He splashed hot water onto his hollow cheeks, lathered a strip of soap above his upper lip, and brushed downward with small strokes, rinsing the razor every now and then.

As he rinsed his toothbrush, a solid knock came on the door and a man's voice followed.

"Jordy, hurry up. It's my turn."

"One second, Mr. Breach."

Jordy placed his toothbrush back in the plastic cup, pulled the sagging wooden door from its swollen frame, and came face to face with his grumpy neighbor.

Mr. Breach — or John, as his drinking buddies called him — was a divorced alcoholic with a restraining order keeping him away from his own kids. He shoved skinny Jordy aside with his thick shoulder and squeezed through the door.

"Takes him half an hour to wash. Get outta here already."

Jordy slipped back into his room and tossed the towel onto the pile of clothes. On his unmade bed lay a packet of single-use Tide pods — courtesy of Auntie Chang while he'd been in the shower. He smiled, remembering how she always grumbled at him when he tried to hug her. Jordy unrolled a trash bag and started tossing clothes from the pile on the floor into it. From his Spider-Man piggy bank — a birthday gift from his mom when he was six — he pulled out twelve quarters, just enough for a wash but no drying. Spring meant the clothes would dry for free outside.

Jordy jumped into his sneakers, popped in his wired earbuds to listen to music on his phone loaded with pirated songs, and slung the laundry bag over his shoulder. Another tough week lay ahead, with six shifts at the store and one online lecture, ending with a long paper. There was no way he'd have time to finish it at home — he'd have to study at work.

"Thanks for the soap, Auntie Chang. When I become a pharmacist, I'll write your prescriptions for free."

"Go on, mèngxiang jiā." *Dreamer.* The seventy-year-old immigrant shook her head.

Jordy ran outside. The wind tossed his hair around his forehead. With his long legs (just like his father's, may he rest in peace), Jordy crossed the street in a few strides, running a red light, and pushed open the glass door of the laundromat.

The smell of detergent and cheap chemicals greeted him. Nine one-eyed washing machines stared out from the lower row, each with a dryer perched above. Two of them were already running. In the corner sat a round woman with a long braid, as round as a swollen watermelon. She was deeply engrossed in a book. She licked her thick, bratwurst-sized index finger as she turned the pages. Jordy caught sight of the spine — *Fifty Shades of Grey*.

"Good morning," he said with a wave.

"Oh, Jordy!" The woman raised all three of her chins to look at him. "You're here again. Need soap?"

"No, I've got my own today," he replied, tossing the black bag in front of the second machine.

"Drying today?"

"It'll dry outside."

She licked her plump lips and winked. "I can throw your stuff in the dryer after it's done washing. On the house."

"Really, Chloe? I feel bad about that."

"Just help me find some cheaper meds through your pharmacy connections. The doctor's giving me some pricey crap, and I'm working a whole week just to pay for it. If you can find something Chinese, cheaper..."

The plastic chair groaned as Chloe hoisted herself up, but it held strong. Jordy squatted, hurriedly stuffing his clothes into the machine, paying no attention to colors. The last thing he threw in were his socks. He crammed everything down, tossed the soap on top, and slammed the door shut. He pulled the quarters from his pocket — one quarter, two, three — and pressed start.

"Thanks, Chloe. What do you need me to find?"

She handed him a scrap of paper, marked up with a pencil. "Come back in a couple of hours. Or later. Don't worry about your things."

Jordy burst out of the soapy-smelling space and into the

fresh air. Without the need to wait forty-five minutes for the drum to spin, he could head straight to the university. Maybe he could drop in on another group's lecture and stop by the restricted section of the library to grab references on component formulas.

A couple of hours later, after attending the seminar on "Neuromuscular Blockers in ARDS" and finding the necessary textbook, Jordy's backpack felt as heavy as his head. He was already behind schedule, waiting for the silver-haired librarian after her lunch break with the key to the closed-off section. Then, he had to wait while she searched for his profile on a computer that looked like it was from the stone age. Lastly, he waited for permission to take the book "on loan."

"I'll return it this week," Jordy pleaded, pressing his hands together.

After finally receiving a stiff nod and the book, he jammed his wired earbuds into his ears, plugged them into his phone, and sprinted toward the subway station. There was still a lot to do before his evening shift at the store, and Chloe was waiting for him. He wouldn't have time to finish the report at home — he'd have to study at work.

The station. The subway. One minute. Jordy ran down the escalator, intentionally stomping loudly. People stepped aside, some smiling as they gave way, others muttering apologies. Why? It was just their habit to apologize.

Although Jordy knew it was his fault. Passive-aggressively, he was trying to catch the train on time. He jumped the last step and shouted triumphantly. The steel subway doors were still open.

Made it.

With long strides, he entered the steel car. Right behind him, a woman, wrapped tightly in a scarf, dashed in. The lower half of her face was hidden beneath the cashmere. Even for the chilly spring, she seemed overly bundled up. Both of them were panting, like they'd just sprinted.

"Harrison Station is next, right?" Jordy asked her.

"No, this train is going to Howard."

His eyes darted toward the platform. Across the tunnel's edge, another train slowed, blurred by motion. A worker in a bright orange vest was blowing a whistle and waving a small white flag on a wooden stick, the kind teachers use when leading students across the street. The faces of the people sitting in the opposite train became clearer and clearer as the train came to a halt.

A sharp warning signal sounded overhead. The train on the opposite side, heading in the right direction, was preparing to depart. Jordy turned his pale face toward the scarf-wrapped woman with flushed cheeks.

"Thanks."

Without waiting for a response, and against the sound of the departing signal, he dashed for the doors. He could feel the rubber seal of the closing doors brushing against his hair, almost squeezing his head like a walnut. His feet landed on the hard platform, knees colliding with the cold floor.

Made it?

A shrill whistle echoed right in his ear. A portly safety officer in an orange vest was running toward him, waving his little white flag, puffing out his round cheeks.

"Idiot! What are you doing?"

Jordy brushed the dust off his knees and clasped his hands in a silent apology. The worker waved the flag near his face, but Jordy was already turning away — the doors of the opposite train were still open, the passengers getting off, new ones stepping in. Jordy touched the floor with his fingertips like a sprinter at the starting line. Another warning signal sounded ahead — the train was ready to leave. The station worker seemed to read his thoughts and blew the whistle even louder. He lunged to grab Jordy by the shirt, but Jordy shot off at the start signal and dashed inside.

Made it!

The train doors closed, and it began to move. Jordy turned around to look at the station worker, who was now flipping him off.

CHAPTER 24

There were only a few people sitting in the entire subway car — a typical sight during lunchtime. As Jordy walked toward the middle, his gaze caught on the woman's hair. The brightness of it drowned out the muted surroundings. It looked just like his mother's, back when he first started school. Blonde, glossy, flowing over her shoulders like a polished wave. Just like his mom's, before it started falling out in clumps. Alive, gently blowing with the draft. Just like hers had been, until she was gone.

A wave of nostalgia hit him.

"The road keeps calling, and something feels heavy inside..."

The lyrics played in his ears, echoing the words his mother used to hum when she could still pull them from the fading corners of her mind.

"I don't know what's next, or if I'm ready for it..."

What a strange coincidence — two memories in the span of a minute. And that dream earlier...Jordy slumped into his seat, pressing his cheek against the scratched window. He turned up the volume. Squeezed his eyes shut.

"Sometimes, you just have to wait...."

***

Many years ago, they rode a train together. Jordy was counting down the days until his twelfth birthday — a significant age, in his eyes. His mom had kicked the drugs for the last (and yet another) time, laughing joyfully. He loved her smile and her fresh, clear eyes. In those moments, he was genuinely happy.

They were talking about his upcoming birthday the next week. This year, his mom hadn't forgotten. She promised that Jordy would get a present, and even swore she'd go to the market to wrap the box in bright paper with little cars on it, just like the boys in his class had. Maybe there'd even be a card.

The past few years, he hadn't received any gifts at all (in fact, he couldn't even remember the last time he had). One year, his mom remembered his birthday too late, but she still hurriedly baked him a sponge cake. Their neighbor even lent her a can of whipped cream — his mom had used it to make fluffy flowers on top. Seven white, cream flowers around the edges. Jordy had licked three of them off with his finger right away, saving the rest for tomorrow. But now, a real present! And for his twelfth birthday, no less! Jordy wiped away a tear of laughter from his eye. Too much laughter meant you'd cry later.

"And we'll celebrate, right, Mom?" he asked hopefully.

"Yes, we'll roast a whole turkey and buy soda."

"Coca-Cola." His eyes lit up. "And...and can I invite my friends?"

Ba-a-ang! His head shrank under his father's hand. A lash fell onto Jordy's cheek.

"Are you outta your mind?" His father's brown eyes reddened with fury. "Who the hell do you think you're inviting?"

"Sorry, Dad," Jordy whispered, pressing his hand to the now-burning spot on the back of his head.

His father's shoulders rose and fell with heavy breathing. Hair peeked out from under his tank top. His crumpled face twitched from a trembling jaw. His eyes were nearly boiling with rage.

Jordy instinctively slid closer to his mom. Just an inch. He glanced at her — she sat with her eyes closed. His father raised his hand again. Little Jordy shut his eyes, as usual, to avoid seeing the blow.

But the hit didn't come. Jordy opened one eye. His father had turned away and was staring at the seat across from them. At a man in a police uniform.

The officer was old. His hair had receded, forming an arch like the McDonald's logo. A faded tie rested on his belly. He clutched his police cap in his hands. Not like the one Jordy's friend had, the one they'd take turns wearing when they played cops in the yard. This one was real — with a "Chicago Police Department" star on it. The officer watched them closely.

His father spread his legs wider, pushed up the sleeves of his shirt, and leaned his elbows on his knees. A blue spider tattoo crawled down his arm, emerging from a web. Peter Evans defiantly raised his chin and gave the officer a sharp nod. *What're you lookin' at, pig?*

Jordy slid even closer to his mom. His thin, childlike leg pressed against her pale one, marked with veins. His dad hated a lot of things (the government, the neighbors, the unemployment office, job fairs, Jordy), but most of all, he hated the cops. Pigs. He'd always sneer and spit on the ground every time he saw them from afar. They had ruined his life. If it weren't for those damn pig rats, the Evans family would already be living like normal people. They'd go on vacations every year. They'd have a car. They'd even have a dog.

***

The first time Peter Evans went to prison was a month before he turned eighteen — he and a friend held up a gas station. They wore balaclavas, each grabbed a gun, and struck at night. But the teenagers hadn't considered that the gray-haired cashier was a Vietnam War veteran. The old man disarmed them, twisted their arms, called 911, and by the time the police arrived, he'd given each boy a good beating. A lasting memory.

He got ten months. His mind wasn't fully formed yet, blood boiling at the slightest provocation. He snapped at everyone and always got more in return. It was a miracle his sentence wasn't extended and he was released on time. Thin, though, and missing three teeth.

When the now-of-age son of the Evans family returned to his childhood home by bus, the only kiss he received was from the new lock on the door. Other people lived there now. Peter's parents had sold the house and moved away without leaving him any contact information. They had simply abandoned their son.

In his head, Peter had already punched the stranger who

now stood in front of him. He managed to restrain himself in front of the people nervously eyeing him at the door, fingers hovering over the number nine on the phone.

"No, the Evans family left nothing for you. No forwarding address for forgotten mail either. And they didn't mention having a son."

Peter thanked them and walked down the street. His lips thinned, his eyes scanning the passersby. They couldn't have just disappeared, right?

"Hey, Evans."

A familiar voice. Peter turned and saw an old friend.

"Yo, Oliver."

Well, at least someone familiar. They approached each other and shook hands. His former classmate smiled, showing all his teeth, wearing — disgustingly — a red University of Chicago hoodie.

"Heard you were in prison?"

"Yesterday's news. Wanna grab a beer?"

Three pints went down easily. By the fourth, some guy in olive pants sat down nearby. After two more pints, the stranger got bold enough to put his hand on Oliver's knee. Oliver told him to fuck off, and Peter decided to prove they didn't tolerate gay men here.

That night, he slept on a prison cot again. He was sentenced to five years in adult prison for second-degree assault.

The adult prison experience was drastically different from juvenile detention: beatings came without warning, from day one. Evans (eventually) learned through his bruises that snapping back wasn't worth it. He figured out who to respect and who to push around.

Peter Evans was released a year early for good behavior. He never wanted to return to prison. He got a job as a security guard at an office building, where they gave him a room in a dormitory. He started taking woodworking classes, learning a new trade. In the summer, he met Lily, a student working part-time in the office — three years younger and a beauty. Two years later, they had a son. And two years after that, methamphetamine became a part of their lives.

They were moved to a slightly larger room in the dormitory when their son was born. Money was tight because of the baby. Jordy cried often, keeping them awake at night. Peter used his prison connections to find a side job with good pay: weekly deliveries to clients' homes. Never beyond the mailbox, no real names, no questions asked. They didn't tell him what he was delivering, but Peter already knew.

One time, Lily broke down from the mounting depression. She hadn't worked since she got pregnant, and she'd had to drop out of university. She only saw Peter at night. She was simply exhausted. When Peter came home after one of his "delivery" shifts, Lily sat on the floor, silently crying. Her husband sat down next to her, wrapping an arm around her shoulders.

"Wanna relax? Right now, the clients are hooked on these magic pills. They're for depression. They work fast, and you're back to normal in an hour. I've got some left over from the last delivery, you know, for sampling."

"Are you sure it's safe?" Lily whispered, her eyes flicking to Jordy's tiny hand hanging over the crib.

"Yeah, yeah..."

One pill. They barely heard when Jordy woke up. Lily stared up at the ceiling, too dazed to get up, while Peter just wished the crying would stop. It was drilling into his ears. He approached the crib. Jordy's little eyes were squeezed shut, his forehead and cheeks flushed from the tantrum. Rubbing the spider tattoo on his arm, Peter turned away. He went to his stash and took another pill. And another. He popped them into his mouth.

He didn't remember when Lily came down from her high. He didn't remember how she soothed Jordy, how she cried and berated herself for trying drugs near her baby. How she swore she'd never, ever trade her child's well-being for a dose again.

Lily didn't get hooked immediately. For a while, she truly did keep her promise and avoided using drugs alongside her husband. But the depression returned, gradually, and sometimes, when Jordy was at daycare, she allowed herself to relax. Just for a couple of hours, while the baby wasn't home. What harm could it do?

One day, she forgot to pick him up. When the clock approached six, the phone rang. She answered. The concerned voice of the daycare janitor asked if the Evans family was coming to pick up the child today. In the background, Jordy was crying.

That's when Lily quit drugs for the first time.

But it was never the last.

***

"How's life, Chief?" asked thirty-eight-year-old Peter Evans, eyeing the balding police officer sitting across from him.

"On duty," the officer replied.

He shifted his gaze from Peter's fiery eyes to the faded spider tattoo on his arm — the mark of a thief. The officer nodded, and as soon as the train doors opened, he stepped off at the station.

Peter Evans smirked with satisfaction, leaned back in his seat, and stretched his arm along the window, his fingers brushing the back of Jordy's head. Filthy rats would never dare tell Peter Evans how to live his life!

***

Jordy snapped out of the rock music blasting in his headphones. He touched the back of his head, still warm from the lingering touch of his childhood. He looked around. The girl with the hair like his mother's had vanished. Or maybe she was just a figment of his imagination. Too many memories.

He got off at his station and rushed to pick up his things. He handed Chloe not one but two prescriptions for cheaper medication alternatives, earning himself a loud kiss on the cheek. He brought his laundry home and then sprinted back to catch the train. His twelve-hour shift started at six p.m. The job wasn't difficult — just working in a small, round-the-clock convenience store in the neighborhood. The selection was modest, but it was enough for the locals. Candy, gum, cigarettes, beer, and other non-perishable items.

The store wasn't in a prime location. Nestled in the middle of a residential block, between private homes, its only customers were locals, with the fewest visitors coming on weekdays. Jordy knew almost everyone by name, and of course, word quickly spread that he was studying medicine. Elderly women would show up at five in the morning to ask him about symptoms of new ailments, despite his protests that he wasn't studying to be a general practitioner and that their knees had nothing to do with his lectures. Still, they came like clockwork. In the evening, teenagers would rush in for light alcohol, which Jordy refused to sell unless someone's older sibling came with an ID. Occasionally, the local homeless man, Gwyn, would drop by, and Jordy would hand him expired food for free.

Jordy burst into the store like a whirlwind, barely making it a few minutes before the start of his shift. After wiping his sneakers on the mat, he sighed and pushed back the hair sticking to his forehead. *There we go again.* The longer his hair, the more he sweated. His predecessor on the shift, the retired Mr. Wolfe, had already changed into his street clothes and was sitting on a stool, sipping tea from a chipped cup. The old man had been retired for three years but worked as a cashier at the store because his pension barely covered his expenses. He had taught Jordy the tricks of the trade and, occasionally, after a drink, would share bits of his experience as a security guard.

"If you see a woman yelling outside, she's either an alcoholic looking for a bottle or a young mother desperate for baby food," Wolfe would mutter in his smoke-laced voice. "Both scream loud, but you let one in and tell the other to get lost."

"How do I know which is which if they're both yelling the same?" Jordy would ask with a smile.

"Look in their eyes — alcoholics have empty eyes," the old man would finish with a raspy cough.

By ten o'clock, Jordy realized that the teenagers would go without alcohol tonight (and there were still hours before the elderly women would arrive), so he locked the front door for safety. The boss allowed it. Jordy sprawled on the duct-taped stool, propped his feet up on the counter, and played an online lecture on his old laptop. He listened to it twice — once all the way through, the second time while taking notes.

...*BANG.* The door took a heavy hit from the outside. Jordy tensed up. Drug addicts didn't have the strength for such a blow, and thieves wouldn't bother breaking into a store like this. Whoever was out there had another reason. He edged sideways toward the window to take a peek.

Who was out there??

Mom?

Jordy turned the lock and pulled the door open.

No. Not his mom...

The girl...

From the train!

She collapsed right onto the floor. Something was wrong. Her legs, arms, fingers — everything was covered in blood. She was barefoot. Trembling and crying. Jordy knelt down in front of her, and she reached out her hands.

"Help me...please," she whispered before passing out.

CHAPTER 25

Jordy knelt beside the girl and gently cupped her pale face in his hands. He placed his long fingers on her neck. There was a pulse. Her fever was high. *Just don't let her die.*

"Okay…I need to lay her down," Jordy muttered to himself.

Slowly, supporting her carefully, he laid the girl down on the floor and rushed behind the counter. Even though Mr. Wolfe was sneaky about napping during shifts, Jordy had seen him dozing off on a pillow. Maybe there was one in the back?

He flung open the cupboards. Where was it? Where did that stubborn old man stash it? Bags, boxes, crates. There was no way Wolfe, with his height, had shoved the pillow up top — it'd make more sense to hide it down below. Jordy crouched and began pulling things out, emptying the bottom shelves. Bags, boxes. *There!* He spotted the corner of the pillow poking out and yanked it free, knocking over a black duffle bag that spilled socks, stretched-out long johns, and a faded towel. Stepping carefully to avoid the mess, Jordy grabbed a plastic crate with his free hand and hurried back to the girl.

She was still unconscious. Jordy lifted her head gently and slid the pillow under her neck, adjusting her position on the floor. Sweat glistened on her face and dripped from her chin to her neck. He wiped his damp hands on his jeans, nudged the crate closer with his foot, and carefully propped her legs on top of it to improve blood flow to her head.

"Let's try waking you up," he mumbled, standing up.

A cold draft brushed against his legs. The door — it was still open. The girl had run from something. Or someone. And that something — or someone — could still be out there.

Jordy crept toward the door. The neighborhood had never been known for its safety, and the locals rarely helped out. Taking a deep breath, he cautiously stuck his head outside. No one. He scanned the area, squinting, holding his breath. As usual, it was empty at this hour.

"But she was running from something," he whispered into the darkness before quietly shutting and locking the door.

The instinct to help took over, outweighing his fleeting fear. Jordy grabbed a tube of antiseptic from the counter, a pack of pink sponge pads, and pushed open the door to the closet-sized restroom without fully stepping inside. Ducking out of habit, he soaked one of the sponges under the tiny faucet.

Being careful not to drip water everywhere, he returned to the store, sanitized his hands, and leaned over the girl's face. Gently, he wiped her forehead with the sponge, tapping her cheeks softly, moving stray strands of her blonde hair away from her face. Then he checked her foot — a deep gash, crusted with dried blood — and began cleaning it.

He reached for his phone, almost dialing 911, when he heard a faint sigh.

The girl opened her eyes and weakly tried to move her head.

"Don't be scared. You're safe," Jordy said in a calm voice. His first aid classes taught him not only how to care for wounds but also how to keep victims from slipping into panic.

Her eyelids fluttered as she tried to focus on her surroundings. She lifted her hand slightly as if to signal something, but it fell limply to the floor. Jordy quickly pocketed his phone, not wanting to provoke any reaction — some people didn't trust the police.

"It's okay," he continued. "I'm Jordy. I work in this shop."

The girl mumbled something and tried again to raise her hand, but her body failed her. Jordy managed to catch her wrist before it hit the ground. He lifted her hand and placed it on his knee. Her fingers clenched slightly, smearing his jeans with dried blood.

He wiped the back of her hand with the sponge, then cleaned each finger — watching as the sponge turned red. Her grip tightened around his hand, their eyes meeting.

"I'll rinse the sponge and get some fresh water for you," Jordy said quickly, standing before she could protest. "It'll help cool you down."

She loosened her hold.

"Don't worry, I just want to help."

Jordy slipped into the small restroom, pulled the door half-closed, turned on the faucet, and took out his phone from his back pocket.

"911, what's your emergency?"

"My name is Jordy. I'm at a shop on 84 Chestwood Avenue. A girl ran in here a few minutes ago and passed out. I'm a medical student, so I provided basic first aid. She's injured, though there's no visible life-threatening wounds. Her feet and hands are bloody, her face too. We need an ambulance."

"Understood. Is she armed?"

"No." Jordy hesitated, peeking through the crack in the door — she was still lying motionless, her eyes shut. "I don't think so."

"An ambulance will be there in about eleven minutes. Call back if anything changes."

Jordy pocketed the phone, tossed the soiled sponge in the trash, grabbed a fresh one, and soaked it in warm water. He returned to the girl, sitting beside her, gently holding her hand again — without fully knowing why.

"Alicia," she whispered, her eyes barely open.

"Jordy," he replied, dabbing her forehead with the sponge. "I'm going to wipe your sweat, alright? You've got a fever."

"It hurts..."

"Where does it hurt?"

"Cold..."

"Hold on." Jordy glanced around and found nothing useful. "You're freezing. I'll go see what else I can find."

He hurried into the back room, sifting through the mess he'd made earlier. Nothing looked right. So much junk — why did they keep all this? Finally, he spotted a towel on the floor, likely fallen from Wolfe's black bag. Jordy picked it up between two fingers and sniffed it cautiously. The towel didn't stink, but it smelled damp.

"Better than nothing," he muttered.

He returned to Alicia, gently wrapping the towel around her feet — careful not to press against the wound.

"Thank you..." she whispered, eyes still closed.

The sound of sirens grew louder. Jordy recognized the ambulance's wail. It was two minutes late. Three medics stepped out of the vehicle and approached the door. Jordy stood, stiff-legged from kneeling, and opened the door for them. Alicia seemed to have fallen asleep.

The medics quickly set to work, dividing tasks: one unfolded a stethoscope, another applied a pressure cuff, and the third spoke to Jordy. He recounted the situation, explaining that he called 911 after giving basic first aid and ensuring she wasn't actively bleeding.

"I made sure her condition didn't worsen. I'm a medical student," Jordy added, slightly embarrassed.

"Did she say anything?"

"Her name — Alicia. I think. She also said she was in pain and cold."

"How about yourself? Are you okay, kid? The medic asked, pulling on a pair of sanitary gloves."

"Yeah, I'm fine. Thanks, sir."

The medic nodded and returned to his colleagues. While they worked — taking notes, measuring vitals, and listening to her heartbeat — Jordy couldn't take his eyes off the pale-faced girl. His emotions were a tangled mess of concern, suspicion, relief, and a strange, familiar feeling. Déjà vu or coincidence — watching paramedics trying to revive a girl who, just earlier today, had sat across from him on the train. The girl whose glowing hair reminded him of his mom. His mom, who paramedics couldn't save after another overdose.

In the distance, the wail of another siren grew louder — this time, the police. The sirens fell silent just before the car rounded the corner. Parking across from the ambulance, two officers — one man and one woman — stepped out of the vehicle and made their way into the shop. Jordy had to move the shelf closer to the wall to make room for everyone. He glanced at the fire safety sign: they were already exceeding the occupancy limit.

The lead medic briefed the police on the situation, ending with the reassurance that no serious injuries or signs of intoxication had been found in the initial assessment. Jordy let out a quiet sigh of relief, as if the weight of an oxygen mask had just been taken off his own face.

"Did she have any ID on her?" the officer asked, turning toward Jordy.

"I don't know...she didn't have a bag with her."

The officer shook his head, pulling out a radio and pressing the button.

"Dispatch, this is Squad 11. Is there a unit nearby for a neighborhood check on Chestwood Avenue? We've got a possible victim of violence and need a sweep of the area."

"Copy that, Squad 11. Dispatching Unit 29 to assist. Hold tight."

"Thanks."

The officer slid the radio back onto his belt and nodded toward his partner.

"Officer Swann, stay here and question the witness while I take a look around."

The female officer with a high ponytail nodded and approached Jordy. Flashing her badge briefly, she got straight to the point.

"Can I see your ID, please?"

"It's in my bag, just in the back," Jordy mumbled, pointing toward the storeroom.

"How do you know the victim?"

"I don't know her. She just ran in here."

"Any security cameras?"

"No, we don't even have a working computer."

Officer Swann shook her head, her ponytail swishing as she moved toward the back room to inspect the premises. Jordy hesitated, glancing nervously at Alicia on the stretcher, then slouched after the officer. As she examined the storage room, the closet, and the restroom for any signs of foul play, Jordy stood silently nearby, clutching his state ID in one hand. Every now and then, Officer Swann's sharp eyes darted toward him, making him increasingly anxious. His father's words about the police buzzed in his head.

Finally, the medics completed the first treatment and began lifting the stretcher to carry Alicia into the ambulance. Jordy snapped out of his trance, feeling like he had just been hypnotized.

"Wait," he called, holding up his state ID as he hurried toward the medics, oblivious to how the officer's hand moved instinctively toward her holster. "Please, can you at least tell me where you're taking her?"

"We're not permitted to disclose that kind of information to non-family members," one of the medics replied.

"Mr. Evans," Officer Swann called from behind. "Please don't interfere with the paramedics and return to the scene."

"What scene?" Jordy frowned. "Am I under suspicion?"

"Please return to the store," she repeated, tapping her fingers against her holster.

"Fine, fine," Jordy muttered, walking back to the shop. "But at least tell her something about me. I helped her, after all."

The paramedic climbed into the ambulance and shut the door with a soft click. Jordy slumped back toward the store under the officer's watchful gaze, his heart pounding in his chest for reasons beyond the situation. Something more than distrust of the police, empathy, or even the nerves from the unexpected situation made his heart race wildly. Just an hour ago, his life had been moving in one direction, and now this stranger had derailed him completely.

He hadn't been able to save his mom the first time.

Maybe today, he was being given a second chance.

CHAPTER 26

Jordy placed the porcelain teapot on the table.

"This one's stronger."

"Don't like it?" Auntie Chang squinted. The wrinkled, raised mole rolled to the corner of her wise eye.

"I like it, I really do," Jordy defended, placing the small cup's lid back on. "It's just, you know, really strong tea."

"Táo qì de nán hái." *Spoiled boy.* Auntie Chang grumbled. She pressed her hands on the table and, groaning, got to her feet. Mumbling in Mandarin under her breath, she took the small clay teapot and, clutching her left side, waddled over to the tiny sink in the corner of the room. Above it hung a once-red talisman of luck, faded from years of sunlight, woven into a feng shui knot.

Jordy removed the lid and inhaled the smell of brewed tea. Whenever he joined his neighbor for a Chinese tea ceremony, it always felt like playing make-believe at a daycare: the tiny cup that barely fit between his fingers, the small board, and the teapot that held just enough for four sips. But the variety of flavors was striking — within a single session, they would sample five different types of tea. Auntie Chang had plenty of relatives back in China who faithfully sent her monthly boxes of herbs — because, of course, America had no Chinatown or real tea. How could they live on just Coca-Colas?

Jordy had been out of work for three days. And without pay. The store had been temporarily closed and sealed off as the police collected information. Like a conscientious citizen, he had given his information to the detective and promised to be responsive if they had any further questions. But so far, no one from the authorities had reached out to Jordy — not the police, not the doctors — and he had heard no news about the girl.

He sipped his jasmine tea and let its bitterness linger on his tongue. What had happened to Alicia? He didn't know. Was she still in the hospital, or had she already been discharged? All Jordy could do was guess, and it gnawed at him. Just a few days ago, her life had literally depended on him, and now he sat in confusion, as if nothing had happened.

Auntie Chang shuffled back, placing the teapot on the worn wooden table. To his surprise, she snatched the cup from Jordy's hands with an unexpectedly firm grip, frowning at him.

"I was almost done." Jordy smiled.

She pretended to slap him on the head but instead gave his long hair a gentle ruffle. Clutching the cup, she returned to the sink, still holding her side.

"When will you start working again?" she asked, drying the inside of the teacup with a towel.

Jordy shrugged.

"Has the boss called you?" she pressed.

"Nope."

"Listen, boy," she said as she threw the towel down. "You

need to hold onto that job if you don't want to get kicked out of university. Be patient, and you'll go back to work like a proper person."

"I know, I know..."

"No, you don't," Auntie Chang snapped. "I see you, always with your head in the clouds. Go to the store and find out what's going on."

"They're waiting for the police to give them permission to reopen."

"Then get a temporary job in the meantime. Ask Chloe at the laundromat, she might have something for you."

Jordy stood up. Even at his height, he still felt like a foolish little boy whenever Auntie Chang glared at him. She barely reached five feet tall, yet she had a presence that could tower over him.

"I just want to find out what happened to that girl first. Maybe she's still in the hospital, and I can visit."

She stood up too, raising her chin to meet Jordy's eyes.

"What do you care about that girl so much for? You talk about her every day. Be glad she didn't accuse you of anything."

"She'd never do that," Jordy said with certainty.

"And how would you know that, boy?"

"She's a good person. She reminds me of —"

"Your late mother, yeah, I've heard." Auntie clapped her hands together in frustration. "You're an adult, Jordy, and this is no fairy tale."

"Maybe it's fate."

"Fate, my foot! I've got things to do. And so do you." She jabbed her short finger at him. "Go find a job, and don't go chasing after that girl. You'll only get yourself in more trouble."

Jordy reached out to hug her. She rolled her eyes, but he bent down and embraced her anyway. Auntie Chang muttered something unintelligible in Mandarin and patted his back.

"It's going to be fine." Jordy smiled as he stepped out into the hallway.

The door slammed behind him. Without lingering in the communal hallway, he crossed quickly to his own room and locked the door from behind him.

Of course, Auntie Chang didn't understand. As an immigrant from the old generation, she always looked at new people with suspicion, and her hard life had stripped away her belief in kindness and selflessness. But Jordy still believed in fate. He was meant to help people. That's why he was studying to be a doctor. That's why so much had happened that day. Maybe now life would turn a new page and sparkle like a rainbow on the fresh pages of a fantasy novel. And in most stories, there's always a happy ending.

The small bed nearly merged with the closet — shelves were mounted in the middle. When Jordy sat up straight, his head would touch the wooden ceiling. But he found something comforting in the coziness of his little corner.

He stretched out on the bed. Was this really his calling? Most likely. It just felt like he'd been helping the wrong people before. A year ago, the reactions to his help were, at best, confusion — gratitude wasn't even on the table. His brown eyes wandered up to the shelf, its surface adorned with stickers: quotes, film decals. Photos from a Polaroid camera were taped above. His high school graduation at sunset. Former classmates at a summer festival, holding hot dogs. His university friend — an ex-girlfriend, though they had managed to remain some sort of friends despite the breakup. A photo of his mother — taken before he was born. She twirled in a bright yellow polka-dot dress, smiling with her eyes beneath thick lashes. Her hair swirled behind her, blurring in the shot. He had no picture of his father, but Jordy always saw him in the scar on his finger — the time his father had stabbed the table with a knife, catching Jordy's hand between his thumb and index finger. It had taken ten minutes to stop the bleeding. Jordy ran that finger over his mother's photo. *She is so beautiful.*

Was.

Alicia crept back into his mind. She had dug in deep. Maybe Auntie Chang was right, after all. The last time Jordy had fallen for the wrong girl, Auntie Chang had tried to warn him, but it was too late — Evelyn had left him. "Such a killjoy," she'd called him in front of her friends, whenever Jordy pulled a joint out of her mouth or flushed a bag of powder down the toilet. It was strange how such opposites had ever started dating: Jordy was always firmly against any drugs, while Evelyn had no patience for those who tossed them.

They'd met during a pharmacology lecture when he had out-argued her in a debate on "Whether Too Many Kids are on Ritalin." Tall and smart, he attended every lecture, and she had an easy time keeping her eyes on him during class. A month later, she asked him to the park, and a week after that, she kissed him. Within three days, they were in her room. Jordy didn't resist the easy win and was glad he hadn't had to try hard. Their relationship felt like an endless debate — they'd spend their free time discussing medical books, articles, and drug discoveries. In their first semester, they both topped the pharmacology course, with Jordy leading by just one point.

Their first real disagreement happened when Evelyn got a tattoo in her dorm room — a serotonin molecule. She'd been drunk and had allowed her roommate to tattoo her arm using a needle from a syringe and eyeliner.

Though the tattoo came out neat, Jordy lost it. In the dorm! While drunk! What an idiot! Evelyn had silently turned and left, not speaking to him for a week.

She forgave him later after several apologies, a bouquet, and a chocolate cake, but after that first fight, the pages of their shared story started to drift apart. Evelyn preferred partying with her roommate's friends, getting drunk and dancing, while Jordy sat on the sidelines, watching in silence. Waiting for the time when he'd have to take her to bed, lay her down, and prepare her pills and water for the night. If it had stopped at alcohol, they might have found a way back to the same page, but Evelyn's friends soon grew bored with just drinking and brought in joints.

Compromises didn't work. Evelyn tried to quit drugs for the sake of their relationship, but her friends didn't share her conviction. A few times, she even stood up for Jordy when he turned off the music, woke up passed-out friends, or dumped bags of drugs into the trash. But her patience ran out. One day, they gave her a choice: break up with Jordy or move out of the dorm and leave their party circle.

And so, for the second time, a woman broke Jordy's heart. As a parting gift, she kissed him on the nose and handed him a postcard of dancing roosters with a neon caption: "Youth forgives everything." He taped it beneath the photo of his ex.

Alicia's face was the brightest thing in his mind. What was he hoping for? What did he want? That some stranger would come back to thank him for saving her life? That the police would hand him a hero's medal? Or that he, a pathetic nobody, could be someone's savior?

No one was going to call him. He'd been forgotten. His part was over.

Auntie Chang was always right. Just like with Evelyn, just like with work. He had to find a way to get rid of the stubborn image of the girl from the shop. Forget her name, forget her smell. And forget any resemblance to his mom.

Jordy got off the bed and reached for his shirt. The idea of asking Chloe for a job was starting to look good — the kind, chubby lady wouldn't say no. Slowly, he buttoned up the shirt, all the way to his collar, and straightened his sleeves. Things would work out eventually. They had to.

Jordy stepped into the hallway, slid the key into the lock, and turned it. He slipped it back into his pocket as his phone rang. An unfamiliar number.

It took a few tries to swipe his finger across the green icon — his thumb kept missing the fingerprint sensor.

"Hello?" he asked on an exhale.

Some shuffling. A rustle.

"Hello? Yes?" he asked louder.

"Jordy?" a woman's voice finally came through.

"Yes."

"This is Alicia."

CHAPTER 27

"Alicia?"

"Yes, Ali. I wanted to thank you for helping me a few days ago. When I...well, got into trouble."

Alicia. Her voice over the phone felt like a push, nearly sending Jordy face-first into the door. Her voice. Her scent. His hand gripping the phone seemed to feel the cold touch of her white hand again. *Was this really happening?*

"Do you know who's calling? Is it a good time to talk?"

"Yeah," Jordy replied, glancing at Auntie Chang's closed door. He would've made a face at her if she were there. "Just one second, please."

He fumbled for the key in his pocket. He didn't want to talk in the hallway, and calling her back wasn't an option — what if the number became inactive, or her phone died, or the phone lines went down? Anything could happen while he searched for that damn key. Finally finding it, he slid it into the lock, turned it. The pins clicked, and the door creaked open. Jordy stepped inside and slumped down against the wall.

"I'm here now. I mean, I'm in my room...I can talk." His tongue stumbled awkwardly over the words.

Jordy heard a mocking laugh in his head — his father's. Peter Evans could still laugh at his son, even from the grave.

"I don't know where to start. I guess I just want to say thank you. You saved me. If it weren't for you, I don't know what would've happened to me." Alicia's voice was hurried but confident. Much more confident than his.

"Yeah, sure, no problem."

As if she had just asked him for directions.

"I must have scared you, though, right? How did you keep from freaking out when I burst into your store?"

You didn't burst in. You collapsed with the door and passed out.

"It's all fine. How are you? How do you feel? Are you still in the hospital?"

Stop it, she's not under interrogation.

"No, I'm home. They discharged me the next day."

A pang in his chest. Then again, she wasn't obligated to call him immediately. She wasn't obligated to tell him anything.

"I'm glad to hear that!"

A little too cheerful.

"Thanks, Jordy."

"How did you get my number?"

"My doctor passed it on to me before I was discharged."

"I'm really glad."

Okay, tone it down a little.

"I'm so grateful to you," Alicia said, her voice thick with emotion. "I'm going through the hardest time of my life right now, and fate sent you to me at the worst moment!"

Fate, she said! Who cared when she called — what mattered

was that she *did*.

"Let's meet up?" Jordy blurted out.

Silence.

His father's voice chimed in again. *Oh, Jordy, you fool. You think anyone wants to go out with you?*

Jordy grabbed a fistful of his hair and squeezed his eyes shut. *Stupid, stupid.*

"Okay."

Okay? Okay. Okay. The word echoed in his chest.

"Are you sure you're alright? Are you really okay?"

"What? Sorry?" Alicia stifled a cough or maybe a laugh.

Pull yourself together! Stop saying dumb things.

"I mean, are you feeling well enough to meet up?"

Of course she's not. What are you hoping for, stupid Jordy?

To his and his imaginary father's surprise, Alicia giggled.

"Yes, I can meet. Thanks for worrying about me. But let's meet somewhere in an open space?"

"Okay, thank you," Jordy responded quickly. "Today?"

"Mmm, I can't today. Or tomorrow. Let's do next week. Weekend?"

"Sure, where?"

"I'm not sure yet, but I'll text you later, alright? Sorry, I have to run."

"I'll be waiting."

Very much so.

"Bye, Jordy."

"Bye, Ali." She hung up before he could finish, but he kept pressing the phone to his ear.

Her voice melted away like sweet ice cream, washing away

the scowl of Peter Evans.

She called.

And screw you, Dad.

***

On a warm Sunday in May — unusually early for Chicago — Jordy was as nervous heading out as a schoolgirl before her first date. His nails, trimmed down to stubs, kept ending up in his mouth — he didn't even try to kick the habit. The perfectly smooth surface of the hair wax was marred by two finger dents. A neatly ironed brown polo shirt from Target hung on the rack, still warm from the iron and smelling faintly of Chinese takeout.

"Boy, you ready?"

The first thing to enter the room was a pair of large blue sails — Jordy's jeans, also from Target. Behind them was Auntie Chang, who took up as much space in the room as those jeans. With her bony hands, she held them up at head level so they wouldn't drag on the floor.

"I pressed every seam."

"They're just jeans; you don't need to press them." Jordy smiled but took the pants and gently laid them on the bed.

"Don't argue, and hurry up — you'll be late for your date."

Jordy ran his hands over his unruly ears, trying again to tuck them under his hair. He liked the smell of the wax — masculinity.

Auntie Chang still hovered by the door. She'd spent too long convincing Jordy to let her help him get ready — ironing his clothes and picking out the right outfit — for him to just flop down on the bed and lazily shove his long legs into his jeans. And definitely not to jump into them, yanking them up by the straps. He had to dress carefully.

"So, what about money?"

That's why she was still standing there, waiting. Not to see how he'd put on the jeans.

"I've got it."

"But you haven't worked all week, which means you haven't been paid." Auntie squinted suspiciously.

"I saved some."

In truth, things weren't going well at the shop. They'd been allowed to reopen on the eighth day, but the locals were wary of coming in. The constant police patrols in the rough neighborhood had scared off the kids who used to hang around with their cheap booze and the students who smoked weed. The moms had switched to grocery delivery through Uber. Sure, things would eventually get back to normal, but for now, Jordy had to make do with instant noodles once a day — especially if he was taking Alicia on a date.

Auntie Chang sidled up to him, holding out a closed fist.

"Take it, you can pay me back later," she said, pushing twenty dollars into his hand.

"No way, I'm not taking money from you."

"Take it, or I'll be offended."

"You didn't even want me talking to her, and now you're giving me money?"

"Well, that's none of my business, boy." She shook her head. "But if you're going, let me at least help."

"Thanks, but..."

"Take it," Auntie grumbled, tapping her varicose veined leg.

She gripped his hand like a hawk, and Jordy finally gave in, lowering his head in surrender.

The windy Chicago air did its best to mess up his hair, but the wax held strong. Jordy wanted to skip — no, run — but the sneaky thought of sweat stains under his arms stopped him. And the smell. Smell was the first thing that mattered if you found someone attractive. Jordy knew that from experience. He'd already lost himself to the scent of someone who had literally fallen into his arms.

He arrived twenty-three minutes early. No way Alicia would get there sooner. He chose a bench and sat on the edge.

Nineteen minutes to go.

He hadn't let Auntie Chang see just how terrified he was. He didn't even know if Alicia had a partner. He didn't know what they would talk about or how to act. Should he bring up that evening, or would that be too insensitive?

Eleven minutes left. *What if she doesn't show?*

Jordy hadn't been with anyone since Evelyn. He knew his own worth — pennies compared to Alicia's six-figure value. Even considering how she looked after the incident, Jordy felt like he didn't even come close. But he hoped. Something pulled him toward this girl, and there was no turning back. Jordy swallowed hard and stood up from the bench. His legs were sweating in his jeans, and his boxers were sticking to him. He glanced back at the spot where he'd been sitting. Dry.

Four minutes to go.

Jordy realized he didn't even know what she really looked

like. *She is like Mom.* No — she *was*, she *was*, he reminded himself. It was bad luck to associate a living person with someone dead.

Ten minutes later, Jordy was tapping his foot. Sweat had spread across his body, and he felt the coolness under his arms when the breeze blew. He didn't want to check how big the circles were. He looked around nervously.

Where are you, Ali?

CHAPTER 28

Alicia stared at the tall, lanky guy who had been nervously looking around for several minutes.

"Jordy?"

His curly hair bounced and twisted clockwise. Big, frightened eyes, a funny nose so long it seemed like it might fall into his mouth. By Alicia's standards, he wouldn't even be nominated for the title of a good-looking guy.

Why did he ask to meet?

In the first few days after the attack, Jordy barely crossed her mind. Endless calls and meetings took up nearly all of her time: the police clung to every detail, calling her constantly; Jack was temporarily handling some of Ali's work responsibilities due to a project with urgent deadlines and requirements. Both of them barely managed to eat, constantly running late for breakfast or dinner at the hotel.

Ali refused to return home. With Katie's help, Jack packed up and moved Alicia's things, so many that they had to rent a two-bedroom hotel suite with a large closet. Although Alicia didn't remember much of it. Flashes of memories flickered in her mind. She first regained consciousness on a blindingly white sheet in a small hospital room. Then off again. Silently, Jack's lips kissed her forehead. Off again, and then back on with sound as the doctor asked for her home address...She told him — no, she shouted to the whole room — that she wasn't going back there. And then off again, just as she noticed the doctor reaching for the IV. When she finally came to fully, Jack was dozing in a soft chair, his body nearly slipping off the edge of the seat. His laptop screen had gone dark. The afternoon sun danced in shadows across the floor through a large window. The IV was gone, as was the headache. Only the cold began creeping into her knuckles as she recalled what had happened the previous night.

The Silent Walker had found her again, and this time he was closer. He almost caught her. She had nearly died. She had no more doubts that he was hunting her, only her. He must have been following her from the police station; how else could he have tracked her in that alley?

Jack quickly booked them into a Novotel just five minutes away, and they headed there directly from the hospital. Check-in, unpacking, lunch — everything happened so quickly Alicia barely had time to speak with Jack. Her brain had temporarily dulled and couldn't focus.

She cried for the first time when Katie arrived. Katie rushed to her friend the moment she stepped through the door, bursting into tears. She gripped Alicia's hand and hysterically promised never to leave her again. Apologies tumbled out for leaving that night, along with bursts of toxic guilt. She swore they'd be best friends forever. Alicia wept until her nose turned red, wiping it on Katie's sweater. "Don't leave me again, best friend forever."

Katie stayed with her when Jack had to leave for obligatory meetings. They lounged around in piles of pillows, watching Disney movies and crunching on ridged chips. On the first night, Katie even stayed over in the second room.

For nearly a week, Alicia hadn't been alone for a minute, and while that sense of safety kept her calm, the lack of privacy had started to weigh on her. When Alicia called Jordy, the main (and perhaps only) reason was to thank him. The guy had literally saved her life. That's why she couldn't refuse when he asked for a face-to-face meeting. Why he needed this meeting was still a question echoing in her mind, but something in his voice — *pity?* — had made her agree. Meeting with Jordy could seem like a welcome break. It took her half an hour to convince Katie not to worry, and another half-hour to send her friend home. After all, he had protected her from the Silent Walker. If he hadn't opened the door, if he hadn't given her first aid, if not for him...

It was impossible to refuse him one simple meeting after all that. An hour of her time was the least she could offer in gratitude for saving her life. A small gesture in exchange for survival.

Now he looked entirely different. Alicia scrutinized him. Was this really the guy who saved her? Maybe he'd look similar if her brain was hazy with panic, she thought. She hid her doubts behind a smile and extended her hand.

"I'm Alicia. You must be Jordy?"

"H-h-hi," he stammered, barely touching her fingertips, shaking her hand as if it were made of crystal.

He's just a kid, probably still in college, Alicia thought.

"Have you been waiting long?" she asked. "Sorry I'm late."

Jordy lowered his gaze to the pavement. Alicia felt an overwhelming urge to lift his chin.

"N-no, I just got here myself," his voice squeaked on the first syllable.

"Do you want to take a walk and grab some coffee?"

"Mm-hm," he nodded.

Alicia gestured toward the nearby coffee shop. She disliked conversations where she had to painfully extract topics like popping a pimple. Why couldn't he at least hold eye contact?

"What kind of coffee do you drink, Jordy?"

"With milk."

"What kind of milk?"

"Cow's...I mean, regular milk," he corrected himself, nervously running a hand through his hair, covering his reddening ears.

"I like soymilk. I'm lactose intolerant."

They approached the café's wooden-framed, floor-to-ceiling windows and stepped through the archway. Behind the counter, a guy wearing a cap with a bread loaf logo was busy restocking shelves. Shiny croissants and a lone apple tart were proudly displayed in the case. Alicia leaned in to inspect the tart's cream.

"So, are you a coffee connoisseur?" Jordy finally asked.

"Well, yes, you could say that," she said, pulling away from the glass, her face almost brushing Jordy's ear as she whispered. "But honestly — between you and me — there's no good coffee in Chicago. If you want the real stuff, you have to go to

California or South America."

Jordy let out a small chuckle and smoothed his jeans. They were still warm, probably from Auntie Chang's ironing.

"I went to Los Angeles recently, and the coffee there was so authentic and delicious," Alicia said.

Somewhere outside, a dog barked *(was it a Shiba Inu?)*, and it seemed the scent of jacaranda filled the air. She hadn't seen fluffy Milo again.

"How did you like Los Angeles?"

"It's lively," Alicia replied honestly.

"I've never been anywhere outside of Illinois."

Alicia pointed to the last tart and asked for it to be packed up, making sure to request three napkins.

"I mean, I only left Chicago once," Jordy muttered.

"And a soymilk cappuccino, please. Don't steam the milk too hot." Alicia winked at the barista.

The cashier handed her the terminal, where a default tip of twenty percent was selected.

"I'll get this, Ali. Same coffee for me — and I'll pay in cash." Jordy hurried to the counter, pulling out his wallet.

Jordy's long fingers fumbled together, and ten-dollar bills slipped from his grip, fluttering to the floor. One bill slid under the counter, while the rest scattered at his feet. Jordy yelped and crouched, reaching under the counter to retrieve it. Something soft and hairy brushed his hand, and he recoiled in disgust. Wiping his dusty fingers on his jeans, Jordy gathered twenty dollars and sighed. That lost ten could've covered two packs of ramen and a cucumber.

Alicia watched in silence.

"How much was it?" Jordy asked in a thin voice.

"Seventeen dollars and eighty cents without the tip."

Jordy handed over two crumpled ten-dollar bills. The guy in the cap eyed the dustball clinging to Jordy's thumb.

"You're short on the tip."

Jordy gulped — he had only coins left.

"No problem, I'll cover it," Alicia said, pulling out a five-dollar bill from her small Gucci coin purse.

"You don't have to..."

"We're holding up the line," she said firmly. Jordy nodded obediently, hoping the fire in his ears wouldn't spread to his cheeks.

With their coffee cups in hand, they stepped outside. Alicia carefully studied her savior: Jordy — a guy from another world. A low-flying bird. If it weren't for The Silent Walker, she never would've crossed paths with him in her normal life. People like him didn't frequent the same places as her.

"Did they catch him? The one who, well...was chasing you? Did they catch that scumbag?" Jordy's last word was laced with anger.

"Are you really interested?" Alicia asked weakly, peering into his eyes.

"Yes. You can trust me," Jordy responded with unusual seriousness.

Something clicked in her mind. The scared boy suddenly seemed stronger, like a reliable wall. She wanted to talk to him. She wanted to tell him everything.

But why?

Then again, why not? What did she have to lose by telling

him?

"I call the maniac 'The Silent Walker.' He's attacked me twice now. I'm so scared," Alicia whispered.

"Tell me everything that's bothering you."

Chapter 29

The taxi had driven just a few blocks when Alicia got a text message.

> Thank you for finding the time and for trusting me with your pain.

Sweet boy. She half-expected her number to be deleted after her two-hour monologue, with no chance of recovery.

> Glad to have met you, Jordy.

The meeting, which should've ended with the last sip of coffee, stretched on for hours. Her impression of Jordy swung back and forth, like a restless child on a playground. He seemed to show his best side when she needed it and a clumsy side when it was least required. His psychological age seemed to fluctuate, too. But most valuable was the respect he gave her — not pity, not a sense of awkwardness, not even mild suspicion. He turned out to be a good listener — understanding, and far from the bumbling person he'd seemed at the café. For the first time, someone listened to her with such respect, without judgment or distrust.

The driver was singing along to something in Arabic, his voice leaping between alto and soprano. Alicia put in her AirPods and turned to look out the window, watching the spring greenery flash by. Her phone started to buzz.

"Hey, Jack, I'm heading back to the hotel," Alicia answered the call.

"I'm still at work. Will you be okay hanging out in the room alone?"

"Work on Sunday?"

"Yeah. Sorry, Ali. How are you?"

"You know, I..." She paused, hearing loud voices in the background. "I'm fine."

"Sorry, some colleagues just came in. I'll call you back later and try to get out early."

When Jack hung up, a new message from Jordy appeared:

`Let me know when you arrive at your hotel.`

Then another right after:

`                    Please.`

Alicia got out of the taxi in front of the hotel and felt a nostalgic craving for something childishly delicious and just as childishly unhealthy. She looked around and found salvation in a nearby 7-Eleven. She went in, passing dried-out hot dogs and frosty Slurpees, and stopped at the wall of rainbow-colored candy. She picked out chocolate dragons, a Kinder egg, and even a choco-cherry Chupa Chups — something she hadn't seen since school.

With a plastic bag full of treats, she stepped back outside

and took in a deep breath of Chicago air.

"DAMN IT!" someone shouted as a scooter nearly knocked her over.

Alicia pressed herself against the mustard-yellow brick wall. A typical Chicago moment — one she'd quickly fallen out of touch with. Nearby, a group of high school kids in blue polos huddled together. Judging by the smell, they were smoking cheap pot. The scent reached the wall, mixing with the pungent stench of urine. A killer aroma.

She opened her eyes, looking at the city, really seeing it this time.

Life in Chicago had hardened her from a young age, building a bubble of indifference around her. This massive city had conditioned her to ignore suspicious people, horrible smells, litter, and noise. It was as if she lived in a bubble with thick walls, filtering reality...until The Silent Walker came along. He shattered that bubble, broke something that used to feel normal.

The bubble had once protected her from society's cast-offs. They were everywhere. On the corner of a residential building, on a stoop, on a bench in a park. Everywhere. Sucking on burnt paper, rocking back and forth like buoys in Lake Michigan. Warming themselves on steam grates in the middle of the road. Pissing on themselves, on each other. Grabbing at hands. Begging for coins. Holding up crudely scrawled cardboard signs. Poking pitch-black fingers with grimy nails. Loud, angry, poor.

She tried to ignore them, like before. *Don't look. Don't pay attention.* It was useless. The stench hit like an uppercut, the sounds hammered at her head, and her steps turned into a sprint, carrying her far away.

She used to erase all of this — like dragging a magnetic lasso in Photoshop. She'd step into the bubble, "lasso" the homeless, and they'd disappear. Trash would disappear. The addicts would disappear. Smells would disappear.

But *he* ruined everything. He had dragged her out of the bubble, taken away her magnetic lasso, and forced her into an unfiltered world.

A haggard figure shuffled past Alicia. She could smell him before she even opened her eyes. A faded cap with rusty spots, visor pulled low over his brow. A joint tucked behind his ear. Empty eyes. A worn-out hoodie tied around his waist. Dirty jeans sagged, exposing a grimy strip of skin. His left sneaker had a hole, his big toe stuck out — just like its junkie owner.

In front of him, he pushed a Walmart cart. A dirty cardboard sign was taped to the blue handle: "Collecting for food, trying to find work." Inside, there were unsettling traces of treasures: an old, moldy blanket, a worn-out glass flask, and a small plastic bag of blue crystals tied off with a rough cord.

The front wheel of the cart jammed, snagging on a tiny pebble, turning sideways. The ragged cart stopped. The man bumped his stomach into the handle, pressing the fabric of his shirt against his ribs. He looked down at the stuck wheel.

Time to go. Fast, back to the hotel. Alicia had never tried meth but had seen its effects on classmates. Even zombies could run. She looked around for other people. No one.

She could dash back into the store, but what if he followed her in? She could slip by him in front, between him and the cart, but her legs shook, unwilling. Too dangerous — he only had to look up to spot her.

Going around from behind seemed better. If she moved slowly, without sudden movements, he might not notice. Zombies didn't have peripheral vision.

And what if he had a weapon? His hoodie pockets bulged with unidentifiable shapes, but it was impossible to make out any kind of weapon.

Suddenly, he screamed, loudly, as if right by her ear. Whether out of rage or frustration, as if hoping to move the cart by force of sound, he screamed one long, flat note at the immobile wheel. Of course, the cart didn't budge.

It was enough for Alicia. She bolted without looking away from his overly dilated pupils, slowly lifting in her direction. Once she was several feet away, she turned back — he merely stared at the wheel. No more yelling.

Alicia glanced around, sprinted across the street at a red light and dashed through the hotel's front doors. Her watch buzzed, congratulating on her "activity." She leaned against a massive column in the lobby, ignoring the receptionist's polite smile, and called the elevator. For the first time in years, she bit a manicured nail. The polish held firm. She tilted her finger and bit at an angle. The nail chipped, and her dry lips spit out the piece.

The old, freshly vacuumed green carpet led her to her room. As she reached for her key card, it brushed against the lock, but before she could swipe it, the door gently cracked open, revealing a sliver of darkness.

"Wait...what?" Alicia tilted her head in confusion. She

waved the card near the lock, and it emitted its usual hum.

Had she left the door open? The same thing had happened to Jack yesterday when he went out to grab some wine. When he got back, he noticed that the door hadn't fully locked — no hum. They'd assumed it was a one-off issue, nothing to report.

But now? She had to check.

"Hello? Anyone there?" She called into the narrow opening, shifting from foot to foot.

Alicia grabbed her phone, trying to hold down her fear. *He* couldn't have followed her here.

First came the beeping ring. Then Jack's polite but detached voicemail kicked in: "I'll get back to you when I can. Thank you."

"Oh, come on, Jack," she whispered desperately. "Pick up."

When his voicemail kicked in again, Alicia's anger shifted to panic. He'd promised he'd be available! Jack still wasn't picking up. Alicia raised her hand to knock on the door of her hotel room but hesitated. She was convinced The Silent Walker was waiting for her inside. She might have smelled him — if fear had a scent. Alicia backed away from the door and glanced at the elevator. Could she make it there? What if he jumped out and pulled her in?

"Everything okay, ma'am?" asked a petite Thai housekeeper. She wore cheap plastic gloves up to her elbows — too flimsy for a place like this, not latex or nitrile, but ordinary plastic bags.

"Yes, yes, yes," Alicia lied, looking from the door to the woman. Then back at the door. And the woman again. Was she imagining things? "Wait," Alicia said, lightly touching the housekeeper's elbow.

The woman flinched and stepped back. Perhaps stranger touch was a cultural taboo?

"Could you check my room, please?" Alicia continued. "I think the lock might be broken; it didn't close when I left a few hours ago. Could you check that no one's in there?"

The housekeeper stared back at her. Silently. Blinking. Language barrier.

"I mean," Alicia said, speaking slowly. "Could you check inside," she gestured with her finger. "In the room. The door was open."

The housekeeper nodded like a bobblehead, set the brake on her cleaning cart, and entered the room. Alicia stood on her tiptoes, peeking over the woman's short head. After a moment, the housekeeper called Alicia in.

"All good, ma'am, yes, ma'am." She clasped her hands in a prayer motion and bowed.

"Um...yes, thank you."

The woman repeated her bow at a precise ninety degrees, released her cleaning cart brake, and moved on.

Ali locked the door, set the chain, double-checked the lock, pulled the door toward her, and finally took out her phone. Nothing from Jack. She texted Jordy.

```
I've arrived. What about you? :)
```

The messages showed a single checkmark, then a green icon appeared next to Jordy's name. All messages marked as read.

```
I just got off the bus a little while
ago. The ride was long, but I managed
                to read.
```

Ali cast a quick look at the message and tossed her phone on the bed, then reached for the TV remote. The iPhone screen lit up again:

```
BTW any plans for next week?
```

CHAPTER 30

The radio was playing a strange blend of Vivaldi's *Summer* concerto mixed with techno beats. Their ongoing argument was more bitter than dollar-store coffee from a gas station. Alicia felt nauseous, maybe from that pitiful attempt at a latte, maybe from the fact that she hadn't eaten anything since yesterday's pastry, or maybe from the lack of sleep. Since Jack had arrived late to the hotel, she'd been yelling, crying, holding her breath, then yelling, crying, yelling, and crying until two in the morning. Jack had been quiet, shouting, slamming doors, going outside to cool down, coming back inside, and eventually going quiet — also until two. By morning, both of them were worn out, and without breakfast, they headed to the police station to meet with the detective. A compromise was reached without a truce. They'd move to a new hotel, but only after Jack's workday, as he had no time for "this useless nonsense and other trivialities."

The detective's office in the morning was lit with the usual cold light, and the ceiling fan spun the yet-to-ferment air. In the corner, a printer hummed quietly. More photos, printed maps, and notes adorned the walls. Red pins marked Perry Avenue,

Chase Alley, and encircled a big question mark in the middle.

Sergio Gibbons, in a new beige shirt with a plaid purple jacket and matching suspenders, traced his finger down a file in front of him. The file had thickened like a hormonal teenager. He didn't lift his hand from the paper when there was a knock at the door. "Come in — Ms. Brooks, Mr. Sylvan."

Alicia felt burdened by an invisible weight, making her look even smaller. The bags under her eyes matched the color of Sergio's jacket. Jack tried to appear more composed, but he looked just as worn. Of the three in the room, the detective looked — and even smelled — the freshest.

"Have a seat; how are you both?" And without waiting for them to answer, he continued. "We've gathered information for this meeting, and we do have some things to discuss."

Alicia scooted her chair closer, her fingers gripping the edge of his desk.

"About time," Jack said bitterly. "Took you putting Alicia's life in danger AGAIN to figure something out."

"If you want to waste precious time being rude, I suggest you go somewhere else," the detective said as he raised an eyebrow. "I don't have a minute to waste on pointless arguments."

Ali pinched her boyfriend's leg, frowning. Jack clenched his hands over his chest and fell silent.

"We have a witness statement — the missing piece we lacked after the first attack. Gwyn Stan — a homeless man who set up camp on Park Street. By sheer luck, he was there when Ms. Brooks was fleeing from her attacker."

"He saw The Silent Walker?" Alicia whispered.

The detective glanced toward the two-way mirror.

"He...wasn't in a clear state of mind at the time of the incident. The officers found the tent almost immediately, and the — er — camp resident was sound asleep. They tried to get coherent statements from him, but he could barely stand upright. So, my partner returned the next day, hoping to find Mr. Stan sober or somewhat coherent. We asked if he'd seen anything suspicious, and showed him a suspect sketch and your photograph, Ms. Brooks. We took his fingerprints, ran them through our database, and compared them to those collected in your house — no matches."

Sergio cleared his throat and reached for a glass bottle of sparkling water. Alicia bit her dry lip.

"Could I have some water, please?"

"Yes, there's a cooler and disposable cups in the lobby," he said, unscrewing the cap and taking several long gulps. Alicia didn't move.

"Mr. Stan wasn't very talkative initially; he insisted he hadn't heard anything," the detective continued. "We left him a card and asked him to contact us anytime if anything came to mind. He did contact us a few days later, showing up at the station himself, neat and completely sober. He said he remembered hearing an unusual noise and decided to peek out of his tent with one eye."

The detective coughed again, raising his finger as he took another sip from the chilled bottle, and Alicia counted silently. Seven seconds. She was really thirsty. Eleven seconds. But more than that, she wanted to know what the police had learned.

"Mr. Stan was too frightened to leave his tent when he saw you, Ms. Brooks. He was afraid of getting into trouble, but he admitted seeing a blonde girl run down the street, followed by a tall man in a cloak and mask."

"I remembered something else. I'm not sure if it will help or just make things more confusing. It's...the smell."

"What smell, Ms. Brooks?"

"The Silent Walker's smell," Alicia mumbled. "He smelled — or rather, reeked — of wood. Not fresh forest wood, but treated and old, like aged timber."

Jack coughed quietly into his hand and stood up.

"Need me to grab you some water?" he asked his girlfriend.

Ali gave him a faint smile and nodded.

"Go ahead without me. I need to make a work call," Jack said and left the room.

Alicia's smile faded. *Work again.* The detective smoothed a crease on his sleeve and reached for his water bottle once more.

"Thank you for recalling this detail, Ms. Brooks. I'll make sure to investigate the scent and keep you updated. Additional witness testimony is always helpful, but witnesses like him often come with compromised credibility. Mr. Stan didn't mention any distinct smell or add much new information. He only confirmed the timeline and our preliminary sketch shown earlier. Given his intoxication on the day of the incident and the hangover the following day, we'll need to verify his testimony thoroughly. We're planning to involve a profiler who will compile a psychological profile of the attacker based on known actions, potential motives, and the sketch. I need to ask you, Alicia, to look at the updated portrait once more."

She flinched at the subtle emphasis on her first name — the detective rarely addressed her that way. It often sent a chill down her spine.

She shook her head. "I don't want to."

"It's necessary."

The detective gently rolled up his shirt sleeve, adjusted a barely visible crease, and pressed a button on the intercom. His associate entered the room. Alicia tuned out his name and face, her attention fixed on the file in the partner's hands. She knew exactly whom she'd see in that file.

The papers covered the table, and Alicia slid back in her chair as far as possible. The darkness stared back at her from every angle: The Silent Walker in front view, profile, full-length — even from behind.

What terrified her most was the full-body portrait of The Silent Walker. His figure was imposing, elongated, disproportionate. Something about his posture — the straight back, shoulders slightly hunched forward, as if ready to step forward — drove Alicia to madness. It felt like he was always nearby. Ready to step out of the photo right now, and no room, door, or even the police station could save her.

Something shook within her like a cold draft in an empty house. This wasn't just a police sketch. It was a nightmare brought to life, standing right in front of her.

A cold glass of water touched her hand, and Jack's warm hand rested on her shoulder. She hadn't even heard him enter.

"Are you okay?"

Ali held onto the cup, the ice-cold water refreshing her mind and thoughts like frozen snow from a freezer. The room came back into focus, and the nightmare turned back into simple drawings.

"Our hunch is that this person knows you personally. It doesn't seem like he just happened to be around a second time. Look closely at the sketches; do you recognize anyone familiar?"

"I don't recognize anyone," she said, shrugging.

"Do you have any enemies?"

Enemies? The word felt childish, jarring in her ears.

"What about that guy from the store? Did he see something, know something? Could he have had some part in this?" Jack interrupted.

"Are you talking about Jordy Evans?"

"Jordy couldn't have done this," Alicia said, shaking her head. "I talked to him afterward, and he...he doesn't match the character or the appearance."

"The police don't have a character profile on Mr. Evans." The detective's eyes glanced at the file. "But Ms. Brooks is correct — he doesn't fit the sketch. The boy is skinny, not physically imposing, and has an alibi — he was in the store when Ms. Brooks successfully escaped from the attacker."

"Fair enough, but enemies..." Jack scratched behind his ear. "Alicia doesn't have any illegal activity on her record, no dangerous business, no obsessive exes. Sounds pretty far-fetched, Detective?"

"Rivals?" Sergio Gibbons suggested.

"We're not drug dealers or anything to warrant that."

"Ja-ack..." Alicia's voice rose as a thought struck her. "What if I have an enemy?"

"Who?" The two men asked in unison.

"Cole. Cole Church."

CHAPTER 31

> If you're free tonight and want to hang
> out — I'm free, too...

I'm free, too? How stupid! Jordy slapped his forehead. His message already had a gray check — sent. No way to edit or take it back.

Across town, Alicia glanced down at the notification. It had come through just as Kendall turned on his father in *Succession*. She turned back to the show. On-screen, Logan gave his enigmatic smile, and the season's final credits started to roll.

Another. Boring. Day. The third one with no plans since that grueling interrogation in the detective's office. They finally had a lead — Cole Church, the one person she could think of who might hold something against her. Now it was up to the good old police to do their job, and she'd wait until they came back with results.

Could it really be Cole? Did she even believe her own theory? Maybe. She wasn't sure. Mostly, she just wanted to escape her thoughts, live someone else's life, and, as always,

TV helped when she was alone. Katie was out — off to a date with a new Tinder guy: spicy tacos and salty margaritas. Alicia was almost relieved; Katie could be unbearable without male attention. She'd have her fun and be back. And Jack? Guess where he was — of course, at work. Another late night; since when was that a surprise?

They'd change hotels tomorrow. Jack found it inconvenient commuting to the office through morning traffic. At this rate, these Chicago staycations were starting to outnumber their actual vacations.

Her back ached from the hotel couch, and the chips were gone. Alicia licked her fingers, watching the names scroll on the screen. She had to admit it — she was sick of the TV. That last episode had hooked her, but her head was pounding, and the thought of binging another season wasn't appealing.

The amber sunlight dusted the window. Paid leave with nothing to do was great — but only for a week. Alicia actually missed work: the frantic deadlines, fierce competition, crazy client ideas, coffee, and thought-provoking conversations over lunch. The Silent Walker had torn at her mind, breaking her down as a professional. Because of him, she'd literally been put on leave.

Could it really be Cole?

Alicia ticked off her usual to-do list in her mind: nails — done; pedi — done; coffee quota — met; still comfortably full from lunch. A bottle of semi-sweet white wine winked at her, but she waved it off — she wasn't going to finish it alone. Going out for an hour wouldn't hurt.

```
Okay. I have an hour.
```

She replied, stretching as her back cracked with relief.

Nine miles away, Jordy gripped his phone with both hands. The screen was shaking.

An hour. An hour with a girl he hadn't even dared to dream about. A girl completely out of his league. She'd replied to his silly message — and so quickly, too. Jordy pumped his fist — yes! — and bolted down the long corridor toward Auntie Chang's room. The scent of incense and the melody of a bamboo flute filtered through her door. He knocked eagerly.

"Who's there?" She opened the door holding a small silicone thimble. "What do you need, Jordy?"

"She agreed to go out with me. Again!" he exclaimed, his eyes shining.

Auntie Chang's expression told him she knew who he meant. He had mentioned a "friend" before — smart, beautiful, even with a respectable job. She seemed older, but with age came wisdom, right? Still, the look in Auntie Chang's eyes told him she wasn't convinced. She wouldn't let her trusting boy walk into something that could hurt him.

"Well, why are you standing here? Go get ready and look like a shuài gē." *Handsome guy.*

"Yes, yes...what should I wear?" Jordy's face fell a little.

"Definitely not those ripped jeans. Where's the date?"

"It's not a date, we're just friends — and we haven't even picked a place yet."

"Mm-hmm." Auntie Chang nodded with a smile. "Are you going to a café?"

"No." Jordy's shoulders drooped. "No paycheck yet. And I have nothing to wear."

"Then listen here," she said and squinted, and Jordy bent toward her — though even then, her gray-haired head didn't reach his chin. "Tonight, go for a walk in the park, breathe some fresh air, and next time you can take her to a café. I'll sew you a nice suit, so nothing hangs or sags like kids wear nowadays."

Jordy clasped his hands in thanks, and Auntie Chang gave his cheek a playful pinch before disappearing back into her room, humming in Mandarin. Once the door closed, he grabbed his phone.

```
Hey, how about we walk in the park
              tonight?
```

He didn't send it. He paused to think, then opened Google, scrolled down the park's page to check closing hours, and returned to his messages. He erased the text and rewrote:

```
Tonight, there's an evening tree
 exhibit at Freedom Park. The lilacs
   look like jacarandas. Meet in 40
              minutes?
```

Ali's phone buzzed. Freedom Park was less than a ten-minute cab ride away. She didn't feel like going all out for a simple park walk — this wasn't a restaurant. Quick makeup, a gray hoodie, hair in a bun — done.

She fished around in her empty bowl, then remembered she'd already finished the chips. She could probably get to the park in forty minutes — or she could relax a bit longer and catch just the first episode of season four to see how Logan's storyline unfolded.

```
Let's meet in an hour and a half.
         I'm busy right now.
```

Ali hit send, stretched out on the couch, and turned on *Succession*.

***

"I can't believe we've been in the park for hours." Alicia laughed, adjusting a lilac blossom in her hair. The mischievous breeze kept trying to steal it. "Thanks for inviting me, Jordy. It's been Groundhog Day in the hotel."

"Are you still not ready to go home?"

They sat on a nearby bench. Plastic rustled — they reached for their ice cream.

"No...no. The thought of it terrifies me."

"Have you always been afraid?" he asked, biting off a chunk of frozen chocolate shell.

Their conversation turned to the topic quickly, and it felt like Jordy was an unofficial therapist. Strange, really — Jack had never asked these kinds of questions. In his world, the past didn't matter, only the future. Sure — if only it worked that way. Alicia sighed, deciding to share a glimpse of her first childhood fear.

"Yes..." She pressed her lips together and let her mind drift back to where it all began.

Her mom had already filled the tub with foamy blue bubbles and stuck rubber seashells all over the tub walls. Little

Alicia was down to her undies when she remembered she'd left her favorite wooden boat in her dad's study. Dad had carved the hull from a piece of wood, fixed a mast, and given Ali the important task of hanging the fabric sail.

Alicia grabbed Mr. Georgie, her teddy bear, promising her mom she'd be right back. Of course, "right back" took several long minutes — time she couldn't count because she hadn't yet learned how to read the clock.

Ali froze before the door. Her bare feet shifted nervously, one over the other, as she stared into the dark room. The boat sat drying somewhere on her dad's desk, just beyond that open doorway filled with shadows.

"Come on, Ali, don't be scared," Mr. Georgie whispered encouragingly.

The little girl glanced around, nervous. What if her mom heard him? In daycare, they'd told her that if adults found out plush toys could talk, the toys would freeze forever and never, ever speak again.

So all the kids in the world kept this secret.

"You can do it; grab the boat, and we'll go back to the bath," her teddy continued, speaking without moving his mouth.

Tiny feet, a child's size nine and a half, stayed frozen in place. From the heart of the room, Darkness smiled at her.

It gazed at the girl through the eyes of a grim wooden mask hanging on the wall. Heavy, rough, and reeking of damp wood. The perpetually squinted holes seemed angry, glaring at Alicia. Her father's prized possession — a mask of some ancient priest of a dragon or something — hung proudly above his desk. During the day, the mask sat motionless, indifferent, but only until Darkness arrived to awaken it once again.

"Ali," Mr. Georgie urged. "The last big blue bubbles are about to pop — you know, the ones you love to float your boat on."

A hiss slithered out from her dad's study, winding its way toward her.

"You can't step in here," the hiss whispered, chilling her spine.

Ali shivered and took a step back.

"Ignore it," her teddy called firmly. "It can only look and scare you."

"You won't dare, will you, little Ali?" Darkness asked.

"Don't be scared — it can only watch."

"Oh, come now, sweet Ali. I'll eat you the moment you step inside. Or don't you believe me?"

Ali could have sworn on Saturday's gummy bears that the Darkness had stuck out its long, pitch-black tongue through the wooden mouth and licked its lips.

"Alicia, I'm here — I'll protect you." Her teddy's soft paw squeezed her tiny hand.

Darkness only smiled wider.

"You're a smart girl, Ali. I can digest plush toys just as well as little kids. Don't you remember what happened to Mr. Georgie's big brother? Where did Bunny Bill go?"

Mr. Georgie fell silent. Alicia's lips trembled. Her plush bunny had disappeared after she'd left him with her cousin on a sleepover and forgotten him alone in a room for a week.

And Darkness had come for him.

"Alicia, where are you? The water's getting cold," her mom

called from the bathroom.

Ali clutched Mr. Georgie in both arms and ran to her mom.

Darkness smiled after her.

CHAPTER 32

"Would a room with one king-size bed be fine?" asked the woman in the white shirt with a Hilton badge on her chest.

"Yes."

"No," Ali blurted at the same time as Jack.

They both stared at Alicia: Jack with a raised eyebrow, and the receptionist with a polite smile.

"I just want to get a good night's sleep in my own bed," Alicia explained quickly. Did they believe her? It didn't matter.

Jack pressed his lips into a thin line and gave the receptionist a slight nod. Her long, manicured nails clacked away at the keyboard.

"Of course, just one moment, please."

Jack glanced at Alicia with a suspicious squint. She could almost hear the thought forming — *What a difficult woman. No matter what he did, it was never enough.*

"Here are your keys." The hotel employee handed over the plastic cards wrapped in paper sleeves labeled with room 317. "Our porter will escort you to your room."

Out of a narrow door, a mustached man in a gray vest, wearing the same Hilton badge, emerged like a giant. He made a somewhat clumsy bow, his nose almost brushing the top of Jack's head, and grabbed their suitcases. The awkwardness, which had nothing to do with the porter, thickened in the air. From the reception to the lobby, three in an elevator (to say nothing of the suitcase), and then Alicia and Jack were finally left alone in Room 317 without the giant — or a Hamilton bill as a tip.

Despite the twilight outside, the room was brightly lit. Ali placed her bag on the floor. Square tiles at the entrance smoothly transitioned into the bedroom area, where a zebra-striped carpet seemed to mock her. Thin stripes: white. Thick stripes: black.

To Alicia's surprise, there were two large beds against the wall, both queen-sized. The receptionist had gone above and beyond, avoiding twin beds and accommodating both of them. Above the beds hung paintings of lions in the wild. One was sleeping, while the other sat, keeping watch. Opposite the lions stood a small sofa, a TV, and a work desk — for Jack and his endless work, of course.

Without taking off her shoes, Alicia marched quickly into the bathroom and closed the door behind her with a loud slam. She hadn't meant to, really. Alicia sat on the toilet lid, hugging herself tightly.

Her phone chimed, and she instinctively glanced down — it was a message from Jordy.

```
Everything okay? How are you?
```

And then another:

How's the new hotel?

A whirlwind of thoughts fought to be heard first. This guy, whom she'd known for less than a month, understood her better than her...who? Fiancé-to-be? Jack wasn't exactly in a rush to propose. Partner? At this rate, they'd soon be sleeping in separate rooms, let alone beds.

Alicia reread Jordy's messages and traced her finger over his picture. It was such a strange feeling, as if her fingertip could somehow feel the roughness of his skin. *Why did it feel so odd? So warm?* He was just a simple guy. And a student, at that.

"Ridiculous," Ali muttered under her breath, getting up from the cold lid.

A massive, round bathtub, large enough to qualify as super king-sized, stood in the bathroom. Almost jacuzzi-like in its proportions. Alicia ran her hand over its smooth rim. No chips, no worn scratches, no dead mold. She pulled the lever and turned on the hot water at full blast.

Steam filled the room in seconds, like a turbulent cloud. The mirror fogged over quickly, obscuring the girl in the reflection. Maybe that was for the best. Alicia slipped her jeans down over her slender hips. She pulled her cardigan and blouse over her head, tossing them to the floor. With two fingers, she unhooked her bra, letting it fall to join the rest. Ali took her firm breasts in her hands, pressing, kneading, and finally slipped into the tub.

Alicia folded a towel under her head and closed her eyes, letting her thoughts drift. No music, no shows. The line between constant fear and reality had become almost transparent, making it hard for her to tell what was real. She no longer trusted her senses. The quiet of the bathroom brought no comfort; it weighed on her like a silent drumbeat, pounding in the emptiness. The water's surface rippled with the shaking of her body...drums, drums in the deep of her chest. She felt it — the shadow moving in the dark. She could not get out. No escape. No refuge.

If only she could start over, stop this avalanche of nightmares, flee the city, and never be alone in that terrifying house. *But what would that change?* The Silent Walker wasn't an ordinary stalker. He was the embodiment of fear. A constant shadow whispering into every crack in her mind. When fear becomes the only air you breathe, is it even possible to take in anything else?

Oddly, the idea of breaking up, quitting, or moving no longer troubled her. Alicia was nearing the point of no return and found herself strangely at peace with it. Perhaps she'd try for a fresh start in another state, or even another country. She smirked, picturing Jack's twisted expression, his voice bouncing off the surrounding walls like a rubber ball.

"Alicia, but what about my work!"

"Ali, how can you irresponsibly abandon major projects for such important people?"

"And my clients?"

"And my reputation?"

"Alicia, what about the house I bought for us."

I wish that house would burn to the ground.

No, she wasn't planning to leave him just yet or burn bridges, but the idea had started to take shape. Once they caught The Silent Walker, she and Jack would sit down for a long, overdue conversation. People come together and part ways, no matter how beautiful the feelings. But right now, in this hotel room, she could taste the change. As soon as they caught The Silent Walker...

Emerging from the bathroom, playing out a third worst-case scenario with Jack in her mind, Alicia noticed him already asleep on the bed under the sleeping lion. The eyes of the second lion met hers. She approached the bed, unable to look away from the painted cat's pupils. The lion continued to watch her, as if with some supernatural ability. Like the Mona Lisa's eyes, always following.

Jack had changed into his pajamas but hadn't slipped under the covers and lay on his side — as though he'd been waiting to talk and had fallen asleep. Did he want her to wake him? Give him a little shake, then run fingers through his hair? Or was he just feeling hot?

She pulled her hand back, barely avoiding his warm shoulder. She shrugged off her robe and tugged at the tightly tucked covers. *Why did they always stuff them so far under the mattress?* She had to pull all the way around the bed's edge. Once she'd wrestled the covers free, she arranged her pillows: two for her head, one for her back, another for her leg. Ali turned off the lamp, and darkness settled in the room.

Sleep wouldn't come; the minutes ticked by. At one a.m., finally surrendering, Alicia grabbed her phone. Jordy was no longer online. Good. No new messages from him, either. Also good. Perhaps he didn't want to intrude. Or had he lost interest in her? *Unlikely.* She knew, she just knew, that even his feelings could break through the walls of the virtual world.

She cast a guilty glance at Jack, who was deeply asleep,

probably already in the middle of a dream. With him, she felt safe — even in silence. He protected her. Took care of her. He drove, fed, and clothed her. He hadn't left her alone yet. And their intimacy was still great. Every thread seemed to lead back to love, unraveling only when she looked at the shadowed outline of Jack, asleep in the darkness.

But why was it Jordy she saw when she closed her eyes?

Alicia held her breath, hoping that the image would pass, that her feelings would freeze. But the world kept spinning, and shameful thoughts gnawed at her like sharp claws, tearing her from the inside. She bit her lip to keep herself from crying. This new feeling, strange and unwelcome, was unbearable. She — an accomplished, successful woman — having feelings for a boy? Yes, things were rough with Jack. They'd drifted apart. Everything felt...materialistic. Jack no longer heard her, no longer understood her inner fears. Their relationship felt like a carefully planned calendar for the coming years: promotions, personal business, house, children. The Silent Walker didn't fit into that plan.

The house — a bitter echo from yet another past argument. Moving. Jack stubbornly refused to leave Chicago, as if this city hadn't already cost enough blood. But Jordy...would Jordy move for her?

Alicia let out a quiet sob, burying her face in her hands. The tears finally broke through her control, like a teenage girl falling in love for the first time. But unlike back in high school, she knew this wasn't true love. It was just attention.

She needed to get through this phase. Therapy, a break. As soon as they caught The Silent Walker...

Alicia nodded to herself with determination. She picked up her phone to set an early alarm before Jack's workday started. She could head out, grab breakfast at the café across the street, maybe a bacon croissant and a large coffee. But her fingers, moving faster than her thoughts, tapped a different contact. Jordy.

The message was sent before she could stop herself:

Want to meet tomorrow?

And another, almost without thinking:

I want to leave Chicago.

CHAPTER 33

"Well, here it is. My place."

Jordy gave an awkward bow, lost his footing, and nearly fell, grabbing onto the doorframe for balance. Alicia laughed, brushing a curled strand of hair off her forehead. She stepped into the room and bumped into a chair standing in the middle of the tiny space. *Even Harry Potter's cupboard had more space than this*, she thought with a smirk.

Jordy quickly grabbed the chair and tried to pull it back, but the legs wouldn't budge, wedged against a towering stack of books nearly Everest-high. The room practically screamed that it hadn't been expecting guests. Jordy hoisted the chair onto the bed in one swift motion — the legs pointed up, nearly hitting the wardrobe that loomed over the bed.

Alicia made her way to the table, clutching a jacaranda bonsai in her hands. The scent of the blossoms was already settling into the room. The wall behind the desk, plastered with cutouts of chemical formulas, sloped up and away with a narrow skylight that let in more cold air than light. Alicia glanced over the cluttered desk: textbooks, notes, a thick, closed laptop, and a black cable held together with electrical tape.

"Jordy, I don't think there's enough room for our jacaranda here," Ali concluded.

Jordy hastily pushed books aside, lifted the laptop, and opened the wardrobe above the bed. A glimpse of a bulky Spider-Man figurine peeked out from a pile of things.

"What do you have there?" Alicia asked with a smile.

"Nothing, nothing," said Jordy, as he struggled to fit the laptop on the shelf.

"Is that Spider-Man?"

"It's a piggy bank. From my mom." The laptop finally gave in, and Jordy shut the door.

"That's adorable. I'd put it on the desk," Ali said genuinely.

Jordy gave her a suspicious look, unsure if she was mocking him. Alicia smiled reassuringly and looked at the window.

"I think the jacaranda needs more light. Let's put it in the common room?"

Jordy quickly shook his head, but Alicia had already stepped out. He dashed after her, hoping his roommate wasn't home.

No such luck. Mr. Breach was sprawled on the couch in the common room, wearing a tank top, his hairy fingers dusted with chip seasoning as he drummed on his belly.

"Alicia, please don't..." Jordy whispered.

Ignoring him, Alicia walked over to the TV stand. In the center, like the Hope Diamond, lay the TV remote, wrapped in plastic wrap and sealed with tape. Alicia picked it up, set it on the table, and placed the jacaranda pot in its place.

"What the hell is that?" boomed Mr. Breach from behind her.

Alicia spun around, her pale hair following her movement

like a crack of thunder.

"Who put that damn thing here?" Breach barked, jabbing a finger at the plant. His intense gaze shifted to Jordy. "You again, kid?"

"Me. So what?" Alicia replied calmly.

"Who the hell are you? Never mind. Get it out of here. Put the remote back."

She took a step toward him, her gaze steady.

"On what grounds?"

"What grounds? "Why the hell would I want some damn bush in here?" Breach snapped.

"This is a shared space, and according to the house agreement, all tenants have the right to decorate common areas with plants as long as they aren't allergenic or dangerous to health. Unless you have a doctor's note proving you have an allergy?"

"What?" Breach flushed a deep shade of red. "I've been living here for god knows how long! What agreement?"

"The rental agreement. Didn't you keep a copy? Don't you remember the clause about not making a mess, avoiding confrontations, and respecting your neighbors? We can go over the rules together if you need a refresher," Alicia said, her voice calm.

Breach blinked, as if slapped. Jordy's eyes widened. In slow motion, Mr. Breach, the abusive menace Jordy constantly had to put up with, seemed to shrink under Alicia's sharp blue gaze.

"What are you, some kind of lawyer?" he grumbled, his voice losing steam.

"No, but I have friends who are," Alicia replied with a wink.

"I'd be happy to introduce you."

"Introduce...what?" mumbled Breach, shrinking away.

As if waking from a trance, Jordy felt a strange heat well up inside him.

"My friend is right, Mr. Breach," Jordy said. "We all have equal rights in this house. The jacaranda plant stays in the common room."

"I'll drop by to enjoy it every now and then. And I expect it'll cheer me up in return. Nice to meet you." Ali extended her hand with a businesslike smile.

Breach looked from Jordy to Alicia, to the plant, and back again. Finally, he wiped his hand on his shorts and gave Alicia a reluctant handshake before leaving the room.

"Ali," Jordy whispered after hearing Breach's door shut.

She brushed a strand of hair from her forehead and put a hand on his shoulder.

"You did well," Alicia said.

Jordy nodded, feeling as if her hand had placed not just reassurance, but a new kind of understanding on his shoulder. For the first time in a long time, he felt strong.

"You read my lease?" he whispered.

"No, silly — I made it up. Those are basic roommate rules. I'm sure the jerk hasn't even read his contract."

The jacaranda's scent replaced the cheap chip smell in the room. *Auntie Chang would be thrilled to see a living plant in the living room,* Jordy thought. With her difficult experience as an immigrant, she'd always feared challenging white Americans, especially burly, intimidating ones like Mr. Breach.

"Alicia, about your message yesterday." Jordy finally

gathered the courage to ask.

Her expression changed. *So he'd asked.* For the first half-hour as they walked around the garden picking out the jacaranda, she'd nervously expected the question, but hoped Jordy wouldn't have the nerve. She'd hoped he'd ignore it, forget about her moment of weakness. Maybe the confrontation with his roommate had given him a boost of confidence.

"Oh, don't mind that; I was just having a low moment."

"It didn't seem like just a moment. You wrote that you wanted to leave."

"Changed my mind."

"Ali, tell me the truth. I can help you. I don't know how yet, but I'll do everything I can to help! I can guard you, walk you home, watch out for The Silent Walker! I could even quit my job and be with you all the time," Jordy's words came out breathlessly, his cheeks flushed.

"Do you have a girlfriend, Jordy?" Alicia interrupted, changing the subject. *A strange question. He didn't, of course.*

"Well, I used to. In university. Just one."

"Why did you break up?"

"We didn't have the same interests."

"Really?" Alicia raised an eyebrow.

"I...I couldn't protect her. She chose drugs and her friends."

Alicia placed her hand on his shoulder again.

"You don't need to save me. There's no reason for you to sacrifice your life for me, Jordy. You have university, a job, and a great future ahead."

"But I didn't mean it that way...I just..."

"Live for yourself, alright?" Alicia smiled and couldn't resist giving him a little pat on the cheek — *such a good guy*. "I'll head back to the hotel. Thanks for the walk. I'll be waiting to hear from the detective. They're questioning Cole today."

Jordy felt warmth spread through him from where her hand had touched his cheek, moving downward. Her touch smelled faintly of jasmine hand cream. He stood still long enough to remember the sensation.

"Are you taking a cab, or should I walk you?" he asked, catching up with her in the hallway.

"Are you ready for university tomorrow? Got that assignment done?" Alicia asked.

"No, I'll manage later."

"What if you don't? You could lose your scholarship. Then what?" She fought the urge to pat his cheek again or flick his forehead, as she might a younger brother. "Go study."

Jordy leaned back against the doorframe, watching as she slipped the backs of her sandals onto her soft heels. Once, he'd nearly been expelled from university — back when Evelyn was kicked out. If it weren't for her father's generous donations, reinstatement wouldn't have been an option. They'd never brought it up after their breakup, but Evelyn still justified her friends who had nearly ruined his career — after a drunken incident, they'd set his dorm room on fire. Only Jordy's good rapport with his resident advisor had saved him from being dragged down with his ex and her circle.

"Walk tomorrow?" he blurted.

"Only if you finish your homework." Alicia winked and slipped out the door.

Jordy touched his cheek. Closed his eyes. Her touch played

on a slow loop in his mind. Evelyn hadn't respected education, but Alicia constantly emphasized it. Evelyn drained energy, while Alicia radiated it. Evelyn was a problem; Alicia, a solution.

"Are you in love, xiao huozi?" *Young man.* He murmured to himself.

CHAPTER 34

On a small, old-fashioned TV, something out of a pawn shop, Alicia studied the figures on screen. Sergio Gibbons sat in a light polka-dot blazer, his posture, so perfect, it seemed to press the wrinkles from his back without an iron. Opposite him sat Cole Church in a thick, slightly pilled hoodie with one large pocket at the front. His shoulders slouched, the stretched fabric hugging his sides and rounded belly.

"Mr. Church," Gibbons's voice came through the speakers surprisingly clearly, which Ali hadn't expected from such an old device. "You are employed as a consultant at LiveSafe, specializing in the construction and architectural field, correct?"

"Yes," Cole mumbled, barely audible, prompting Alicia to lean closer to the screen.

"You worked alongside Ms. Brooks for several months on a project?"

"Yes, on Mr. Wales's project."

"But recently, you've been the sole consultant on that project?"

"Yes."

"So you no longer have any competition?"

"Well, not at the moment. Alicia, it seems, went on leave due to health reasons."

"Does Ms. Brooks's absence affect your typical workday?"

"There are no irreplaceable people." Cole shrugged with his crescent-shaped shoulders. "I manage the project on my own just fine."

"Do you work with wooden materials, Mr. Church?"

"In what sense?"

"Have you recently used any wood in connection with your work?"

"I don't do hands-on work. At most, I'll inspect contractors at warehouses or take part in an audit."

"What about the past two weeks?"

"Well, I visited a logging site."

"How long were you there?" the detective asked, flipping back a few pages in his notebook.

"I went, conducted the inspection, and left. Maybe an hour, at most."

"Do you remember the exact day of that visit?"

"I'd need to check my calendar. I don't recall."

"Mr. Church." Gibbons narrowed his eyes. "Did you know Ms. Brooks was attacked multiple times?"

Cole jolted, his belly quivering like unset jelly. He cleared his throat before responding. "Attacked? That's terrible! No, I wasn't told any details. Who attacked her?"

"Did you discuss Ms. Brooks's possible return with any of her close contacts — Mr. Jack Sylvan or Ms. Catherine Black?"

"I don't remember."

"Mr. Church," Gibbons said, his voice remaining level, though his shoulders leaned forward slightly, as if waiting to catch any small reaction from Cole. "An anonymous source claims that after you assumed full responsibility for the project, you said, 'Finally, that bitch is gone — now I'm in charge.' Is that accurate?"

Alicia's eyes widened as she glanced from the TV to the detective sitting beside her — now jacketless, but in a fresh short-sleeved shirt. Sergio gave a small shrug, gesturing to the recorded interrogation from yesterday, where Cole fidgeted in his chair. That self-assurance Alicia had always loathed had clearly left the room.

"No! I mean...maybe I said something, but not like that..."

"Were you pleased that Ms. Brooks left the company?"

"What do you want from me?? Am I here as a witness or a suspect?"

Gibbons held his gaze for a moment, watching Cole's labored breathing before speaking again.

"Mr. Church, before we proceed, I must remind you that you have the right to remain silent. Anything you say can be used against you in court. You also have the right to an attorney. If you cannot afford one, the state will provide one for you. Do you understand your rights?"

Cole paled, swallowed nervously, and nodded quietly. "I want a lawyer," he said, calmer than before. He took a deep breath and met Gibbons's eyes. "I won't say anything else without a lawyer."

The recording paused, and the detective turned off the TV.

"Funny how our budget gets distributed," he joked, patting

the TV.

"I'm going to step out for a moment, okay? I need some air."

How had Cole behaved? Suspiciously? Fearfully? Or completely innocently? How well did she actually know him? Did he have a family? A pet? An elderly mother?

Alicia nudged the door open with one finger and wrinkled her nose. The women's restroom at the station had certainly been neglected in terms of budget, cleanliness, and comfort. Graffiti-covered walls bore the signatures of generations past. A bar of soap was threaded onto a metal rod jutting from the wall to prevent theft. The single toilet paper roll for the five stalls was also locked in place. Alicia tore off a few pieces, dampened them under the faucet, and wiped under her eyes. Lately, she'd been neglecting her usual makeup routine. In her previous life, she'd never have allowed herself to leave the house half-prepared. Now, she felt too tired for primer, too tired for foundation, too tired for setting spray. Instead, she found herself wiping away smudged makeup more and more often.

```
What are your plans today, Jordy?
        When are you free?
```

His response arrived almost immediately, before she could even pocket her phone.

```
        Im free now
```

Ali smiled. As a teenager, she'd enjoyed attention from boys and never turned down gestures when they dropped everything just for her. But not with Jordy. Not under these circumstances, not given where he lived. He needed to focus on building his life — studying, earning his degree, landing a solid job, and leaving that toxic environment behind.

> Send me a screenshot of your class
> schedule. And don't try to fool me.

Color-coded rectangles popped up on her screen moments after — "Pharmacy Operations" and "Pharmacognosy."

> I'll be at the university parking lot
> at 3:10 p.m.

Alicia returned to the office. The detective's sharp eyes seemed to bore through the fourth wall. She rarely could read his mood, but now the entire room felt charged with a hunter's energy. The scent of pursuit hung in the air.

"That'll be all for today, Ms. Brooks. We'll continue by coordinating with Mr. Church's attorney. We're planning to review his location history to verify his alibi, take fingerprints, and run DNA tests. He certainly has a motive, but I have one last question for you. Think about it, and give me your answer by the end of the day. Do you feel the presence of The Silent Walker in Cole Church?"

***

Bugs Bunny's face squeezed between them, his whiskers just out of frame. The performer in costume held up a big, white-gloved thumb.

"Smile," Ali sang out. "And...one more time!"

The bunny twitched his ears and hopped away to a horde of screaming kids, who instantly mobbed the performer, climbing up his legs and tearing at bits of the cheap costume.

On a weekday, Six Flags Great America was nearly empty. European tourists often avoided renting cars to get to the park, and the locals hadn't yet started the amusement park season. Alicia and Jordy had gone on all the thrilling rides (Batman three times), tasted the adrenaline with ice cream, got soaked on the lumberjack ride and topped it off with Justice League temporary tattoos — he picked Superman; she, Wonder Woman.

They passed through a giant metal flag under the turnstile at the exit and sat on a cold stone, which stole warmth and promised a few pimples in a couple of hours. The sun dipped behind the trees, and rays stretched like spider webs across the blue sky.

"You know, as a kid, I always dreamed of spending my birthday at an amusement park. But my dad would never have allowed it. Until today, I never realized how much fun it could be. You gave me a special day, Ali!" Jordy patted her shoulder and turned away; his ears flushed with the color of the setting sun.

"I hate your father. Without him and The Silent Walker, the world would be a much better place."

"My childhood doesn't compare to what you're going through now."

"Don't say that."

"But it's true. Your life has changed completely, and I'm sorry we didn't meet earlier, before you had...you know."

Alicia wiped away a stray tear and placed her hand on his knee.

"Everything's different now. At work, at home, with Jack, with friends. I don't remember what my life was like before. Without that damn maniac in his damn mask. I wish I could see him as Mr. Dogshit instead of The Silent Walker. A couple of days ago, I just stared out into the hotel courtyard. I haven't told you this, but I hate streetlights and the shadows they cast. I thought I saw something move...like he was there... like in horror movies, when they flash by, quick and loud yet unnoticed. I would've sat there until dawn if it hadn't been for Jack. You know, The Silent Walker is always on my mind. Not a day goes by without me thinking of him. That sharp knife in his hand. The sweep of his black cloak. And his smell, Jordy! I feel like I've known it before, but I can't remember when."

Jordy placed his hand over hers and squeezed. If she realized how he felt now, it didn't matter. His feelings didn't matter in this moment.

"And yesterday, I went to the pool, and after swimming, I got stuck in a changing stall. I was almost done when someone came into the room. Slowly, quietly — just the sound of approaching steps. What if it was him? What if he'd followed me to the gym, waited until I was alone, come to finish what he started? I froze." Alicia remembered how rough the scratched-up door felt under her fingers, sticky with old gum, and shivered. "This person went into the stall next to mine. Right next to me, Jordy, even though there were, like, ten other stalls! I could barely breathe, just half-breaths so they wouldn't hear me. Fear twisted and coiled inside, gaining energy until...I burst. I flew out, shoved the door, and ran. Crying like a lunatic. I didn't stop until I reached the first bench."

Her voice cracked with shaky breaths, and Jordy felt his cheeks grow damp. He couldn't hold back his tears. Their hands intertwined; their emotions synced.

"Jordy, what if he is part of me? They think it's Cole. But when the detective asked me today...I don't know! He's already part of me! But I'm not insane! I'm normal, right, Jordy?"

"You're not insane!"

"If only they all knew how hard it is to live like this. They go to bed, and I wait out the night. They walk in the park, I run out of the park. When dogs bark, I'm afraid to look out the window. But I'm scared not to look, too. What if he's under the window? Then I need to check to be sure he's not there...And if he is? Standing there, on the trimmed lawn, staring up at me, breathing so heavily I can feel it under my skin."

"They will catch him." Jordy's voice trembled too.

"When? How much longer, Jordy? I don't want to go outside alone, but I can't stay home. I can't sleep alone. I can't look in the mirror. What if he's behind me? What if I close the closet door, and he's there? Have you seen those kinds of movies? I'm living that damn movie every day. It's like a tumor that can't be cut out."

The sunlight disappeared from this part of the continent. The streetlights flicked on. Two figures sat on the cold stone, hand in hand. The day sank, streaked with drops of color, leaving a dark canvas for the night.

"You know, Jordy, a great person once said, 'A horrible end is better than endless horror.' I agree. I choose a horrible end."

"Please don't say that," Jordy whispered. "Don't say it."
He kissed her.

CHAPTER 35

Alicia ran her hand along the wooden desk, letting her index finger linger over a dark swirl — the natural design in the wood, once part of a living oak. She didn't know the official term for these patterns, so she called them "underbark eyes," a name she'd made up as a child.

"Alicia, once they catch the maniac..." Jack's voice trailed off.

"The Silent Walker."

"Right. Once they catch The Silent Walker, the office will welcome you back with open arms. Especially Mr. Wales," Jack finished, trying to sound confident.

She nodded out of habit. A notification pinged — a message from Jordy. Alicia flipped her phone over, screen-side down, a bit too forcefully for Jack not to notice.

"Spam?" he asked.

"Something like that. Katie. Practically spam."

She and Jordy hadn't spoken since the previous evening. That kiss lingered on her lips with a strange aftertaste of disappointment. She hadn't given Jordy any indication of a romantic connection, ever. The betrayal wasn't external — it was internal, silent, and crept in precisely when she was most vulnerable. Why had he done it? Had he taken advantage of her fragility, her fear, to get closer? Was it love — or just a way to exploit a broken girl?

She hadn't looked back when he called out to her, hadn't answered his calls, hadn't read his messages. She wanted to know the reason yet wasn't ready to hear it. Time. Only time could heal this. Loneliness pressed down on her, heavy and sticky, wrapping around her chest. She felt as if she had nothing left. Nothing but time.

"I even miss my desk. Is that strange?" Alicia looked at Jack, her eyes misty.

He knelt by her desk, holding her cold hands in his. He was shaving less often now, and his stubble prickled against her fingers.

"It's completely normal. Nobody envies your situation; everyone understands and is just waiting for you to come back. Your office is still your office. Don't let it get you down, okay? Now, I need to stop by the director's office before we leave." He glanced at his watch, kissed her hand, and straightened up. "I'll meet you in the lobby? Maybe go gossip with Jacqueline if you've missed her. She'll cheer you up."

"Oh, Jackie." Alicia smiled. "You can be as sarcastic as you want, but I do miss the office gossip."

Jack winked and left the room. The scorching summer heat seeped in through the glass. Her office looked untouched but clean. The water cooler in the corner was gone — no reason to refresh the water in an empty office. They probably came in once a week to dust and air out the room, but Jack was right — no one had laid claim to her space. The whiteboard that had helped her secure a lead role on her last project stood untouched, waiting, as though the very construction project itself was on hold, awaiting her return. Ali rose from her desk, grabbed her purse, and took one last — final — look at the room. *See you soon.*

All that was left was to catch the bastard who had wrecked her life.

The public restroom in the office always irritated her — on every floor, really. Three clean but pale-gray stalls faced equally drab walls; no plants, a dark-gray soap dispenser; and a small square mirror above the sink that only reflected the top half of her head. And the ridiculous half-door stalls, three feet long, made privacy a joke — everyone could guess who was "serenading" from behind those flimsy doors by looking at their shoes.

Alicia entered the stall furthest from the entrance, hanging her purse on the metal hook. She tore off a decent length of toilet paper, sprayed it with sanitizer, and wiped down the seat. Then she sat down, finally feeling a bit of relief.

The silence pressed on her like a suffocating shadow. Life had turned into a game of hide-and-seek. From The Silent Walker. From Jordy. From Jack. From life itself. She took a shaky breath, feeling as though the silence was consuming her. *I've lost everything,* she thought. Even the damn desk with its little "underbark eyes."

Someone entered the restroom. Alicia jolted out of her reverie. The person chose the middle stall — a strange selection. *At least people here respected each other's space,* Alicia thought.

Why squeeze in when there's a free stall in between?

But really...why?

Alicia held her breath. Normally, she rarely shared the restroom with her colleagues — the few other women in the department worked on lower floors. Besides her, only two other women worked on this floor. The unspoken rule was clear: don't take the stall right next to someone else if others are free. Respect each other's space.

Alicia didn't see the person's feet. She tilted her head, moving her hair to one side, and carefully leaned down, holding her hair back so the tips wouldn't brush the floor. A little more...

Someone next door shifted a foot.

Her hand slackened, and her hair swept the floor.

The smell drifting over the partition was familiar. Hauntingly familiar.

He had found her. Again.

Alicia shot to her feet, hurriedly yanking up her pants and underwear. The waistband twisted at her hip. Her trembling fingers grabbed the latch. *Just don't faint. Not now.* The shoe behind the partition moved again, giving her the strength to push the lock open. Alicia nudged the door with her knee and bolted out of the room without looking back.

The corridor seemed longer than usual. Had she never noticed this before? Wasn't it just ten steps from her office to the elevator? Why did the distance feel so enormous now?

She reached the elevator, frantically jabbing the down button. Over and over. The elevator was still on the first floor. Alicia started pounding the "up" button. The elevator wouldn't move. No time left.

The restroom door opened. The dark form of The Silent Walker pulled her in like a magnet.

A dusty cloak. A sagging mask. Dark eyeholes stared at her. With each encounter, he grew larger. Broader. Darker. The world around Alicia shrank, leaving just the two of them.

Alicia clasped her hands together, pleading.

"What do you want from me?"

The Silent Walker twisted his knife, like a kid showing off a new toy in preschool. His shoulders twitched with delight. He tilted his head to the side. Alicia whimpered and bolted for the emergency stairwell.

The sensor light between the nineteenth and twentieth floors flicked on, illuminating the stairs above. The way down was swallowed in darkness. Panic overrode logic. Panic caused mistakes. Like a moth to flame, Alicia turned and ran up the stairs. She wasn't thinking rationally. Logic, along with her purse, had stayed behind in the restroom stall.

The stone steps seemed to grow larger, and Alicia raced up, taking them two at a time, her breathing frantic, her cheeks streaked with tears. She stopped at a door one floor up, tugged at the handle.

"A-ahhh!" she screamed, throwing herself against the door. The magnetic lock flashed red. It was easy to get onto the fire escape, but returning to the office without an access card was impossible.

The door slammed shut below. Heavy footsteps followed. Alicia squeaked and dashed upwards. There was no turning back now. The roof was only a few flights away.

She didn't even try to open the next door properly, just

jiggled the handle out of desperation — no luck. The magnetic lock (unlike her luck) worked flawlessly. The stairwell's soundproofing held as well; her cries stayed trapped inside. Alicia leaned on the railing, glancing down at the staircase. Darkness filled the distance below. Footsteps echoed. Thud. Thud. The cloak rustled. He wasn't in a hurry.

Blonde strands of hair clung to her forehead. Sweat formed above her lip, mingling with tears and trickling onto her tongue. Alicia swallowed the salty mixture and looked up. One floor remained until the roof.

She dashed up the last flight like an antelope, taking the steps three at a time, barely touching the railing. Her heart raced like a turbine. The final door — this one without a magnet — opened easily.

A strong wind tore her damp hair from her face, lifting her shirt from her body. The amount of air felt overwhelming. Blazing sunlight blinded her, and the gust pounded her ears, making her feel deaf. The wind seemed determined to push her toward the edge of the roof. A summer blend, so intense she could barely breathe.

Alicia let go of the door, and it slammed shut, sealing off the world behind her like a coffin lid. She screamed with all her might, but the wind swallowed her hysteria. There was no future. It was impossible to see through the haze of tears. Alicia screamed at the city, telling it how much she hated it. Chicago had ruined her life. Chicago had stabbed her in the back. Chicago hid behind a mask, stalking her with a knife, waiting to slam her door shut.

The scream brought her back to herself. Alicia scanned

the roof. The wide, open space was crowded with industrial equipment. To her right stood massive ventilation ducts, with thick clouds of steam pouring out. Nearby, concrete dividers created narrow passages, like a maze for a mouse.

Alicia caught her breath. The stairs might have been a mistake, but the rooftop was her last chance — her only hope of hiding. She darted behind the tallest vent, crouching low to the ground. Only a few feet separated her from the edge, and for someone who had never feared heights, her throat tightened with nausea. The only path led down.

Ahead, a skyline of skyscrapers loomed. The towering buildings around her often adorned dollar-store tourist postcards. The business center of Chicago shimmered with sunlight on sealed windows. The walls of glass, metal, and brick loomed above her, pressing her down against the cold metal of the vent.

The door slammed shut. Alicia covered her mouth with her hands. Death was closing in from both sides, squeezing her like a concrete press. She glanced down — the fall would take only a few seconds. *What if she just let go?* Die in the air or be slaughtered like livestock?

Footsteps grew closer. She was too afraid to turn around. Too afraid to be seen. It wouldn't take long for The Silent Walker to find her — just as long as it would take her body to hit the ground. Alicia looked down again: the city continued its indifferent life below. Tiny people, like ants, planned identical vacations, rushing and scrambling to keep up with one another.

She was exhausted. *What if this was just a bad dream,* she thought. Then everything would end instantly, and she'd wake up in her bed, drenched in sweat, but alive...

Alicia crawled closer to the edge on her knees and grabbed onto the ledge with her hands. The wind lashed her fingers mercilessly. She leaned her head over the edge, her mind refusing to function, her head filled with static like a broken radio in a car.

The horrible end had never felt so close.

Chapter 36

Alicia swallowed...but couldn't find the strength to jump. She drew her head back and rested her forehead on the sun-warmed rooftop. Her fingers continued to grip the ledge she couldn't bring herself to cross. She lay there in child's pose, and her life flashed before her eyes like a series of colorful slides: parents, whom she never found time to call; the scruffy mutt, Dill, who used to wake her with a scratchy tongue before school; grandmother's pancakes, which she hadn't tasted in over five years; first kiss, school prom, a funeral. Faceless figures by a gravestone flickered in her mind. "Alicia Brooks — born wanted, lived brightly, died worthless."

"Alicia," a muffled voice called, and she felt the end approaching. *They say you always hear the voices of loved ones just before death.*

She swallowed hard, closed her eyes tightly, and prayed it would all pass quickly. Suddenly, warm arms wrapped around her waist.

"Alicia, my girl."

Someone pulled her upward and lifted her into their arms. The familiar scent made Alicia open her eyes. Jack? She blinked. He was there. On the rooftop. With her. The wind had whipped him too; his tie was awkwardly tucked under his arm, his hair stood in windswept disarray, and his cheeks shone with tears that had dried instantly in the breeze.

"What happened?" he shouted.

"Jackie, he came, he's here," Alicia said faintly.

"What? I can't hear you!"

"He's in the office!" Alicia shouted.

"Who?"

"The Silent Walker!"

Jack's eyes widened, and he almost dropped Alicia. He squatted down, gently setting her on the ground, and put a finger to his lips. Ali nodded weakly. Jack pulled out his phone, quickly dialed a number, and covered his mouth with his hand to muffle the sound.

Alicia watched as if in slow motion, with the sound turned down. The effect was like when she tried mushroom therapy. The nearby buildings blurred like a carousel. The edge of the roof seemed impossibly far away, and she couldn't believe she'd been lying there just minutes before.

"W-e...d u e-e?"

"Hm?" Alicia squinted, trying to focus.

"Where. Did. You. See him?" Jack asked, enunciating each word over the wind.

She pointed a trembling finger toward the door. Jack nodded and kept speaking into the phone, shielding it with his hand.

Everything spun around her, as if she were in a third-person video game. A security team arrived. Three men in heavy uniforms and helmets burst onto the roof. They silently split up and began methodically searching the area. After each man signaled "clear," they approached her and Jack. The tallest introduced himself with some title and some name she barely registered, then told them to follow him. Jack held Alicia, who seemed empty, by the arms. Together with two security guards, they descended flight after flight until they finally reached Jack's office.

Alicia lay down on the couch and closed her eyes.

***

The sun was setting over the city, illuminating the streetlights as office workers headed home to their families. But in the building of LiveSafe, no one was allowed to leave yet. Employees remained in their offices, permitted only to go to the restroom. A police officer was stationed on each floor. Some muttered in irritation over spoiled plans; others were relieved at the chance to avoid work; a few women huddled together, frightened by the alarm they'd heard. Only a few people knew the truth of what was happening and now sat around the conference room's round table, waiting in tense silence.

The door finally opened, and Detective Gibbons entered with his partner, carrying a laptop under his arm.

"Detective Gibbons," the company's director, David Wood, spoke firmly. "We greatly respect our collaboration with the Chicago police, but we would like to know how long we'll be locked in here, waiting to resume our work."

"As you suggested, Detective," said the head of HR. "We

haven't mentioned the armed intruder, but the employees need to know something. When can we lower the alarm?"

Sergio Gibbons took a seat at an empty chair and rubbed his eyes. "Thank you for your understanding, gentlemen. There are a few things we need to discuss, but you're right — we should first address the staff. Every corner of the office building has been searched, and we found no evidence of an armed intruder in the building. This means the office is safe again. Employees may return to work or leave the premises. However," he paused, scanning the faces in the room and stopping at Alicia. "I want to ask everyone here to keep all information confidential until the case is fully resolved."

Several directors exhaled and began to rise from their chairs, but Mr. Wood raised his hand, and they obediently sat back down.

"Detective Gibbons, where could the suspect have gone? And most importantly, how did he get into this secure building?"

The detective pressed his lips together, his voice momentarily caught before he gathered his thoughts. "The police reserve the right to withhold necessary information during an investigation, but I can assure you that the office is entirely safe. Guards will remain on duty until the end of the day, and I recommend increased security and stricter ID checks at the entrance starting next week."

"What about the armed intruder?"

"Confidential."

"How did he get into secure areas?"

"I can't disclose that."

"What do we tell the staff?"

"Blame it on a false alarm. Say it was triggered by a stray cat, or anything but the truth." The detective's gaze moved from one face to another. "Now, if no one objects, I'd like to continue working with Ms. Brooks and Mr. Sylvan."

David Wood nodded and rose from the table — the other directors followed suit, each taking a turn to shake hands with the detective, patting Jack on the back, and offering Alicia hollow words of support before leaving.

The detective's partner placed a tray with four cups of green tea on the table. Jack nudged one over to himself and another toward Alicia.

"Alicia, how are you feeling?"

Her hands lay clenched in her lap, as if holding on to her last shred of sanity. She shrugged awkwardly, as if he'd asked her about her favorite color.

"How do you think she feels?" Jack said with a scoff. "That lunatic somehow got into the office today, of all days. How did he know she'd be here? Where'd he get an access card? Who told him?"

"Cole? It has to be him," Alicia gasped.

"As for our suspect, Cole Church..." The detective sighed. "His lawyer provided sufficient evidence of his alibi during the first attack. It turns out Mr. Church actively participates in private role-play clubs. Specifically, he's involved in one of those eccentric subcultures where people dress up as animals and let others 'control' them. He had probably been too embarrassed to admit his alibi right away." The detective shrugged.

"Something like...animal fetish play?" Jack said, raising an eyebrow.

"Not necessarily," the detective's partner chimed in for the first time. "The club is officially registered, although it has attracted some scrutiny from the tax authorities."

"That's not relevant to this case," Sergio said, cutting him off. "We have records of Mr. Church participating in legal events, and other club members can confirm his absence from the scene, during the attack."

"You told me yourself it's possible to hire someone on the dark web to do your dirty work. Cole could have easily paid someone and gone about his day," Alicia said.

"That's theoretically possible, but we need facts, not theories. We're following every lead. So far, we have no evidence tying Cole to the dark web in this case. As for the second attack, while we don't have exact eyewitnesses for his alibi, there's activity logged on his HBO account at his home address. But as you know, that's not a full alibi."

"Where was Cole today?" Alicia asked.

The partner started to respond, but Gibbons silenced him with a gesture. He took a sip of tea and replied. "We can fully rule out Cole Church for today's incident. At the time of the incident, he was meeting with his lawyer, which the police have personally confirmed."

"You've been running in circles after the only suspect all this time and got absolutely nowhere!" Jack pointed a finger at the detective. "Three attacks and not a single lead!"

Gibbons stared out the window. The sun was nearing the horizon.

"And I just don't understand," Jack continued, raising his

voice. "Why, after two months, you still haven't made any progress? You're just sitting here, waiting for us to hand over names on a platter. Three attacks, no breakthroughs!"

"Jackie," Alicia whispered. "I think the detective wants to tell us something."

Gibbons looked into her eyes. She saw a sadness there that had never been there before.

"I'm terribly sorry you're going through this nightmare for the third time," the detective said, slipping into a more familiar tone. "It's hard for me to say this, but we searched the rooftop, the fire stairs, the hallway, and even the restroom. We found... nothing. No signs, no evidence of anyone else being there."

Jack slammed his fist on the table, sending the teacups rattling and spilling pale green genmaicha. Alicia let out a quiet sob as a tear spilled over her lip.

"Sorry," Jack said, putting a hand on her shoulder. "I'm just so tired."

"We also reviewed the security footage, and..." The detective nodded to his partner, who set the laptop in front of Alicia and Jack.

"No, no, no," Alicia muttered. "I can't — I don't want to see The Silent Walker again!"

"Alicia, you won't see him," said the detective, pressing play.

The video displayed a grainy, black-and-white feed from an overhead camera. The corridor was empty at first, seconds ticking away in the corner of the screen. Then the restroom door burst open, and Alicia rushed out. Even on the wide-angle shot, her panic was evident. She pounded the elevator button, clasped her hands together in a silent plea, then said something to the empty space around her before disappearing into the stairwell. The screen went still, the seconds continuing to tick.

A few more minutes passed before Gibbons's partner closed the laptop.

"He wasn't there," Alicia said quietly, her gaze fixed on the table where the laptop had been. "No one followed me."

Jack shook his head. "I don't understand."

"He…isn't on the CCTV footage."

"So someone tampered with the video?" Jack asked, narrowing his eyes.

"No," said the detective's young partner. "That's unlikely."

"There's no sign of interference with the surveillance system. I was the first to request access to the footage. Once we reviewed it, everything changed. Our suspicions only deepened." The detective frowned. "Our team went to the location of the second attack to question the sole witness, Gwyn Stan. We found him in his tent — and let's just say, in an intoxicated state. Under a little pressure, he admitted he lied. He confessed that his friends, who had criminal records, warned him that if he didn't confirm another person's presence, the case would be pinned on him. He panicked and gave false testimony, claiming to have seen someone and even describing our suspect sketch. This country is full of idiots." The detective exhaled bitterly. "We've arrested him for providing false information, and now he faces charges for interfering with an investigation. But this significantly changes our case."

"What does this mean for me?" Alicia pressed her trembling hands to her cheeks, which trembled beneath them.

"We've conducted a thorough analysis, Alicia," the

detective said, choosing his words carefully. "Given all the data and statements, we strongly recommend you undergo a full medical evaluation. Specialists can help rule out any potential psychosomatic factors. This is standard practice in cases like this, especially when perceptual distortions may be involved."

"You're saying," Alicia said, struggling to comprehend. "That The Silent Walker exists only in my head? That I'm schizophrenic?"

She looked to Jack, hoping for his reassurance, but he didn't contradict the detective. Her boyfriend stared silently at his hands. Alicia glanced at the detective's partner, whose name she'd forgotten, but he too avoided her gaze. Only Sergio looked back at her, sympathy etched into his expression.

"Alicia, no one is diagnosing you. This is just a precaution. We all want to be certain that what you're experiencing...is entirely explainable."

CHAPTER 37

"It's a pleasure to work with you, Mr. Evans," the tall man with a neatly trimmed beard said as he extended his hand. "I was surprised by your application, which came in just half an hour before the deadline, but I'm glad I didn't defer it to the next round."

Jordy shook his hand slowly, feeling the heat in his suit like he was in a greenhouse, trying his best not to move too much so he wouldn't sweat. Even with the sweat pads Auntie Chang had sewn in, he could already feel dampness under his arms. He gave a slight bow out of habit, then scolded himself for it, took his folder of documents, and left the admissions office.

His folder bore the word "Accepted" stamped with a bright green seal from the Massachusetts College of Pharmacy and Health Sciences. It was a graduate program and an internship at one of the country's best universities. The five stages of acceptance and eight days had passed since the unfortunate kiss. Actions spoke louder than words, and now Jordy had something real to show Alicia. As soon as he could reach her... But if at first, she'd only ignored his calls and messages, now her phone responded with an automated operator voice, and her online status simply read, "Recently Online." Would she have changed her number because of him? She'd most likely blocked Jordy through the operator and just hidden her status.

Auntie Chang sat patiently on a bench, looking like a porcelain figurine beneath the young maple tree. Jordy waved to her. The adrenaline from the meeting slowly gave way to satisfaction. He'd done it, not without her support. Endless jasmine tea to calm his nerves, warm food delivered straight to his laptop, clean clothes always waiting in his closet. She had become his family long ago. Had he always noticed just how much she did for him? Come to think of it, she was closer to him than anyone else.

He hugged her tightly. Her small frame felt so fragile in his arms. For the first time, Jordy realized just how much of his pain she had taken on, and how little she'd given back in return.

"Aiya xiaozi!" *Oh, you troublemaker!* She muttered. "You're going to break my ribs — I'm an old lady now!"

Jordy relaxed his grip and, unable to contain his excitement, loudly said with a smile. "It worked out! They're taking me!"

"All the way in Boston?"

"Yes!" He closed his eyes in bliss. Happiness burned so brightly that he feared it might blind him.

A fire of hope kindled in him during the second sleepless night. "Do something," a spark whispered, then faded. As Jordy tossed and turned in bed, more sparks ignited until one of them burst into flame. He sat up suddenly, carefully attuned to that inner fire. *Do something for her that her always-too-busy, always-at-work, don't-bother-me Jack would never do.*

Jordy knew the kiss had been a mistake. He hadn't explained

his feelings and had gone straight for her lips. Alicia had shared her deepest fears with him, and he'd acted on impulse. He needed to act, not wait for forgiveness — to show his feelings through actions, to declare his love. Screw Jack, screw their relationship. Ali had told him to live for himself — it was time to be selfish.

"But where will you live in Boston, Jordy? I bet the prices there are sky-high." Auntie Chang shook her head.

"The graduate program provides either a single room on campus or a financial equivalent if I rent a place off-campus. I looked into it — I could rent a two-bedroom apartment just a half-hour commute away! With my own bathroom and shower! No more schedules!"

"Jordy," Auntie Chang went up on tiptoes to smooth his suit on his shoulders. "You've done so well."

"I know," he said as he took her worn hands in his. "And you're coming with me."

"Wā ō." *Whoa!* "You're a fool! What kind of nonsense is that? Aren't you planning to move in with that young lady? What use would you have for an old granny?"

"You're my family. My only family."

Auntie Chang quickly pulled her hands free to wipe a tear from beneath one of her wrinkles before he could see it.

"I'm going to ask Alicia to move with me," Jordy continued. "It might be a bit tight at first, but once she finds a new job, we'll manage. The salary's good, plus what we pay for rent in Chicago...If Alicia truly wants to leave Chicago, she'll come with us. I know she will. I feel it so deeply...I'll show her an act worthy of the girl I love."

"Jordy," Auntie Chang said cautiously. "Are you doing all this just for her? Leaving the city where you grew up, moving to one you've never seen. New job, new apartment, university. I'm happy to see how she's inspiring you, but be careful you don't get burned if she says no."

Jordy looked into his heart for the answer. He drew closer to the flame and grasped it with his bare hands. He didn't get burned.

"No, Auntie Chang. I'm going either way. I will work my way up from pharmacy assistant to lead — I'm doing this for myself. Even if I can't help Alicia..."

"You don't have to help anyone, my boy," Auntie Chang whispered. "You're not responsible for your mother's death."

"I know. But Alicia helped me realize that. She brought love into my life — for her and for myself. And if she returns my feelings, I'll help her start fresh. And if not...whether it's with or without Alicia, we're moving to Boston after my graduation."

"Oh, oh, graduation is only a week away, and I haven't finished your suit."

"There's nothing you can't do." Jordy said with a smile. "I also want to invite Ali to my graduation. As soon as I find out where she's staying, as soon as I can meet with her and explain everything."

"And when do you have to be in Boston?"

"The documents are ready, so I start work in a month."

"That's so soon..."

"Will you come with me? Please?"

Auntie Chang leaned into Jordy. Her time-worn shoulders trembled, and tears ran down her wrinkled face, tangling in her graying hair.

"I'll come," she whispered through tears. "Thank you, my dear boy."

***

"Hello, Jack Sylvan speaking."

"Hello? Jack? This is Jordy. Jordy Evans. I'm a friend of Ali — Alicia."

Despite practicing a calm greeting several times, Jordy's voice still wavered. *Damn it!* Alicia's phone was still out of reach, even when he tried from another number. The last remaining option lay through the main obstacle — Jack. Jordy had gotten his number from Alicia as an emergency contact. "Just in case of an unlikely event," she'd said with a nervous giggle.

Still, Jordy needed to speak to him only long enough to set his plan in motion: find out the hotel address from Jack and wait outside with flowers, his folder, and the green seal.

"Jordy? Oh — yeah, hey."

"Listen, Jack, I lost contact with Alicia over the past few days. I just wanted to check in, you know, see how she's doing? Maybe pass something along." Jordy clenched his fist, holding back everything else he wanted to say.

"Jordy, you don't know? Alicia didn't tell you?"

"What??"

"Alicia is..." Shuffling and muffled background noise made Jack's voice both fainter and clearer. "Listen, I really can't talk right now. If you want, swing by my office, and I'll step out so we can chat."

"What? Wait — what?"

"Look, I seriously have to go. I've got an important meeting. If you want to stop by, I'll be there at noon. I'll text you the address. We can grab a bite and talk."

The call ended. The screen went dark. Jordy's fingers clenched tightly, and his knuckles turned white. He felt an overwhelming urge to punch something. His phone lit up.

```
55 Monroe St., 60603.
       12:00 p.m.
```

The arrogant jerk hadn't even bothered with a brief explanation. Jordy felt sick and dropped to a crouch. Had he been too quick to turn selfish? He hadn't once considered that something might have actually happened to Alicia. He'd assumed she was ignoring him because of the kiss. Jordy smacked his forehead — what an idiot! How could he forget The Silent Walker?

Jordy arrived at the office almost an hour early — waiting was unbearable. The soulless glass building blended in with its look-alike neighbors. He checked the address — 55 Monroe. He moved closer to the revolving doors, pressed his forehead against the glass, and peered inside. A turnstile stood in the lobby, allowing entry only with access cards. Some pulled cards from their pockets; others wore them on lanyards. "To keep the herd in line," Jordy thought with a smirk. He turned his head and locked eyes with a guard in a short-sleeve jacket and a holster. The guard narrowed his eyes suspiciously and approached. Jordy raised his eyebrows and forced a smile, quickly stepping back to a safe (but not suspicious) distance, then leaned on a flowerbed to wait.

Time dragged by, and for the first time, Jordy regretted not being a smoker. At 11:45 a.m., he caved and texted Jack, claiming he had "accidentally" arrived a little early.

Jack emerged at 12:10 p.m.

Jordy recognized Jack instantly.

Jack wore an expensive cream-colored shirt and a dark suit — clearly not made by Auntie Chang from Chinese contraband fabrics. From the impeccably trimmed stubble to his lacquered shoes — he irritated Jordy. Jack scanned the faces around him and glanced at his watch.

Jack didn't recognize Jordy.

CHAPTER 38

"I'll have the salmon bento and a miso soup, please," Jack Sylvan said, smiling at the waitress with pink hair.

"What's going on with Alicia?" Jordy couldn't hold back any longer.

"Have you eaten?"

"I don't want to."

"That will be all, then." Jack said, handing the menu back to the waitress.

She tucked her notepad into her apron and walked off to place the order. Besides her, there were only the chef and his assistant working in the cozy Japanese restaurant. Though the place was hidden away, every seat was taken — yet their table felt sealed in a bubble. The noise of passing traffic, background music, and the clinking of utensils all faded away.

Jack lifted the water pitcher and filled their glasses — first Jordy's, then his own. "I understand you want to know where Alicia is. The police have currently put the investigation on hold."

"On hold?" Jordy narrowed his eyes in disbelief. "They just froze everything?"

"There was another incident at the office..."

"Another one? When?"

"Last week. Friday..."

Jordy jumped up from the table, shattering the bubble of silence. People at nearby tables turned to look at him, and the waitress adjusted her pink bangs before indifferently turning away.

"Is she alive?"

"Jordy, sit down."

"What happened to Alicia?"

"Sit down, have some water, and I'll explain."

Jordy's lungs hammered for air, and he lowered himself into his seat. He nodded, grabbed the glass of water, and drained it. He exhaled, nodded again, and clasped his hands on the table.

"Alicia's unharmed," Jack replied. "Physically..."

"I haven't spoken to her in over a week — I didn't even know..."

"I'm not surprised. I doubt she wants to talk about any of it. Jordy, Alicia's in the hospital — in the psych ward."

Questions boiled over, simmered, then bubbled up again as Jack brought Jordy up to speed. Half of it sounded absurd, and the other half was terrifying. He almost wanted to look over his shoulder to check if Alicia was there, recording his reaction with a hidden camera. How could this even be possible?

"At this point, the leading theory is that The Silent Walker existed only in her mind. No one was caught on camera. No one was seen entering or exiting the office building, no trace left behind."

Jack paused when the pink-haired waitress brought his

order. A rectangular bento box arrived, divided into four compartments: white rice, teriyaki salmon, finely shredded fresh cabbage, and avocado maki. Steam rose from the miso soup, carrying the pleasant aroma of seaweed. Jack opened a drawer on the table, took out wooden chopsticks and a white ceramic spoon.

"I don't understand," Jordy muttered, watching Jack pour soy sauce over the rice. "The police actually think Alicia's unstable?"

"They didn't say it outright, but when no evidence turns up three times in a row — neither on camera nor physically — the police start to doubt. And the third incident happened in broad daylight. The camera caught Alicia running down the corridor to the stairwell, but no one was chasing her. It was empty. No one at all."

"And you believe this?" Jordy asked. "That she's unstable?"

"I know Alicia has always struggled with fear." Jack sighed. "I'm not saying she's sick, but she's been battling this since I've known her."

"That's nonsense! She's not insane!" Jordy raised his voice again.

"I didn't say she was," Jack replied calmly, pushing the empty soup bowl to the side. "But at this point, it's the only explanation that makes sense. Illness can come on when you least expect it — cancer, for example. That's why psychological evaluation is essential. This is standard procedure. She's in one of the best departments in the city — safe and professional. While she's there, she can't use her phone or social media. Limited contacts, to avoid stress. The doctor said the evaluation could take a couple of weeks. After that, the police would decide if it made any sense to keep chasing someone who might not even exist."

Jordy clenched his jaw and gripped the back of his chair, resisting the urge to ball his hands into fists. He tried to ignore his simmering anger as Jack carefully picked up grains of rice with his chopsticks. Jordy felt like he truly knew Alicia, and the thought that The Silent Walker was an illusion felt like a trap. Either the police were deceived, or Jack was lying. But it definitely didn't feel like the truth.

"And you're okay with this?" Jordy asked through gritted teeth. "She's locked up in a psych ward, and you're here savoring rice?"

Jack coughed and wiped his mouth with a paper napkin. "I don't know how close you were with Alicia, but it seems you're overstepping a bit. We're not friends, Jordy, so let's keep things civil, all right?"

"Sorry. I'm just on edge..."

"So am I. I've been living with this for a week."

Jordy barely restrained himself from making a snide comment. Jack didn't look remotely like someone on edge. Instead, Jordy asked, "Can I visit her at the hospital?"

"Visiting day is Wednesday, but you'll need approval from her guardian."

"From whom?"

"From me."

Jordy straightened in his chair, locking eyes with Jack. Did he expect Jordy to beg for permission? Or was this just how he looked, always arrogant and unblinking?

"What do I need to do for that?"

Jack gestured to the waitress. She spent a long time scrolling through her phone, as if she was at home instead of at work, before finally walking over with the bill.

"Check, please. I'll pay by card."

She nodded lazily and went to get the terminal.

"Well?" Jordy had to fight the urge to grab the soy sauce and pour it all over Jack's pristine shirt.

"I'll get you a one-time pass." Jack took his phone from his jacket pocket, pressed his thumb to the sensor, and frowned at the screen. After a few seconds, his expression smoothed. "Ah, how convenient. I'll be in L.A. from Tuesday to Friday. Sure, I'll arrange for you to visit her on Wednesday. So she'll at least have someone come by."

Jordy gave a curt nod, clenching his hands tighter to resist smashing Jack's iPhone (undoubtedly the latest model) into his face.

"Text me today with your full name, address, and job — unless you're unemployed," Jack added. He tapped his card against the terminal, added a thirty percent tip, and stood up from the table. "If I don't respond by Monday, text me again. I'm a busy man."

"Is a trip to L.A. really more important than Alicia?" Jordy blurted out and immediately regretted it.

Jack tilted his head and raised an eyebrow, considering the jab carefully. His face became calm, cold, and he replied quietly.

"I'm not sure who you think you are, but you just missed your one chance to see Alicia. You believe you two were close? That you *really* knew her? She barely mentioned your name once or twice. I had to dig through my memory when you called. Get over yourself, kid. Your role in her life is done."

Jack stood, smoothed his jacket, and without another word, headed for the door. Jordy watched as his last hope of seeing Alicia walked away. He cursed himself for his outburst.

"Damn it!" Jordy slammed his fist on the table.

The waitress snapped out of her phone daze and hurried over. Jordy jumped up and bolted from the restaurant, almost bumping into her — like a schoolboy running from his first girlfriend.

Once outside, he slowed his pace. The LiveSafe office building loomed before him as employees rushed back from lunch, and somewhere behind that glass sat that pompous jerk.

"Screw you, Jack. I'll ask her myself whether my role in her life is really done."

Chapter 39

A man with a prosthetic leg smoked a cigarette. The wind slowly lifted the smoke, carrying the ash away toward the hospital walls. He took long drags, savoring the bitter, acrid taste in his mouth. When the cigarette burned down to the filter, he didn't toss it into the bin. Instead, he stood there rolling the stub between his fingers until the filter singed his skin. Finally, he dropped the smoldering butt onto the ground, crushed it with his one foot, and looked up toward the window.

A little girl was watching him, gripping the iron bars with her small hands, her lips moving in silent song. The thick windowpane didn't let any sound escape, yet the man could already hear her melody in his mind. She was laughing, and his eyes filled with tears. Every time they sang their made-up song together, her face lit up — though it happened less often now, the wandering light in her eyes flickering more and more.

The man took out a pack of Marlboros from his pocket. He pulled out another cigarette, lit it, and offered one to the young man nearby. Jordy shook his head, tossed his coffee cup into the trash, and stepped through the hospital's wide doors.

***

Alicia didn't want to open her eyes. The dream was fading, lingering in her memory for a few final moments. Since starting the new medication, her dreams had become vivid, ridiculously absurd but amusing. They were the kind of dreams that made her dread returning to the room in the psychiatric hospital.

But eventually, she had to get up. She felt it again — that creeping sensation that he was here. Alicia bolted upright in bed. No one. She lay back down but kept her eyes open, not willing to risk slipping back into sleep.

Nurse Maggie — just Maggie, no Mrs., Ms., or Dame — usually brought breakfast at eight a.m., but Alicia had woken up early again. When a glum Jack mentioned his business trip, which meant he couldn't visit her at the hospital that week, she'd felt indifferent. Well, almost indifferent. She'd lost track of the days — Maggie was the one who kept the calendar for her. Breakfast, injections, devices with suction cups, other tests, lunch. Then came afternoon therapy sessions and a choice of three activities during personal time: a few TV channels, a small library, and a gym. Dinner. The food was decent, but the endless tests were driving her mad.

***

Jordy stood at the marble reception desk, nervously shifting from foot to foot as he rehearsed the fabricated story in his mind. The woman in front of him was laughing loudly, telling a story about her cat — he'd climbed up a ten-foot apple tree in her yard — while the freckle-faced receptionist smiled politely, her eyes flicking to the growing line. Finally, the story ended — the cat climbed down in the evening — and the receptionist, clearly a little regretful, said she needed to assist other visitors.

The hospital admitted the upper crust of society. The bright walls adorned with abstract paintings, scattered potted plants, and the soft gleam of glass doors — everything seemed flawless to Jordy. The rooms lay beyond a door painted in a rainbow. The air didn't smell of bleach or sanitizer, as he remembered from childhood; it smelled of green tea, mint, and money. Jack hadn't lied — there probably wasn't a better hospital anywhere.

***

Alicia studied her reflection in the mirror. The cotton pajama with alpacas hung off her like a rag. She ate every meal, yet she kept losing weight. Or was it the daily workouts in the gym?

Exercise was the only thing that kept her sane in the hospital. Or perhaps she had already lost her mind, and all that remained was for the diagnosis to be confirmed. Alicia's thoughts swung back and forth, and several times a day she changed her mind about whether The Silent Walker was real. She'd asked Maggie for advice, but the nurse never gave a clear answer.

"Only a doctor can make that diagnosis," Maggie would always reply.

Sometimes, at night, Alicia heard the rustle of a cloak. She saw a dark figure by the window. She felt the touch of a blade. The Silent Walker never left her mind, but did she truly believe that her mind had created him?

***

"How can I help you?" the receptionist asked with a polite smile.

"I'm here to visit my girlfriend, Alicia Brooks," Jordy lied, forcing a steady tone.

"Alicia Brooks...Alicia Brooks..." The receptionist scanned the screen, scrolling down with the mouse. "Ah, from room 1-927?"

"Mm-hmm." Jordy cleared his throat, trying to sound vague.

"Your name?"

"Jack Sylvan."

The receptionist glanced from the screen to Jordy and back to the screen, squinting slightly as she looked at him again.

"Do you have an ID?"

"Left it in the car," Jordy replied in a breathless murmur.

Despite his best attempts to wear a suit and style his hair like Jack's, the resemblance was minimal. The receptionist might even remember Jack's face, or worse — they could have his photo on file. Jordy felt his cheeks reddening.

"Look, Alicia's been waiting for me all morning!"

The receptionist picked up the desk phone. "Dr. Granger, we have a visitor for Miss Brooks. He claims he's the patient's boyfriend."

Stupid mistake — of course they knew what Jack looked like. Jordy realized his plan was already falling apart, but he wasn't going to give up. Casting a glance at the rainbow-colored doors that led to the patient rooms, Jordy bolted. His own footsteps and pounding heart echoed in his ears — someone already chasing after him.

***

Every time she tried to sleep in the dark, the image of The Silent Walker appeared before her. She was terrified at the thought that he might truly exist, but equally frightened at the possibility that he was just a figment of her imagination. When it became unbearable, Alicia pressed the small button by her bed, and Maggie came with a thin syringe to give her the "funny sleep" injection.

A sharp pain pierced her head. She rubbed her temple — the migraines had become more frequent. Maggie was already fifteen minutes late with breakfast, and Alicia's stomach — trained by routine — grumbled in discontent. Had something happened to her? But if Maggie had run into trouble, Dr. Granger surely would have come by to inform Alicia during breakfast.

***

Room 1-917...1-919...1-921...

Jordy sprinted down the endless corridor, barely keeping his footing on the slick floor. The walls and doors blurred together in a stretched, distorted smear. The receptionist's voice trailed after him as she called for security. There wasn't much time, but if he reached Alicia before they reached him, he would win. He didn't care if she was mentally unstable; he still wanted to take her to Boston, where the doctors in Massachusetts were the best — they would definitely help her.

***

Footsteps echoed from behind the door. Was it for her? Maggie? The doctor? There was a knock — no one had ever knocked in the hospital before. Biting her lip, she climbed onto the wide bed, clutching the blankets. What if it was The Silent Walker? What if he'd sneaked into the hospital, attacked Maggie, and now found her room?

She could no longer trust her own senses. She felt him again.

The door burst open. A shadow flickered — barely noticeable, but enough to make her breath hitch. It was him.

It *really* was The Silent Walker.

He slowly advanced toward the bed. Alicia pressed her back against the cold wall, biting the blanket. *Just imaginary! He's not real, not real!*

The Silent Walker put his hand in his pocket. His eyes merged with the mask in the darkness, darkening the bright walls, casting shadows across the windows. Darkness gazed out from under the fabric once more.

Alicia opened her mouth, but The Silent Walker was faster.

He grabbed her by the neck.

The scream dissolved, trapped in her throat.

***

1-927…Jordy burst into the room.

"Ali!" he called, breathless.

No one. The bed was neatly made, the windows shut, and no clothes hung from the corner hooks.

An empty room. Was he too late? Had he misheard the number?

A firm hand landed on his shoulder.

"I don't know what you're up to or why you lied," said the security guard, "but Ms. Brooks is no longer registered at this hospital. Leave the premises now, or we'll call the police."

***

Jordy exhaled, practically spitting out the smoke, as he waited for the harsh scratch in his throat. Nothing — no cough, no dirty-sock taste. He took another deep drag. Deeper. Exhaled without a cough. Another movie lie: people don't hack up their lungs on the first cigarette like that. But on the third drag, his head started to spin. *Good. It's working.*

"Well, at least they didn't call the cops on you," the man snorted, brushing ash off his prosthetic knee. He reached into his pack of Marlboros and pulled out the second-to-last cigarette.

"Isn't it bad to smoke that much?"

"Who cares. No point living long, anyway."

The smoke muted the pain in his head. For the second time in his life, Jordy regretted not starting smoking earlier. Cigarettes smothered his thoughts, pushed them into a dark corner.

"Did anyone at the hospital say where she went?" the man asked.

"No. Either she ran off, or they discharged her, or… something worse. They didn't say a word," Jordy muttered, clumsily flicking ash off with his other hand.

"What are you going to do now?"

"What am I going to do…I'm going to Boston."

"Are you going to look for her?" The man lit his own cigarette with a giraffe-patterned lighter.

Jordy's lips held the filter, and the flame was already close to the yellow paper. Irreversible.

"No…After all, her role in my life is done." Jordy clenched his jaw, choking on the smoke in his mouth. A cough tore from his throat. Finally.

"Can I have one more?" Jordy asked, wiping the stub on the wall. The black mark it left behind formed a triangle.

The man silently held out the pack, a single cigarette poking out.

"Last one?"

"Take it."

Jordy took the cigarette between his lips. The man flicked the lighter, creating a small flame. Jordy shielded it from the wind with his hands and leaned in.

Their cigarettes were fading into silence at the entrance to the psychiatric hospital. When only the burning filter remained, Jordy added two more lines to the triangle.

"Goodbye," he said, tossing the butt to the ground.

The letter "A" on the wall watched him as he walked away.

Epilogue

It had been a tough, risky decision to dedicate a third of the pharmacy space to a mini tailoring shop. Customers came for round ibuprofen tablets, soothing oils, and condoms — never expecting to see a sewing corner right at the entrance.

They'd had to work hard to push the shelves of medicines to the back and set up a podium for the sewing machine. To visually separate the atelier and pharmacy, Tom had brought in a ten-foot Japanese-style screen he found on the street in one of Boston's expensive neighborhoods. Red and blue koi fish swam from one corner, disappearing behind another. Once they had the screen, they decided to add more Asian elements to the atelier corner and had to work even harder to persuade the seamstress to accept the style.

"Boss, I'm heading out for lunch," Tom said, his head appearing in the doorway.

Jordy looked up from his spreadsheets. He glanced at the clock in the corner and closed his MacBook's silver lid.

"I'll go myself. The usual for you?"

"The usual if the boss is paying, or half a portion if I'm paying myself," Tom said, grinning widely.

He pressed his hands together in mock pleading and pouted. Tom had joined the pharmacy a year and a half ago, initially just for the summer, but the flexible hours and conditions tempted him into a permanent position.

Tom enjoyed working for Jordy — a guy from the bottom who managed to open his own small business in Boston. A year ago, Jordy had helped Tom with lab work at the Massachusetts College of Pharmacy and Health Sciences — for free. With the opening of the atelier, the boss had less time, but Tom still appreciated the opportunity to work together and gain background knowledge along the way.

"Auntie, what should I bring you for lunch?" Jordy peeked behind the screen.

Auntie Chang was bent over her table, meticulously running her fingers along a seam. She raised a finger in a "wait" gesture, laid the fabric on the table, and traced the seam with a tailor's chalk. Then, she scribbled something on a piece of paper, set the fabric aside, and switched off her small headlamp.

"Waste of money," she chided, tilting her head. "Tonight, I'll make enough home-cooked food for the whole week."

"I don't want to burden you; you have plenty of orders. It's time to hire an assistant for you."

"Oh, I don't want one..."

"We have clients booking two months in advance. Let's bring in another tailor, you'll train her and then retire. Spend your summers sunbathing in the yard, and in winter, I'll take you to Florida."

"Florida, you say? So I'll be driving Lamborghinis and wearing gold chains?" Auntie Chang laughed with a raspy chuckle.

Jordy smiled. The years had taken their toll, but life in Boston suited her. Two years ago he persuaded her to get her thyroid checked; a year ago he arranged new dentures for her; more recently, he bought her an electric scooter with a grocery cart.

"So, Thai food for everyone?" He asked, raising an eyebrow.

She waved her hand dismissively and turned the headlamp back on.

Jordy stepped outside to the corner of the pharmacy-atelier and pulled out a pack of Marlboros. He lit a cigarette.

A white Toyota Corolla pulled up in front of the pharmacy — the typical choice for an immigrant Uber driver on a student visa. The car was dust-covered from the dry weather, and the Uber sticker was peeling off in the upper corner.

The taxi logo reminded him of an overdue task on his to-do list — they'd long needed to enter the delivery market. Some regular customers were already sending cars to pick up their orders and complained about the lack of delivery service. *I'll deal with it after lunch*, Jordy thought.

He'd installed a large aluminum trash can outside at his own expense because his pocket ashtray filled up too quickly. To prevent anyone from stealing it, Tom had chained it to a metal hook on the wall.

Jordy crouched to stub out his cigarette on the pavement. The wind whipped up a street-cocktail of smells, stirred it well, and flung it straight at him, slicing through the curtain of smoke. Within it, Jordy caught a familiar trace — bittersweet enough to give him goosebumps, torn straight from his heart — but *how? Here, in Boston?*

Soft, measured footsteps stopped a few feet away.

"Jordy? I finally found you!"

He lifted his head and squinted. The sunlight bounced off golden hair, blinding his face.

"Alicia?"

Acknowledgements

To every reader who picked up this book — thank you. You believed in me and this story, and that means more than I can put into words. Whether you bought the book, borrowed it, or simply took a chance on a new voice, I'm endlessly grateful.

Writing a book may start alone, but finishing one never is. Every person mentioned here helped me in ways big and small — and without them, my fears would still live deep inside me, unnamed and unwritten.

To my lovely husband Anton: thank you for being with me from Day One — literally, from that night in 2021 in Singapore when I said, "I think I want to write a book about someone living in fear." Since then, you've been my number one editor, alpha reader, therapist, photographer, marketer, critic, stakeholder, and the most relentless believer in me. Thank you for holding the dream when I doubted it.

To my beta readers — my mom and The Princess — thank you for bravely reading an unsolicited manuscript before it ever touched a professional editor's desk. Your long feedback was golden (and yes, I know — we all miss the fuzzy Crocs). I took your words seriously and polished every corner with love.

A special thank you to Lotta, who I can't quite call a beta reader, but maybe a skim-reader mentor? Your feedback on my synopsis (yes, that monstrous 40,000-character beast) was invaluable and kept me focused when it mattered most.

To Halley Sutton, my professional copyeditor — you didn't just refine my words, you taught me so much about writing and storytelling across cultures. From tiny commas to head hopping, you treated every detail with care. I knew we were a perfect match from the moment I saw your sample edit, and I'm beyond proud to say this book was copyedited by you.

To Yulia Zaitseva, my book cover designer — OMG, my face when I saw the final version! It was so beautiful, I couldn't believe it came from my story. Thank you for being so patient with all the changes, and for crafting something I couldn't even imagine myself. This cover is our shared baby, and it's filled with infinite love.

To Ekaterina Hoarau, author and creative writing tutor — your *Hard One to Write!* book scared me at first (so much to learn!), but both courses I took in 2023 and 2024 turned out to be two of the most meaningful and productive experiences of my creative life. Thanks to all the mentors in the courses who reviewed my passages and offered deep editorial insights — I received a treasure chest of smart voices, generous lessons, and international insight I didn't even know I needed. Thank you for building such an inspiring space.

To my fellow writers from the course: my Ukrainian group "Skarbniki" — thank you for reading my raw passages and providing honest feedback, and warm support. And to my favourite mastermind group formed after the course, which we call "Ekaterina's Incubator," thank you for helping me move forward when I felt stuck — and for helping me answer questions I might not have thought to ask without our brainstorming.

To everyone else who lent their skills along the way: Alina and Heorh2, thank you for your thoughts and input on the book cover. Christina, Anna, Masha, and Nicola — thank you for your review of the sample English translation.

And finally — to Naruto. Yes, really. Your story, your mindset, your ninja path. I would've given up more than once without your stubborn kind of hope. "Believe it," right? Let's just say...I carry your hand of support with me. Always.

ABOUT THE AUTHOR

Marina Meier is the author of *Then I Choose a Horrible End*, a psychological thriller that dives deep into fear and blurred reality. Originally from Ukraine, Marina now lives abroad and writes across languages and borders.

She completed *The Magic of Editing* and *Editorial Magic*, two intensive writing and editing programs focused on structure and character development — and later returned as a mentor, offering editorial feedback to writers working in three languages.

Marina believes Stephen King is responsible for at least half of her fears — and still considers him one of her greatest inspirations. She writes to understand fear. To show how it shapes our minds, words, and actions. Almost like her protagonist, she lives with it — not as intensely, but closely enough to understand it. She finds it easier to write about than to speak aloud about it. This novel is her way of showing how isolating fear can feel, and how vital support is when it begins to take over.

svitlopress.com/#marina_meier

References & Inspirations

Even Harry Potter's cupboard had more space than this, she thought with a smirk.

Not exactly subtle, but a very direct nod to something I simply couldn't leave out. Harry Potter isn't just a book, movie, or game for me. It's a part of my life.

***

The water's surface rippled with the shaking of her body...drums, drums in the deep of her chest. She felt it — the shadow moving in the dark. She could not get out. No escape. No refuge.

A reference to The Lord of the Rings: The Fellowship of the Ring — my quiet tribute to the great master J.R.R. Tolkien.
The original line: "Drums, drums in the deep."
His words and that sense of an approaching, unstoppable threat helped shape the fear running through this scene.

"Nightmares exist outside of logic," a
great man once said.

This is a nod to the king of horror himself — Stephen King — the man who gave form to many of my fears.

The full original quote: "Nightmares exist outside of logic, and there's little fun to be had in explanations; they're antithetical to the poetry of fear."

***

April 28, the date when Alicia was first attacked, is not random.

That date holds personal meaning for me — a reminder of things I'd rather not forget.

***

Some numbers and names might have their special meaning...or they might not.

I'll leave that to your imagination, dear reader.

www.ingramcontent.com/pod-product-compliance
Ingram Content Group UK Ltd.
Pitfield, Milton Keynes, MK11 3LW, UK
UKHW042319260925

463342UK00001B/7

9 781764 121118